11/19

Advance I

"Martino explores [...] Milan's white aristocracy with technically accomplished descriptions of privilege, luxury, and teenage longing." ~ Kirkus Reviews

"I read this novel in a single sitting! The story of sisters Emilia and Maria Salvini is riveting, rich, and like a lovely piece of music, impossible to forget." ~ Louise Hawes, author of *The Language of Stars* and *The Vanishing Point* and founding faculty member of the Vermont College of Fine Arts MFA Program in Writing for Children and Young Adults

"A virtuoso performance by Carmela Martino. You'll love Emilia Salvini in her impossible quest to be herself at a time and place when girls had no choices." ~ Mary Jane Beaufrand, author of *Primavera* and *Useless Bay*

"In *Playing by Heart*, Carmela Martino transports readers to the palazzos and salons of eighteenth-century Italy, revealing from one sublimely crafted and evocatively detailed page to the next the lives of two passionate and inspiring sisters—women who are both far ahead of their time and absolutely believable, and who, thanks to Martino's rich characterization, linger in the mind as dear friends might, long after this beautiful, compelling, and ultimately hopeful novel draws to its rewarding end." ~ Karen Halvorsen Schreck, author of *Broken Ground* and *Sing for Me*

"*Playing by Heart* is as lyrical as the gifted musicians that inhabit its pages. Carmela Martino, in an impeccably-written story, captures both the grace and refinement of 18th-century Italy and the timeless dilemmas to which the modern reader can relate—the pressure of familial expectations and obligations, living in the shadow of a sibling, the desire to direct one's own destiny, and love tested by time, distance, parental resistance, and class." ~ Carolyn Astfalk, author of *Ornamental Graces* and *Rightfully Ours*

"Strong, intelligent female characters and meticulously re-searched detail drew me into this novel of 18ᵗʰ-century Italy. Intrigue, music, and love are all ingredients in this tale of up-per-class teen girls seeking to steer their adult lives. This is an Italian tapestry come to life." ~ Mary Ann Rodman, author of *Yankee Girl* and *Jimmy's Stars*

"A beautifully composed tale of love, faith, and family! *Playing by Heart* is sure to win the affection of its readers." ~ A. J. Cattapan, award-winning author of *Angelhood* and *7 Riddles to Nowhere*

"*Playing by Heart* is a lyrical story that captures the reader from the first page. The words literally sing. Authentic, strong char-acter voice, rich and detailed historical setting, and an intri-guing plot all come together to create a can't-put-it-down book. The story provides a look into the fascinating world of 18th-century Italy in a way that no history book ever could. The fact that it is based on the lives of extraordinary real women who were quite ahead of their time makes it a must-read addition for school libraries everywhere. Carmela Mar-tino's writing style blends the historical facts with the emo-tional family life details in a way that creates a dramatic, beautifully written novel that will capture the hearts of readers of all ages." ~ Roxanne F. Owens, PhD, Chair, Teacher Edu-cation, DePaul University

"[Martino's] brought history alive through masterful storytell-ing. Her teenage Sisters Salvini breathe on every page. You ex-perience their joys and pains as they make their ways in a restrictive society that won't understand or appreciate their ex-traordinary talents. You cheer them on as they confront their own, internal limitations with a growing maturity, mind, and yes, heart. Indeed, *Playing by Heart* achieves what we look for in good historical fiction: Teach us something about today through yesterday—and entertain us in the process." ~ Marie Ann Donovan, EdD, Associate Professor of Teacher Educa-tion, DePaul University

"This beautiful story takes place over 200 years ago, yet its lessons are timeless. Emilia and Maria have so much to teach us about balancing one's calling, one's gifts, and what brings one joy. Both young women navigate these decisions with grace, beauty, determination, and compassion. And, in our current age where instant gratification seems to be expected, Carmela Martino gives us the gift of watching true love blossom slowly." ~ Peggy Goralski, Director, Middle School Faith Formation, St. Thomas the Apostle Parish

"Set in 18th-century Milan, *Playing by Heart* is a symphony of romance and faith with an undercurrent of social commentary. Carmela Martino's novel for teen readers explores family ties, vocations, and discernment of the best ways to use God-given gifts. Cue up some Vivaldi or Pachelbel and settle in for an intriguing tale." ~ Barb Szyszkiewicz, writer at *Today's Catholic Teacher* magazine and Editor at CatholicMom.com

"Carmela Martino has created a historical heroine contemporary readers can relate to. The fact that Martino was able to do this while immersing the reader in Milan in the eighteenth century is astounding. Little tidbits of detail reveal the extensive research that must have gone into the writing. A glossary aides in understanding this remarkable time and place." ~ Gayl Smith, MLS, Retired K-12 Teacher/Librarian

"This is a heartfelt romance, very much a period piece but it would resonate with women in our day. It documents the struggles of any gifted woman trying to overcome gender bias. The relationships between the sisters and their eventual fates is quite captivating as they unfold. And it tells a tale of love, which is complicated by the age in which Emilia and Bellini lived, but love stories are timeless." ~ Dorothy Strening, Retired Parish Liturgy/Music Director

Other Books by Carmela A. Martino

Rosa, Sola

For John, who makes my heart sing

Playing by Heart

CARMELA A. MARTINO

Vinspire Publishing
www.vinspirepublishing.com

ISBN: 978-1546799450

Published by Vinspire Publishing, LLC

First Movement

December 1736 -

January 1737

Chapter One
Iron Bars

The day I decided to take my fate into my own hands began much like any other. As soon as I was dressed, I headed to the harpsichord salon to practice. The maestro had finally returned from Venice and would arrive shortly. I was anxious to show him how much I'd learned in his absence. But when I turned the corner near Mamma's sitting room, a clash of angry voices stopped me. Mamma was arguing with Father, something she never did. And something she shouldn't be doing now, as she was heavy with child.

I tiptoed to the sitting room door. With one hand on the wall, I leaned close. The edges of the decorative plasterwork dug into my fingers as Mamma said, "Did Maria request this herself?"

My hand relaxed. They weren't arguing about me. But knowing my sister's fate was intertwined with mine, I pressed forward again.

"No," Father replied. "It was *my* decision, one I would have carried out long ago if not for the Sardinian occupation. It's time she had a tutor who specializes in mathematics, one who can nurture her natural aptitude for the subject. He will teach her astronomy as well."

"Astronomy!" Mamma screeched. "Maria already spends too much time with books. Haven't you noticed her pallor? The throat illness took a greater toll on her than the other girls."

I pictured Mamma seated in the high-backed armchair near the window, her legs resting atop the footstool cushion she herself had embroidered. No doubt her normally calm blue-gray eyes flashed steely as she said, "Maria needs fresh air and physical activity, not more studies."

"Very well," Father said. "We will increase the frequency of her dance lessons. And I will order her to keep a window open in her study at all times. Come spring, I'll have her tutors move her lessons to the garden."

"They will simply stuff her head with more book learning," Mamma said. "What of her *real* education, the one she would have received at convent school? Maria should be cultivating practical skills, such as sewing and embroidery, and how to manage a home—skills she will need to be a useful wife and mother."

"There will be time enough for that," Father said. "She is young."

"Young? Perhaps her quiet manner has led you to forget that your eldest daughter is fourteen! Instead of hiring more tutors, you should be making arrangements for her future. For her betrothal, and Emilia's, too."

My betrothal! I clasped my hands to my bodice. It was the subject I'd both longed for and feared, especially since seeing Zia Delia last week.

At thirteen, I'd never heard either of my parents speak of my betrothal before. But that hadn't kept me from painting a portrait of my future husband in my mind.

He'd be as tall as Father, if not taller, with mysterious dark brown eyes. And even more important, he'd love music as I did and encourage my meager talent.

I turned my ear to the wall so as not to miss a word.

"Though, I dare say," Mamma went on, "given Maria's religious devotion, she'd be happier as a nun."

"Don't even suggest such a thing!" Father's voice crescendoed. "I will not have her extraordinary talents hidden away in a convent."

A chair scraped. Father must have stood up. "Do not concern yourself about our daughters' futures, Woman. That is *my* responsibility. I assure you I will do what is best for them *and* for the family."

Father's staccato footsteps approached. I gathered my skirts and hurried away on tiptoe.

When I was out of earshot, I let my heels drop and continued down the drafty corridor to the harpsichord salon. Father's words echoed in my mind. He'd promised to do what was best for his daughters *and* for the family.

Of the seven children in our family, four were girls, with perhaps another on the way. It would be burdensome—if not impossible—to provide marriage dowries for that many daughters. At least two of us would end up nuns, whether we had a calling or not. Such had been the fate of Zia Delia, Mamma's youngest sister.

In my mind, I saw again the long, narrow convent parlor where Mamma and I had visited Zia Delia last week. The parlor was separated from the nuns' quarters by two large windows. Iron bars covered the window openings, crisscrossing the space where glass should be. A linen drape hung over the bars on the nuns' side.

When we'd arrived that day, Mamma had eased herself into a wicker chair facing the first window, directly across from Zia Delia. We couldn't actually *see* my aunt, only her shadow on the drape. I had stood with my hand on the back of Mamma's chair as she'd tried to make conversation. The other nuns talked and laughed with their visitors. Zia Delia said nothing.

Mamma began describing Father's recent name-day celebration to Zia. "After the meal, we adjourned to the harpsichord salon. There, we listened to Maria recite two epic Greek poems she'd translated herself. Carlo said it was the best present she could have bestowed upon him." Mamma gave an exasperated sigh. "Really, he praises that girl too much! If heaven hadn't blessed Maria with such a humble nature, she'd be unbearably prideful by now." Mamma shook her head. "Afterward, Emilia gave a spectacular performance on the harpsichord, but Carlo barely thanked *her.*"

So Mamma had noticed, too.

As I recalled Father's disappointment, the room started to spin. I gripped the wicker chair tighter and breathed in deeply until my bodice stays dug into my ribs.

"Carlo's behavior was terribly rude," Mamma went on, "especially compared to Count Riccardi's impeccable manners. *He* praised Emilia profusely, saying how he'd never heard anyone her age play so beautifully, boy or girl."

I took another deep breath. Mamma didn't understand. The count was just being polite.

Zia Delia's shadow shifted. "What did you play, Emilia?"

Surprised by her question, I released my grip on the chair. "Three of Scarlatti's sonatas and Rameau's Suite in A Minor."

Zia bowed her head. "Secular music is strictly forbidden within these walls." Her voice held both sorrow and longing.

How could such beautiful music be forbidden? I shivered at the thought.

I stepped forward and pressed my hand against the iron grille. On the opposite side, Zia stood and raised her hand to mine. She pressed hard, as though she could make our fingers touch through the linen drape. But I felt only the cold iron bars.

Zia whispered, "Don't let them do this to *you.*" Her shadow gestured behind her, toward the nuns' quarters. "Don't let them lock you away from the music."

I shivered again then shook my head. *Father would never do that to* me.

Now, as I neared the harpsichord salon, I wasn't so sure. Especially not after what I'd just overheard. Or rather, what I *hadn't* overheard.

When Mamma had mentioned arranging for Maria's betrothal and mine, Father had said nothing of me. He'd spoken only of Maria. A spark of envy flared in my chest. *Heaven forgive me*, I prayed silently as I took a quick breath to extinguish the flame. Even if envy wasn't a sin, I owed Maria too much to blame her for Father's favoritism.

I pushed my thoughts aside. Time was running short. I had to prepare for my lesson—my first with the maestro in nearly three years.

Not long after the Sardinian invasion, Maestro Tomassini had accepted a temporary assignment in Venice. The maestro was a stern taskmaster, but I'd sorely missed his instruction. His return made me grateful Milan was again under Hapsburg rule. I'd be doubly grateful if the maestro's time away had somehow softened his disposition.

I hurried into the harpsichord salon. Paintings of various sizes covered the walls here as in the other rooms. Most depicted scenes from the Bible, though there were also a few landscapes, seascapes, and still lifes. But this room held a work of art not found elsewhere in our palazzo—a harpsichord.

This morning, sunlight from the window fell directly on the harpsichord's open lid, illuminating the painting there of a small white ship sailing across a blue-green sea. The waves carved onto the harpsichord's side panels continued the nautical theme, as did the lovely mermaid figures hugging the base of each of the three legs.

Naldo, our manservant, must have been here already, for fires burned brightly in both hearths, chasing away the December chill. I sat down and began as I always did, by pressing the high-C key. As the note rang out, it merged with the sensation of the quill plucking the string to send a quiver of delight through me. I loved both the sound and the feel of the instrument.

Instead of starting with one of my usual practice pieces, I played the opening allemande of Rameau's Suite in A Minor. I'd hoped the challenging opening would distract me from the dark thoughts hovering at the back of my mind. But playing Rameau only reminded me of Zia's words, "Don't let them lock you away from the music." Which would be worse, to be deprived of music or of love?

My fingers slipped, striking an ugly chord that set my teeth on edge. I dropped my hands to my lap.

I didn't understand—why couldn't Father let Maria take the veil? She would truly welcome a life of devotion to God. Yet

Father'd been angered by the mere suggestion. *I will not have her extraordinary talents hidden away in a convent.*

The chiming of the Basilica bells pulled me into the present. Maestro Tomassini would be here any moment. I raised my hands to the keys and began my first practice piece—a piece the maestro used to have me play blindfolded.

Suddenly, I knew what I must do. I had to make Father feel the same way about *my* talents as he did Maria's.

My fingers stumbled again as a voice in my head said, *But you're not good enough.*

To which my heart replied, *then I must become good enough.*

Chapter Two
The Challenge

The maestro strode in just then. "Well, you've obviously been neglecting your practice in my absence."

"Maestro Tomassini!" I jumped up. "I, I, I—"

Maestro Tomassini set his leather satchel on a chair. "Bah! Stop babbling, Girl."

Girl. My shoulders sagged under the weight of the word. I was the maestro's only female student and, as far as I could tell, his least favorite. His time away obviously hadn't changed that. Or his disposition.

The maestro moved to the far end of the harpsichord and waved his long fingers at me. "Come, come. I don't have all day."

My heart still racing, I sat down and began again. But I couldn't find the right tempo. How could I hope to impress Father with my talents if I couldn't even play a practice piece properly?

I breathed in so deeply my bodice stays pinched. *I can play this piece blindfolded*, I reminded myself. Then I did the next best thing—I closed my eyes. I imagined I was alone in the room. The beating of my heart gradually slowed and I settled into the music.

When I finished, I opened my eyes.

The maestro still stood at the end of the harpsichord, but he was frowning at the floor.

I continued with my normal practice routine. Now that I'd found my rhythm, I moved easily from one piece to the next. In between, I stole glances at the maestro. He kept staring at the floor with one ear cocked toward me, his sharp profile dark against the light from the window.

The maestro's time in Venice had left little mark on his appearance—he was as tall and thin as ever, though the silver streaks in his black hair seemed to have multiplied. He wore his hair tied back at the neck with a ribbon, as always. I'd never seen him in a wig. Perhaps he thought a wig inappropriate for a priest, even one who was now *maestro di cappella* at three different churches and who not only directed the choirs but composed most of their songs, too.

As I worked through the last three practice pieces, I realized the maestro had never heard me play them before. He'd sent them from Venice along with the new music he'd wanted me to learn in his absence.

When I'd finished the final piece, I let my hands fall to my lap. The closing chords faded away. I waited for the maestro's inevitable criticism. But none came. He must have been intent on keeping the session short, for he said only, "Now let me hear how much of the Rameau Suite you've managed to learn."

He pointed his long chin toward the harpsichord bench, which held a storage compartment. "I trust you have the music."

"*Sì*, Maestro." I stood and took out the sheet music. Rameau's Suite in A Minor was the most recent piece he'd sent and the most difficult. I handed the music to him then sat down again and started playing. I'd barely begun when he stopped me.

He held out the sheet music. "Don't you need this?"

"No, Maestro. I know it by heart."

"You mean to say you've memorized the opening allemande?"

"No, Maestro. I mean I've memorized the whole thing. I played it for Father's name day."

The maestro's eyes widened ever so slightly. "Very well then," he said, taking a seat. "Let me hear it." The words sounded like a challenge.

It was a challenge I happily accepted. I loved the Rameau Suite.

I had to concentrate to do justice to the long opening allemande, but I was rewarded for my efforts. Soon, I was being swept away by the great arpeggios of the second movement. I lost myself in the music, playing one movement after another until I reached the end of the seventh and final movement.

I smiled in satisfaction. Then I remembered the maestro.

He sat poring over the sheet music, his eyes scanning left to right across the page. Had I misinterpreted the music? Was he looking for the place where I'd gone astray, to point out my mistake?

Maestro Tomassini stood and placed the pages before me on the harpsichord. I sat up straighter, bracing for the reprimand, but I wasn't prepared for what he said next.

"Have you been working with someone else?"

"Excuse me, Maestro?"

He frowned then said slowly, as though talking to a child, "Has another tutor been instructing you in my absence?"

"No, Maestro. I've had no other tutor." I could see in his eyes he didn't believe me.

"Hmpmf," was all he said. He walked to the chair and removed some sheet music from his satchel. "See what you can make of this." The maestro practically threw the music at me. "That's all the time I have." And then he was gone.

Had I disappointed Maestro Tomassini that badly? Perhaps the time away had changed him after all. Now, instead of ranting over my failings, he expected me to find them for myself.

I stood and slipped the new music into the harpsichord bench. As much as I longed to learn something new, I couldn't even think about it until I'd uncovered and corrected my errors in playing Rameau's Suite.

I don't know how much time passed before Nina, our maidservant, came in. "I'm sorry to disturb you, Miss," she said. "Your mother wishes for you to join her in her sitting room to work on your stitchery."

I groaned. All I wanted to do was practice. But I didn't dare disobey. I went to my bedroom to get my embroidery.

Maria was already there, pulling her own project from the wooden *cassone* that held her future trousseau. When she looked up, the paleness of her cheeks made her brown eyes seem even darker than usual.

"Oh, Emmi, it's you." She sounded relieved. "Did Mamma call for you, too?"

"Yes. I just came for my needlework."

"Praise heaven! I thought I'd done something wrong." Maria straightened up. "It's unlike Mamma to call us at this hour. Father won't be happy when he learns she sent my tutor away."

I thought of the argument I'd overheard but decided against telling Maria about it. She hated any kind of discord.

"Don't worry yourself." I opened my own *cassone*, which stood beside Maria's, and grabbed my needlework. "Come. We'd better not keep Mamma waiting."

"You're right. She'll be displeased enough when she sees this." Maria held up her embroidery.

Her project was a purse made of drawn-thread work. Between the embroidered sections, it was supposed to have tiny windows of open space. But Maria's windows were filled with loose threads. My sister had an amazing gift for languages and could solve complicated geometry problems, yet when it came to embroidery, she was hopeless. I couldn't help feeling sorry for her.

I took Maria's hand, which was cold, as always, and pulled her to the hallway. "Let's hope Isabella's already there to distract Mamma."

Isabella *was* there, seated beneath a large portrait of Santa Clara. Our little sister's bouncing legs and restless spirit contrasted sharply with the tranquility on the saint's face in the painting.

"Look, Emmi." Isabella held up a piece of burgundy and black brocade. "I'm making a new gown for Lina."

Lina was Isabella's favorite *bambolina*. At eleven, my sister was still fascinated with dolls, and she managed to beg the finest fabric scraps from Mamma to clothe them. "Isn't it beautiful?"

"It is," I answered. Isabella and I were the only ones who had inherited Mamma's blue-gray eyes. But my sister's eyes were bluer than mine, especially when she smiled, as she did now. "Lina will be the best-dressed doll in all Milan, maybe even all of Italy."

"And Isabella will be the most proficient young seamstress," Mamma said, "once she learns to keep her stitches of even length." Mamma sat working on a beaded pillow cover stretched across a standing embroidery frame. "Now back to work, Isabella."

Mamma often addressed us by our Christian names, something Father rarely did. And when he wasn't present, she encouraged us to call her simply "Mamma." If Father knew, he'd be furious. Before the Sardinian occupation, he'd been scheming for our family to be added to the ranks of the nobility. With the Hapsburgs again in power, Father was so confident of success that he insisted we call him *Signor Padre*—my lord father—instead of simply *Padre*, as if he'd already been granted a title.

Maria and I sat down on the sofa and began to work. I was embroidering a border of flower petals and leaves onto a set of white handkerchiefs. Mamma had given me a simple pattern of cross and satin stitches, infinitely easier than Maria's purse of drawn-thread.

The four of us stitched in silence for some time. While Maria embroidered in white thread on a white background, I worked with many colors—pink, red, and gold for the flower petals, and green for the leaves.

I was finishing the last of the leaves on one of my handkerchiefs when Mamma stood to stretch. With the baby's birth expected in less than a month, Mamma was heavy with child and unable to sit for long.

Isabella, whose legs had never stopped bouncing, stood and skipped about the room.

Mamma came over to inspect my work. "Excellent progress. *Brava*, Emilia."

"*Grazie*, Mamma." I smiled up at her. She smiled back, a rare occurrence lately.

"Let me see yours, Maria." Mamma held out her hand.

Dread filled Maria's eyes as she offered up her embroidery hoop.

Mamma held the hoop toward the window and peered through the cutouts in the fabric. "What's this?" she said. "Your threads are showing. You have to stitch *exactly* as I taught you and bundle the stray thread as you work."

Maria bowed her head. "I'm sorry, Mamma."

"Go back and gather the loose threads." Mamma dropped the hoop into Maria's lap, startling her. Mamma spoke her next words quietly, as though they were meant for Maria alone, but I couldn't help overhearing. "Your father is forever boasting of your intelligence, yet I do not see it in your needlework."

Maria's cheeks flushed pink.

As Mamma returned to her chair, I squeezed the sleeve of Maria's blue velvet gown. I could barely feel her slender arm in the folds of the heavy fabric. I don't know if my touch brought any comfort. Maria was already intent on fixing the mess she'd made of her needlework.

By now Isabella stood at the balcony doors, tracing the ice patterns on the glass with her fingers. Mamma called, "Come along, Isabella."

Isabella sat down and took up her sewing again. Mamma slowly lowered herself into her armchair. She pulled her standing embroidery frame as close as she could and leaned forward.

"Maria," Mamma said, "if you spent half as much time on your needlework as you do on your studies, you'd improve much more quickly." Mamma stitched as she spoke, something I couldn't do without losing count of my threads. I let go of Maria's arm and went back to my own work, switching to the pink thread for the flower petals.

"At your age," Mamma went on, "I was proficient not only in embroidery but in weaving and lace-making, too. I had also learned to read and write and to do sums well enough to run a household." She pointed her needle at Maria. "I didn't waste hours a day on books as you do. What value is there in learning

Greek and Hebrew? How will it serve you as a wife and mother?"

Mamma shook her head, then added, "Presuming your father will even be able to find you a suitable husband. Rare is the man who desires a learned wife."

Maria was bent over her needlework so I couldn't see her reaction to these words. It couldn't be easy for her to hold her tongue. Maria loved studying and saw no reason why girls shouldn't learn the same things as boys. But she always said it was best to keep silent during one of Mamma's lectures. No good could come of disagreeing with her, especially when she was with child. This was a perilous time for both Mamma and the baby.

"At least Emilia's musical training has practical value," Mamma said, her voice suddenly lighter. "She'll be able to entertain her future husband with her talents."

My heart warmed at Mamma's words. I held my needle against the tip of a tiny pink petal and offered a silent prayer. *Dear God, please help me prove to Father that my talents really are as extraordinary as Maria's.*

Otherwise, I may never have a husband at all.

Chapter Three

Summons

The next few days, I worked longer and harder at my lessons than ever before. When I was finally satisfied with my ability to play Rameau's Suite, I began learning the new music the maestro had given me, a Sonata in A Major by Pergolesi.

One afternoon while I was practicing, Father sent Nina to fetch me. A summons from Father was not to be taken lightly. I hurried from the room.

I stopped to catch my breath outside Father's study. Through the open door, I saw him at his desk, writing a letter.

I took another breath, then knocked. "You sent for me, Signor Padre?"

"Enter, Daughter." He pointed his feather quill at the chair facing him. "Sit while I finish."

I watched Father's quill bob back and forth as he continued the letter. *Scritch-scratch. Scratch-scritch.* The sound of his writing filled the room. I wondered if the letter had something to do with why Father had summoned me. I sat up taller, stretching my neck, but I couldn't make out the upside-down words.

Father wrote methodically, pausing only to dip the quill's tip into his silver inkpot. He seemed to have forgotten me. But that was impossible. Father never forgets anything.

Scritch-scratch-scritch. The sound scraped at my nerves. With my hands resting in my lap, I rubbed the tip of my right index finger around the pad of my thumb, over and over, a nervous habit Mamma was always trying to break me of.

Finally, Father reached the end of the letter. He signed his name with a flourish. "There, that's done." He set down the quill, uncovered his silver pounce pot, and sprinkled sand onto the page. "I have news that concerns you, Emilia."

My fingers froze. Father had used my Christian name.

Looking directly at me for the first time, he said, "The new interim governor is due in Milan any day." Father's normally stern expression softened, and the corners of his mouth turned up slightly. "Count Riccardi is planning a special celebration in the governor's honor."

I nodded. Emperor Charles VI had appointed one of his generals to rule the Duchy of Milan as a reward for distinguished service against the Sardinians. What could the new governor's arrival have to do with me?

Father's dark brown eyes glittered as he went on. "Count Riccardi wishes to use this opportunity to show the governor how cultured and sophisticated we Milanese are. To that end, he has requested that you and your sister perform at the reception."

"Perform?" My voice came out in a squeak. "For the governor?" How could Father want me to play at such an important event when he'd been so disappointed in my last performance? Without thinking, I blurted out, "Why me?"

The hint of smile vanished. "Count Riccardi is a nobleman of the most refined tastes." Father raised his chin. "Obviously, he believes you capable of impressing the new governor, and I trust his judgment."

"*Sì*, Signor Padre." Count Riccardi always had lavish praise for my performances. I'd thought he was simply being kind. Could it be he really did admire my abilities?

Father lifted the letter and carefully poured the sand back into the pounce pot. "This letter expresses my gratitude to the count and assures him that *both* you and your sister will be well-prepared to perform for the new governor."

My hands went cold. I sensed an unspoken threat underlying Father's words. If I failed, I'd end up like Zia Delia.

But this could also be my chance. If I managed to impress the new governor, Father would finally value my talents as he did Maria's, and my future would be secure.

I rubbed my hands together to warm them. "*Sì*, Signor Padre."

Father lowered his chin in a half-nod. "I will send word to Maestro Tomassini to begin preparing you immediately. The reception will take place on the Feast of Epiphany."

Epiphany! That was less than a month away. I opened my mouth to speak then stopped. It would do no good to protest.

"That is all," Father said, with the same gesture he'd use to shoo away a fly. "Shut the door behind you."

My hands trembled as I closed the study door. I leaned my forehead against the wood.

I'd never performed outside our palazzo.

Or on a strange harpsichord.

Or in front of a governor.

The reception could be my salvation or my downfall. I had to make sure it wasn't the latter.

I thought of Maria—she was experienced in such performances. Before the Sardinian invasion, Father had often hosted academic meetings to show off her gift for languages. Surely, she could help me prepare. I dashed down the hall to her study.

The usual jumble of books and papers lay strewn across Maria's desk, but her chair was empty. She stood beside a table at the far wall, her back to me. I envied how her brown hair lay perfectly in place. My unruly curls always managed to escape no matter how I tried to secure them.

"Taking a break, Maria?"

"Oh, Emmi." She waved me over. "Come see what's just arrived."

The fire crackled as I crossed the room. Maria's study was much warmer than Father's.

Before her, on the table, stood a brass armillary sphere nearly two feet tall. The instrument consisted of a small globe surrounded by a series of interlocking rings. Father had one like it in his study. I doubted he ever used it, though, except to rest his hand on while posing for a portrait.

"Isn't it marvelous?" Maria said.

"Yes. But why do you need an armillary sphere? Don't tell me Father is having *your* portrait painted, too?"

Maria giggled. I smiled to hear such a childlike sound from her. Although only thirteen months my elder, she usually seemed much older.

"No, you goose." Maria gave my hands a quick squeeze. Despite the warmth of the room, her hands were even colder than mine. "Father has hired a new tutor. I'm to study the motion of the planets." She touched one of the armillary sphere's outer rings, shifting the alignment of the earth and stars.

Of course. The astronomy tutor Father and Mamma had argued about. "No wonder you're excited."

"That's not all," Maria said. "I'm to study advanced mathematics, too. Oh, Emmi, God is so good to me!" She clapped her hands like a child who'd just received a new toy.

"I'm glad to see you happy, Maria, though I don't understand how learning such things can bring you pleasure. Studying Latin with Abbot Zanetti was torture for me. Of course, it was none too easy on him, either." I laughed. "Does this mean the old abbot will be quitting as your teacher?"

"Oh, no. He'll continue tutoring me in languages and history." Maria's eyes glittered even more brightly. Her resemblance to Father was uncanny. The similarity always struck me as odd, considering the difference in their temperaments. But perhaps it was one of the reasons Father favored her so.

"The abbot has me translating another section of Homer's *Iliad*, this time into German," Maria went on. "Father wants me to present it at a reception to honor the new governor."

Father had spoken to Maria first. I shouldn't have been surprised. Even so, envy flickered in my chest. I pressed a hand to my bodice to smother the feeling.

"Did Father mention I'm to perform for the governor, too?"

"No, he didn't. How wonderful!" Maria grabbed my arms. "Now the attention won't all be on me."

"I don't understand. You've been performing at Father's meetings for years. I thought you'd be used to it by now."

Maria shook her head. "I don't think I'll ever get used to it." She sat down at her desk. "I love learning. But standing up to demonstrate my knowledge before an audience of scholars and noblemen …" Her voice trailed off. She grasped the gold cross she always wore around her neck.

My stomach tightened. If Maria, with all her practice, dreaded such performances, how would *I* ever manage?

"Is it that unnerving?"

"It's more than unnerving," Maria said. "It's immodest. I spoke to Padre Gilberto about it. He said it would be a far greater sin to disobey Father's wishes."

My stomach relaxed. Only my pious sister would consult our family confessor about such a thing. "God is the one who blessed you with your amazing gifts, Maria. Surely, Our Heavenly Father wouldn't disapprove of your sharing them with others."

Maria smiled. "That's what Padre Gilberto said." She reached up to take my hand. "Oh, Emmi, I'm glad you'll be performing at the reception, too, and not only for my sake. You glorify God with your musical brilliance."

My sister's praise felt like sunshine on my face. If only I could get Father to agree with her.

‗‗‗

At supper that evening, Father sat at the head of the table, as always. Since Giovanni and Alessandro were away at boarding school, Maria sat at Father's right and I at his left. Isabella and our youngest sister, Paola, flanked Mamma at the foot of the table. Little Vincenzo was already in bed.

Father said to Mamma, "Our daughters will need new gowns for the reception for Governor von Traun."

Mamma paused, holding a forkful of risotto in midair. Gray shadows haunted her eyes. The baby she carried seemed a greater burden than Vincenzo had been. Or perhaps she'd been having troubling dreams again. Mamma had the gift of *prescienza*—prophetic dreams. She'd foreseen the Sardinian invasion weeks before the forces descended upon the city. And she'd predicted the return of the Hapsburgs almost to the day, a good three years in advance.

"I have already ordered new gowns for Christmas," she said to Father. "The girls can wear them for the reception, too." Mamma put the risotto in her mouth.

"No, they cannot." Father's brows knitted together. "Maria and Emilia will be under the scrutiny of not only the new governor but also Milan's highest aristocracy. I will not have them seen wearing the same gowns twice in a fortnight."

Mamma took her time chewing. Finally, she said, "As you wish, Husband. I merely thought to spare the extra expense."

"Consider it an investment in our future," Father said. "In order to be admitted to the ranks of the nobility, we must demonstrate that we belong among them." Father seemed more anxious than ever to become a *don*. I wondered if it had something to do with the new governor's arrival.

Sitting beside Maria, Paola asked, "When we're nobility, will I be a princess?"

I couldn't help smiling. Five-year-old Paola was obsessed with tales of princes and princesses.

"I want to be a princess, too," Isabella piped up next to me. "Then I'll wear the loveliest gowns and precious jewels in my hair and ..."

Mamma silenced Isabella with a look then gave Paola a tired smile. "You are already *my* princess, dear."

Paola beamed at Mamma.

"Do not encourage her childishness," Father said.

"But she *is* a child," Mamma said. "How would you have me treat her?" Mamma was careful to keep her tone respectful, but anger flashed in her blue-gray eyes.

"You must answer her earnestly, yet in terms she can understand. Like so." Father said to Paola, "Regarding your question, Daughter, when we are nobility, you will not be a princess, you will be a *lady*."

"A lady?" Paola scrunched her forehead. "But Signor Padre, how can I be a lady when I'm only five?"

I covered my mouth to keep from giggling, as did Isabella beside me. Across from us, Maria looked down at the risotto on her plate to hide her own amusement.

Father, however, was not amused. "You are confusing the title 'Lady' with the word for 'woman.'"

"I still don't understand." Paola turned back to Mamma. "What's the difference?"

"The main difference," Mamma said, "is how people address you. If we become nobility—"

"Not 'if, '" Father interrupted. "*When*."

"Very well," Mamma said. "*When* we become nobility, the servants will have to address you as 'my lady' instead of 'Miss' as they do now."

Father drew up his neck. "There's much more to it! Being nobility means commanding greater respect not only from those beneath us but from those above us as well. After I am made a nobleman, those in authority will esteem me in a way they do not now."

"Yes, of course," Mamma said. "But Paola is too young to understand all that."

"Ha!" Father said. I'm sure he would have gone on if the kitchen maid hadn't come in just then.

~

As I lay in bed beside Maria that night, I wondered just how my life would be different if, or as Father said, *when* we became nobility. We already lived in a fine palazzo filled with lovely furnishings. We had liveried servants who drove us about in our own carriage. And we were being educated by the best tutors in the city.

One difference might have to do with our clothing, as Father had suggested at supper. I closed my eyes and pictured the noblewomen who attended Mass at the Basilica. They dressed in the latest Parisian fashions and wore an abundance of gems and pearls, as did their daughters. Their husbands and sons were always elegantly attired, too.

It suddenly occurred to me: If I were a noble *donna*, Father would betroth me to a *don*, unless he sent me off to a convent first.

All the times I'd imagined my future husband, I'd simply pictured him as tall, with brown hair and eyes. I'd never considered he might be a nobleman. Of course, I wouldn't *mind* if he were a nobleman as long as he loved music as I did.

I opened my eyes and stared into the darkness. I was getting ahead of myself. First, I had to impress the new governor with my performance on Epiphany. The maestro had already sent over three new *saltarelli* for me to learn, with a note saying they were popular as dance pieces in Venice. He'd chosen them particularly with Governor von Traun in mind—the governor was said to favor lively music. If that was true, then mastering the *saltarelli* could be the key to winning his approval, and Father's with it.

But the quick tempo and challenging fingerings of the pieces wouldn't be easy to perfect. And I had only a few weeks.

Chapter Four
Palazzo Riccardi

Snow muffled the *clomp-clomp-clomp* of the horses' hooves as we rode to Palazzo Riccardi the evening of Epiphany. Maria and I sat in silence across from Father. Mamma was feeling unwell and had stayed home in bed. I'm ashamed to say that in my anxiety about my performance, I gave little thought to Mamma's health.

Cold seeped into the carriage. Even with all my layers of clothing—a wool cape, velvet gown, and silk petticoats, I felt chilled. I pressed against Maria for warmth. Thankfully, we didn't have far to travel.

At the palazzo, our carriage was greeted by a footman wearing gray livery adorned with the red and white stripes of the Riccardi coat of arms. Banners fluttering on either side of the doorway bore the actual arms—a golden lion on a field of red and white stripes. The same image was carved in stone above the door. How many generations of Riccardis had lived here? We were the first Salvinis in our home, and since we weren't nobility, we had no coat of arms.

The footman held the palazzo's massive oak door open for us. In the front hallway, a *presepio* stood on an immense table. The baby Jesus in the manger was surrounded by porcelain figures of the Blessed Mother, her husband Joseph, shepherds, and the three wise men. An angel wearing a blue sash sat atop the stable's roof. The star hanging above the angel gleamed in the candlelight. My eyes widened. The star appeared to be made of gold!

After handing my cloak to a manservant, I brushed the snow from the hem of my skirts. My new velvet gown was a rich mahogany color, with a bodice of green and gold swirls embroidered on a cream background. My dark skirts contrasted sharply with Maria's rose-colored ones, but the lighter hue suited her better, bringing life to her pale cheeks.

The manservant held up a large candelabrum to light our way. He led us up a marble staircase twice as wide as our main stairway at home. At the top of the stairs, we turned right. Candlelight danced in beautiful crystal wall sconces as we proceeded down the broad corridor.

When we reached the end of the hallway, I heard someone tuning a violin. I didn't know other musicians would be performing today. My mouth went dry. What if their musical ability surpassed mine?

The servant showed us into a vast salon lit by three massive chandeliers. Candles in wall sconces added to the light here, too, as did the trio of blazing fireplaces. I couldn't help thinking: *This is how nobility lives.*

The servant bowed. "Lord Riccardi will be with you shortly."

Father had arranged for our early arrival so I could practice on the Riccardis' harpsichord. I was surprised, then, to see two men dressed in black standing in the corner. To my relief, I realized one was Maestro Tomassini. The other was nearly as thin as the maestro but considerably shorter. He held a violin in his left hand.

Father crossed the room quickly. Maria and I followed. "Maestro Tomassini," Father said, with a slight bow. "You are here early."

As the maestro bowed to Father, the other man turned toward us. He looked young, close to my own age, in fact. The old-fashioned style of both his suit and his white wig had made him appear older. Perhaps that had been his intent.

"Signor Salvini," Maestro said to Father. "I wanted to give my nephew here the opportunity to become familiar with the room's acoustics." Maestro Tomassini actually smiled as he put his hand on the young man's shoulder. "Allow me to present my sister's son, Antonio Bellini, one of my best students." I bristled at the maestro's words. He never said anything like that about me.

Bellini tucked his violin under his arm and bowed stiffly to Father. "A pleasure to meet you, Signor Salvini." The young man's posture contradicted his statement. He didn't even have the courtesy to look up after completing his bow.

"Bellini?" Father said. "Any relation to Marquis don Vittore Bellini?"

At the marquis's name, Antonio Bellini raised his chin, but he still didn't meet Father's eyes. "He is my father's uncle."

Bellini's square, cleft chin did indeed give him a noble air. I wondered if his stiff posture meant he thought his family better than ours. Perhaps he would be inheriting his great-uncle's title and was already practicing to be the next Marquis Bellini. That could explain his aloof manners but not his attire. I'd expect a wealthy nobleman to wear something more like Father's charcoal-gray velvet jacket, which was cut in the longer Parisian fashion.

Father introduced Maria and me. Bellini bowed to us both. When his gaze met mine, I was struck by his eyes—I'd never met anyone with eyes such a vivid blue, the color of Lake Como on a clear summer day. I felt myself drawn in, wanting to know what lay in their depths. I saw pride and sadness and something else. What was it?

"Come, Girl," the maestro said, breaking the spell. "There's no time to waste." He gestured toward the harpsichord in the center of the room. "I've already tuned the instrument, but its feel is quite different from what you're accustomed."

The harpsichord looked finer than ours. I guessed its reddish-brown frame was made of cherry wood. The inside of the lid bore a painting of gods and goddesses in long white robes dining at a banquet table set on an emerald green hillside. Carvings of nymphs picking flowers adorned the side panels.

As I sat down at the keyboard, my stomach lurched. Would I even be able to play such an instrument?

Then I noticed the inscription just above the keys: *MUSICA LIETA DONO DIVINO*. I knew enough Latin to translate: *Joyful music is a divine gift*. I took the words as a good omen, given the joyful *saltarelli* I'd be playing today. My stomach relaxed a bit. I sat down and played a C-major chord. The clear, pure sound filled the air. But the maestro was right—the keys felt tighter than I was used to.

Father led Maria to the far end of the salon to listen to her recitation once more. In the opposite corner, Antonio Bellini warmed up on his violin.

I said to Maestro Tomassini, "I didn't know another musician would be performing today."

"My nephew's presence is of little consequence to you. He will provide some light entertainment while the guests arrive." The maestro pointed his long chin at the keyboard as if to say, "What are you waiting for?"

I began with a series of scales and chords. It took some time to get the feel of the harpsichord and the acoustics of the vast room. I worked through all the pieces I'd be playing. Despite the familiarity of the music, I fumbled a bit. With Bellini playing so proficiently in the background, my mistakes seemed magnified.

"Bah!" the maestro said. "If you don't do better than that, you'll embarrass us both, Girl."

The scornful way he said *girl* hit me like a splash of cold water. *I can do this*, I told myself. I *must* do this to prove myself to Father.

I began again. When I came to the middle of my program, I stopped and did my vocal warm-ups then accompanied myself as I practiced singing the *Magnificat*. I rehearsed the remaining pieces, ending with the *saltarelli*. Finally, I ran through the whole program once more without stopping.

I looked up. Maestro Tomassini was frowning. "Music is more than precision, Girl."

I resisted the urge to smile. His words were a compliment of sorts. They meant I'd played adequately. Now I needed to work only on expressing the emotion within the music.

But I was out of time. Count Riccardi and his family had arrived.

Chapter Five
Governor von Traun

Count Riccardi had a round face matched by an even rounder belly. Despite his size, he carried himself with the air of a true nobleman. Today he wore a burgundy-colored suit embroidered in a floral pattern of peach and pale green. A fashionable white powdered wig covered his head. Countess Riccardi, unlike her husband, was quite slender. She too was elegantly dressed, in a pale green gown that perfectly complemented the count's suit. I stood and curtsied.

"Ah, Signorina Salvini," the count said. "I don't believe you know my children. Allow me to present you to my son, Lord Raffaele, and my daughter, Lady Gabriella."

I curtsied again. Lord Raffaele bowed politely. He was taller than his father and nearly as thin as his mother. He wore a dark gray suit trimmed in the same burgundy as the count's. Lord Raffaele's wig was dark brown and tied back in a queue.

Lady Gabriella, who favored her father, had on a beautiful brocade of red and gold. I felt grateful Father had insisted on my having a new gown. Otherwise, I might have looked shabby beside such a bright bird.

The maestro called his nephew over to the harpsichord. Father and Maria joined us, too. Count Riccardi went through more introductions then asked Maria about her current studies.

Lady Gabriella pulled me aside. She immediately began twittering away about how happy she was to be home for the holidays—she was usually off at a convent school where the nuns "kept her under lock and key."

I thought of Zia Delia and cringed. If my performance didn't go well, I could be sent away to a convent, too. And not just as a student.

"Father has praised you so highly," Lady Gabriella said, "I expected you to have a halo and wings." The gleam in her eyes contradicted the mask of seriousness she'd suddenly put on. "I'm relieved to see no trace of either."

"Lady Gabriella—"

She placed her hand on my arm. "Please, call me Gabriella."

"Very well then, *Gabriella.*" Her mask melted, and she smiled as I continued. "I was about to explain that you must have me confused with my sister. She's the one who wears the halo in our family."

I nodded toward Maria. She stood in a circle made up of the count and countess, Lord Raffaele, Father, and the maestro. That's when I noticed Antonio Bellini had slipped back to his corner of the room. He sat again tuning his violin.

Gabriella followed my gaze. "That Bellini is an odd one. Do you know much about him?"

I shook my head. "I've only just met him."

"A shame he's so cold," Gabriella said. "I'd like to be able to stare into those azure eyes of his." Gabriella giggled, and I couldn't help giggling, too. I soon learned Lady Gabriella was fifteen, and her father was working on a marriage match for her. No wonder she had boys on her mind! But I had to admit, there *was* something about Bellini's eyes.

When the first guests arrived, Maestro Tomassini signaled his nephew. Bellini put his violin to his shoulder and began to play. Behind my clasped hands, I traced circles on my thumb with my index finger—it would soon be my turn.

Gabriella called my attention to the other side of the salon, where the count and countess were greeting their guests.

"That's Marquis don Cesare Volpi," Gabriella said, indicating an elderly man who was just arriving. "He is one of the richest noblemen in all of Lombardy."

Although the marquis's face was lined with age, he had the gait of a much younger man. He seemed to have little need for the ebony walking stick he wielded.

Gabriella drew closer and whispered, "His son and heir is as handsome as the old man is conceited. Lord Lodovico Volpi would be an excellent match, one I hope Father is considering for me."

"Has your father said anything?"

"Not yet. But Mother has been nudging him in that direction." Gabriella snapped open her fan. "Imagine the wedding we would have. I would be the envy of all Milan." She made a show of fluttering her fan haughtily. We both laughed.

I couldn't resist glancing back at Bellini. His eyes were closed as he focused on his playing. And such playing. I didn't recognize the piece, but parts of it reminded of the murmuring streams of Vivaldi's *Primavera* concerto. A strange feeling stirred within me.

Gabriella tapped my arm to draw my attention to the next group of arriving guests. She delighted in sharing bits of gossip about each person. The distraction of her chatter kept me from fretting too much about my impending performance.

By the time the governor appeared in the doorway, the salon had grown crowded. Governor Otto Ferdinand von Traun cut an imposing figure. He wore a pearl gray military uniform decorated with gold and silver medals, a dress sword, and white canvas gaiters that extended from above his knees to his boot heels. As interim governor of the Duchy of Milan, he ruled the city proper and the surrounding region of Lombardy, extending all the way north to Switzerland. He was also commander-in-chief of the Hapsburg forces in the region.

Four tall uniformed men followed the governor into the salon then stationed themselves beside the doors.

Governor von Traun greeted Gabriella's parents. After a brief conversation, he surveyed the room. The governor stood with his right hand on the hilt of his sword, his lips pursed.

My throat tightened. "He doesn't look happy to be here," I said, my words a hoarse whisper.

"That's just his normal expression," Gabriella said with a flip of her fan. "Probably from so many years as a general. He's really not as stern as he seems. I've made him laugh many times."

"I'll be glad to make him smile."

"Oh, you needn't worry," Gabriella said. "He loves music." Her words gave me little reassurance.

Count Riccardi led the governor to the seat of honor—a high-backed armchair upholstered in red velvet and positioned near the center of the room. Once the governor was settled, the count nodded to Maestro Tomassini. The maestro signaled his nephew to stop playing.

Father appeared at my side. "It is time, Daughter. Are you ready?"

I answered, "*Sì*, Signor Padre," though I felt far from ready. I wished I'd been able to practice my whole performance one more time.

"Dear friends," Count Riccardi called out, raising his hands for quiet. The gesture reminded me of Father, the day Maria made her speaking debut.

As the count waited for his guests to settle themselves, I recalled the hot summer evening when Maria first spoke at one of Father's meetings. He had invited scholars and noblemen from across the Duchy to gather in our garden. They'd chattered away as Father stood on the wooden stage erected especially for the occasion. That's when he had motioned with his hands for quiet.

Father had held his chin high while my sister took her place beside him. He was no doubt confident everyone would be impressed by how well Maria, who was only nine at the time, could speak Latin. Maria, on the other hand, wore a tight, worried expression and clutched the gold cross at her neck. No women (or girls) had been invited to the meeting so I watched from a hiding spot behind our hedge of blooming red oleander. I was there for Maria's sake, to give her moral support.

After introducing Maria, Father stepped down from the stage. My sister looked out at the audience seated before her—some of the most important men in the Duchy—and froze.

You can do this, Maria, I thought, but she didn't move. The audience grew restless. I peeked out from the hedge and waved. When Maria spotted me, I smiled my encouragement. She gave a slight nod, took a breath, and began.

She spoke entirely in Latin, which I knew little of back then. But she'd told me the speech was about the importance of educating girls.

When Maria finally finished, the audience applauded enthusiastically. My heart swelled with pride. My sister had shown them what an educated girl could do!

Later that evening, after Maria and I had climbed into bed, she shared some of the details of her talk. Most of it had to do with the reasons why girls should be allowed to study subjects usually reserved for boys, such as history, astronomy, and mathematics. At eight years old, I had no interest in such subjects. I fought to keep my eyes open as Maria rambled on about the accomplishments of learned women.

Then Maria sighed and said, "Oh, Emmi, you and I and Isabella and baby Paola are so blessed."

"Blessed?" I perked up. "How?"

She found my arm in the darkness and clutched it. "Blessed to have a father who is an enlightened thinker. He told me tonight that instead of sending us to convent school, he plans to hire the best tutors for us. If we work hard and excel, we'll be allowed to study the same subjects as Giovanni."

"What!" I wriggled from her grasp. "I don't want to study any of those things. All I want to learn is music."

"Music?"

I didn't know how to explain it to Maria. I heard music everywhere—in the whispering of the wind and the rustling of the trees. Even in the footfalls of our sister Isabella when she ran down the hall. I felt as though I'd been born to make music.

"Yes," I answered. "I want to play the harpsichord. Giovanni taught me what he knows, but it's not enough." In truth, I could already play more proficiently than our older brother.

Maria was quiet for a moment. Finally, she said, "Then you should have a music tutor." My heart quivered with hope at the conviction in her voice. "I will speak to Father about it tomorrow."

Maria was true to her word, and for that I'd forever be in her debt. Father would never have hired Maestro Tomassini otherwise. Of course, Father had required me to study Latin, too. But Abbot Zanetti eventually convinced him my time would be better spent developing my "stupendous" musical talent. Back then, I'd assumed the abbot had exaggerated my abilities just to be rid of me.

Now, as Count Riccardi prepared to introduce me to his guests, I told myself he, too, must believe my talent stupendous, or he wouldn't have asked that I perform tonight.

This was my chance to prove him right.

Chapter Six
Musica Lieta

With the guests finally settled in their seats, Count Riccardi spread his arms wide, as though embracing the whole palazzo. "I am immensely grateful that all of you could join us tonight on this Feast of Epiphany to welcome our illustrious new governor to Milan." Count Riccardi bowed to Governor von Traun. The governor gave a slight nod but kept his lips pressed together in a tight line.

Count Riccardi said to his guests, "I have arranged a fabulous program for this evening, thanks to my friend Carlo Salvini. He has agreed to allow his two eldest daughters to demonstrate their amazing talents for us. I have no doubt you will be impressed." A murmur went through the crowd. I clutched my hands together.

"We will begin with his second daughter, the wonderfully gifted musician, Emilia Teresa Salvini." The count gestured toward me.

Father nudged my elbow.

I made my way to the harpsichord. As soon as I was settled on the bench, the maestro tipped his pointy chin at me. It was time.

I took a deep breath. My fingers trembled as I touched the keys. I prayed silently, *Jesus, Joseph, and Mary, help me.* I took another breath. Then I played the opening notes of Pachelbel's Canon in D.

Despite my practice, the keys on Count Riccardi's harpsichord still felt strange. Fortunately, the canon's stately *adagio* opening gave me time to adjust. *I can do this,* I reminded myself. The keys gradually grew more comfortable, and the piece's repeating patterns calmed my nerves.

The music seemed to calm the audience, too, for their murmuring stopped. When I reached the end, they applauded enthusiastically. They responded equally well to the Handel suite I played next.

Buoyed by the approval, I began the Pergolesi sonata, the most familiar part of my program. But the familiarity did more harm than good, for I fell into my old habit of playing it too *allegro.* I dared not look at the maestro. He was no doubt scowling.

The audience's applause was not as enthusiastic this time. Maestro Tomassini had said the governor favored lively music. Perhaps *he* didn't mind that I'd played a little too quickly. I glanced his way. The governor's lips were still pursed. My chest tightened.

Then I remembered what Gabriella had said about making the governor laugh. I hoped the sprightly *saltarelli* would at least bring a smile to his face. But first I had to sing. I cleared my throat.

I knew several versions of the *Magnificat*, but the maestro's new arrangement was especially lovely. The Latin lyrics were the Virgin Mary's own words after learning she would be the mother of Our Savior. Her heartfelt words combined with the moving music to fill me with awe and reverence. I tried to convey those feelings as I sang:

> *"My soul proclaims the greatness of the Lord*
> *and my spirit rejoices in God, my salvation.*
> *For He has shown me such favor—*
> *me, His lowly handmaiden.*
> *Now all generations will call me blessed,*

because the mighty one has done great things for me.
His name is holy,
His mercy lasts for generation after generation
for those who revere him."

A hush fell over the room. As I sang the last measures, a sense of overwhelming gratitude for the talent God had given me, however meager it was, washed over me. I blinked back tears.

The audience must have been touched, too, for they applauded vigorously. I said a silent prayer of thanksgiving.

Now, it was time for the *saltarelli*. I took a deep breath to gather all my energy for the tricky fingerings.

My eyes fell on the Latin inscription just above the keys: *MUSICA LIETA DONO DIVINO. Joyful music is a divine gift.* During our rehearsals, the maestro had said the *saltarelli* were, at their heart, joyful. Expressing that joy was as important as getting the fingerings right.

My hands sprang to action. I resisted the urge to play too *allegro*, as I'd done with the Pergolesi sonata. *Focus on the joy*, I told myself. I imagined the music so moving the guests that they stood and danced. The thought gave me new energy.

I took a quick breath at the end of the first *saltarello* before diving into the second. By the time I began the third, I felt myself perspiring in very unladylike fashion. I'd found the music's heart!

When I reached the end, I finished with a flourish then dropped my hands to my lap.

The sudden applause startled me. My pleasure in playing had made me forget the audience. I glanced at the governor. He was smiling! Everywhere around the room I saw smiles, even on Father's face.

Count Riccardi came to stand beside me. "Thank you, my dear. That was quite wonderful!" The genuineness of his compliment added to the joy in my heart.

I curtsied to the count. "Thank you, my lord."

He gestured for me to curtsy to his guests. Their renewed applause sent shivers of happiness down my spine.

When the applause finally died down, Count Riccardi said to everyone, "Let us pause now for some refreshment." He waved toward a long table at the far end of the salon. "In a few moments, we will have our second performance."

Then he said to me. "Pardon me, my dear. I need to attend to the governor." Count Riccardi walked away wearing a broad smile.

Gabriella approached at the same time as Maestro Tomassini.

"That was splendid!" Gabriella said. "How did you learn to play so beautifully?"

I held my hand out toward the maestro. "The credit goes to my excellent teacher."

Maestro Tomassini's eyes widened at the compliment. "Yes, well ..." He seemed at a loss for words. "At least you did not embarrass either of us."

I resisted the urge to laugh with joy. Coming from the maestro, that was great praise. Then I recalled what he'd said about his nephew being one of his best students. I looked around. Bellini was nowhere in sight. I sighed in disappointment. I'd thought he might comment on my playing, as one musician to another.

Count Riccardi, who stood beside the governor now, waved for me to join him. Just then, Father appeared at my side. "I believe the governor wishes to speak with you."

As I followed Father across the room, I hoped for a word of praise or approval, but he said nothing. His eyes were fixed on the governor.

To my great relief, Governor von Traun was still smiling. He didn't seem so intimidating now. After Count Riccardi introduced us, the governor said, "Thank you for a most charming performance, Signorina."

At least, that's what I think he said. He spoke with such a heavy German accent that I had a hard time understanding.

He added, "I especially enjoyed the *saltarelli* you played at the end. They were well executed."

I silently praised God for the gift of *musica lieta*. "Thank you, Lord Governor." I curtsied as deeply as I could.

He said to Father, "I congratulate you, Salvini. Your daughter does you proud."

"Thank you, Lord Governor." Father bowed low. "I hope you will be as pleased with her elder sister's performance." Father nodded toward Maria.

"I can hardly wait."

The governor insisted Father and I sit close by to watch Maria with him. As a servant brought over two chairs, I held my breath. Now, at last, Father would surely express his opinion of my performance.

He remained silent until we were settled in our seats, then said, "Well, Daughter, you've succeeded in impressing the governor."

I waited for something more. What had *he* thought of my playing?

Father gave a small, satisfied smile.

I let go of the breath I'd been holding. *He's pleased with my performance*, I told myself. But was he pleased enough to spare me from the convent?

Chapter Seven
Prodigy

Now it was Maria's turn. She stood in front of the harpsichord as Count Riccardi introduced her to the guests. He called her a "language prodigy," saying, "She is a shining star, much like the light that guided the magi to the infant Jesus on the first Epiphany." The count bowed to Maria, then returned to his seat beside Governor von Traun.

Maria cleared her throat and took a deep breath before addressing the room. "Today I will recite a selection from Homer's *Iliad*. It is the story of Hector, a brave Trojan warrior who gives his life in defense of his city." She turned to the governor. "I have translated the poem from the original Greek into German. I hope I have done the story justice."

Maria's voice faltered at first. Her cheeks were even paler than usual as she struggled to find the rhythm of the German words. She glanced at Abbot Zanetti. Her tutor lifted his chin while gesturing with his right hand. Maria raised her hand in imitation and began using it to emphasize her words. She gradually gained confidence.

I knew a little German but not enough to follow what she was saying. Judging from the bored expressions, few of those in the audience understood. The monk sitting across from me frowned. Behind the monk, a foppishly dressed young man stifled a yawn. The broad-shouldered woman beside him fidgeted with her fan.

Father's gaze was fixed on Maria. He nodded, occasionally murmuring her words to himself. Maria's voice rose and fell then rose again. She had found her rhythm.

Unlike Father, the governor did not nod or speak. He only listened.

As my sister's voice grew more commanding, the governor sat up taller. From Maria's expression and gestures, I guessed she was in the midst of describing a battle scene. Her cheeks now flushed with color.

The monk across from me stopped frowning. The fop became attentive. The woman stilled her fan.

Maria's voice came to a crescendo with a staccato of sharp words. I imagined Hector, the noble warrior, fighting fiercely before dying a brave death.

After the story's climax, Maria's hand dropped. The tempo of her words slowed. I glanced at the governor again. His eyes now glistened. He appeared to be on the verge of tears. Maria's voice fell one last time as she came to the story's conclusion.

The audience instantly broke into applause. Several men called out, "*Brava!*" I wondered if they had actually understood the poem or were simply praising my sister's performance.

The soldiers stationed at the doors seemed especially moved. They applauded long and hard. The governor rose to his feet. The other guests joined him. I stood, too, my chin raised in pride for my sister.

Then it occurred to me—no one had stood to applaud my performance. Maria had outshone me.

Envy flared up in my chest. I pressed my hand against the embroidered bodice of my gown, but this time I couldn't quell the flames.

Maria blushed as the applause continued. Count Riccardi walked over to say something to her. Maria curtsied to the count. Then he led her to the governor. The applause finally died down.

Governor von Traun said to Maria, "That was outstanding! I have heard the tale of Hector many times, but no other translation has moved me so powerfully. And your German is impeccable."

Maria curtsied deeply and thanked the governor.

He said something to Maria in German. She answered in the same language then added in Italian, "My tutor deserves the real credit." She held out her hand toward Abbot Zanetti. The old abbot hobbled over, sweeping the polished marble floor with the hem of his long black cassock. He bowed as Father presented him formally to the governor.

Taking his seat once more, Governor von Traun asked Abbot Zanetti, "How many languages have you taught her?"

"Five, Lord Governor."

"*Five?*"

"Yes, Lord Governor," the abbot said. "When I began tutoring her, she already spoke French quite beautifully. I've instructed her in Latin, Greek, German, Spanish, and Hebrew, bringing the total, counting Italian, to seven languages."

"And she can read and write in all seven?" the governor asked.

"Indeed, Lord Governor," Abbot Zanetti said. "She can also readily translate from one to another."

The governor shook his head in amazement.

He and Maria spoke back and forth in German for several minutes. Finally, Governor von Traun said to Father, "Your daughter tells me she is also studying history with the abbot here and astronomy and mathematics with another tutor."

"Yes, Lord Governor," Father said. "Her new tutor says she exhibits a great aptitude for mathematics in general and geometry in particular."

"I must admit," the governor said, "when Count Riccardi first told me of your daughter, I was rather skeptical. In my experience, the word 'prodigy' is bandied about much too loosely. However, it is clear that she is indeed a prodigy. The first I have ever met. And a girl, no less!"

Envy blazed in my heart. I longed to be called a prodigy, too.

"You honor her greatly by your praise, Lord Governor," Father said with a bow.

Count Riccardi said, "So, Lord Governor, you concede, then, that I did *not* exaggerate."

"Indeed, Count," the governor said. "If anything, you failed to extol this girl's talents strongly enough."

I couldn't bear to hear any more. I pushed my way through the throng of my sister's admirers and into the hallway. I tried to remind myself of how much I owed Maria. If not for her, I'd never have had a music tutor. Yet I couldn't stop thinking of how she had outshone me. The governor obviously considered her talents as "extraordinary" as Father did. Mine were trivial in comparison.

When we returned home from the governor's reception, Maria immediately headed for our room. Father, on the other hand, strode off to his study. No doubt he wanted to begin planning his next academic meeting. He'd promised Count Riccardi that the meetings would resume as soon as possible and that Maria would again be a regular participant. Father didn't mention me at all.

I dragged myself up the stairs. Part of me couldn't help thinking: if not for Maria, *I* would have been the evening's "shining star." Yet another part of me blamed myself—my performance had been merely satisfactory, not outstanding.

In my distraction, I nearly bumped into our maidservant Nina at the top of the stairs. "Pardon me, Miss," she said with a curtsy.

"You're up late, Nina. Is something wrong?"

"The mistress asked for some tea. She's having trouble sleeping."

Mamma. I hadn't thought of her all evening. "Perhaps I should look in on her."

"I'm sure she'd like that, Miss."

I knocked on Mamma's door. "It's Emilia, Mamma. May I come in?"

"Please do." She sounded more awake than I'd expected.

Mamma was sitting up in bed against a stack of pillows. The heavy winter bed curtains were pulled open and the candelabra on both nightstands burned brightly. She held a cup in one hand.

"Come." Mamma waved me over with her free hand. "I want to hear all about the reception." Her cheerful tone contradicted her appearance. Mamma's chestnut-colored hair was disheveled about her face, and the shadows under her eyes seemed darker than ever.

I took a breath to calm the concern that rose in my chest. "Did you sleep at all?"

"A little, until a disturbing dream woke me. I haven't been able to get back to sleep." She set her cup on the bed tray. "I had Nina bring some valerian tea. Would you like some?"

"No, thank you." I resisted the urge to wrinkle my nose. Valerian was known for its calming properties, but it smelled horrid and didn't taste much better.

Mamma patted the bed beside her. "Sit down and tell me everything."

I did as she requested, describing everything from the *presepio* in Palazzo Riccardi's front hall to the expression on the governor's face when he learned Maria was fluent in seven languages. The flame of envy flickered within me again as I recalled the scene.

Finally, I said, "Father was so pleased with Maria's performance that he forgot all about mine."

"Come now," Mamma said. "Your father never forgets anything. And I know for a fact he is quite pleased with your progress on both the harpsichord and your singing. He told me so himself."

"But he favors Maria," I said.

"I'm afraid he does." Mamma patted my hand. Her touch felt soft and warm. "However, exchanging places with your sister would not bring you happiness. Your father's demands are a terrible burden." She sighed. "I worry for Maria's health. She is not as strong as you, Emilia."

I'd never thought of myself as strong. Then I recalled what I'd overheard Mamma say to Father about the terrible throat-and-fever sickness that struck last winter. By spring, Isabella and I had recovered completely, but Maria had remained ill for weeks afterward. She never regained her normal appetite.

Mamma went on, "I have been considering how I have ill-treated Maria. I often scold her more harshly than necessary, especially with regard to her needlework. I fear I've favored you in the same way that your father favors Maria."

I wanted to tell Mamma she was wrong. She was nothing like Father. But just then Nina returned and asked, "Will there be anything else, Mistress?"

Mamma said to me. "Would you like anything, Emilia?"

"No thank you, Mamma."

She signaled for Nina to take away the tray.

When we were again alone, Mamma said, "God has blessed you with an amazing gift, Emilia." She stroked my hand. "You are destined to use it for great things. But difficult times lie ahead." Her brow wrinkled in a worried look. "The dream that woke me ..." Her voice trailed off.

I thought of how Mamma had foreseen both the Sardinian occupation and the return of the Hapsburg forces. Her prophetic dreams had an uncanny way of coming true. "What is it, Mamma? Will there be another invasion?"

"No," Mamma said. "It's not that." She shook her head. "This time I dreamed of you and Maria. She is going to need you." Mamma looked right at me then. A terrible sadness overshadowed the tiredness in her blue-gray eyes. "In truth, you will need each other. But *you* are stronger, in both body and spirit." Mamma took my hands in hers. "Maria's destiny will one day rest in your hands, Emilia. Will you be able to put aside your envy to help her?"

Heat rose to my face. Had the dream told her of my envy, or had she seen it for herself in my eyes?

I turned away and stared at the brass candelabrum to the right of Mamma's headboard. The melting wax had formed an ugly lump on the candle nearest me. I felt as loathsome as that lump.

Instead of answering Mamma's question, I asked, "But you'll be here to help us, won't you, Mamma?"

This time, Mamma was the one to look away, fixing her eyes on the farthest bedpost. "Parts of the dream were unclear." She swallowed hard, then sat in silence for a moment. Finally, her gaze met mine.

"I can promise you one thing. I will help you in any way I am able." Mamma squeezed my hands. "Will you make me the same promise? Will you promise that when your sister needs you, you will do whatever you can for her?"

I hesitated. My own sense of inadequacy fanned the flame of envy already burning inside me. But I couldn't refuse Mamma. "I promise."

Later, as I lay in bed, I prayed it was a promise I would be able to keep.

~

The next morning, Maria and I joined Mamma for hot chocolate in her sitting room, as had become our habit lately. Mamma said our younger siblings had grown too boisterous for her to tolerate early in the day. I had noticed no change in Paola and Vincenzo's behavior. Rather, I believe it was Mamma who had grown less patient. Whatever the reason, I cherished the intimacy of our time together.

Sleet pelted the windows, but the sitting room was warm and cozy. Mamma sat in her high-backed armchair wearing a gown of deep cerulean blue, one of her favorite colors. With her hair neatly arranged atop her head and a soft smile on her face, she looked much better than the night before.

She was particularly attentive to Maria this morning. I might have felt envious again if not for what Mamma had told me about her dream.

"Eat something, Maria," she said, pointing at the plate of pastries on the table. Ever since the throat-and-fever illness, Mamma never missed an opportunity to feed Maria.

My sister took a small sliver of *panettone* then passed the plate to me. As much as I enjoyed the raisin egg bread, I really wasn't hungry. I set the plate down without taking any.

"I understand a celebration is in order," Mamma said to Maria. "Your father told me the new governor was quite impressed with your performance."

Maria blushed at the compliment. "*Grazie*, Mamma." She stared down at her bread then took a nibble.

"And Emilia," Mamma said, "your father told me Governor von Traun particularly enjoyed the *saltarelli* you played."

"Really? Father said that?"

Mamma nodded. "He also said he is planning for both of you to perform at his next meeting."

Praise be to heaven! Father valued my talents, too. I might be spared from the convent after all!

I raised my glass to my lips to hide my grin and inhaled the wonderful scent of hot chocolate. I sipped slowly, relishing the rich flavor as its warmth filled me.

Maria set her barely-touched *panettone* down on her plate and said to Mamma, "I pray Father won't schedule the meeting too soon for he'll surely want me to prepare something new."

The anxiety in her voice reminded me of what Mamma had said last night. Father's demands really were hard on Maria.

"Do not fret," Mamma said. "I shall convince him to wait until after the baby's birth." Mamma placed a hand on her abdomen. "It won't be long now." I expected Mamma to smile. Instead, she winced as though in pain.

"Is something wrong, Mamma?" I asked.

"It's nothing," she said. "You girls go off to your lessons." She waved us away.

I should have known then something was wrong—Mamma never encouraged our lessons or at least not Maria's. But I went to the harpsichord salon without giving it a thought.

Chapter Eight
Quivering Flames

I had finished my lesson with Maestro Tomassini and was practicing a new piece he'd given me when Isabella rushed into the harpsichord salon. "Have you heard, Emmi?" Isabella said. "The midwife is here."

My hands slipped, and I struck a bad chord. "What?"

"The midwife is here," my sister repeated. "That means the baby's coming, right? Nina won't let me in to ask Mamma." Isabella could hardly wait for the birth of our newest sibling. She hoped for another little sister to dress up like one of her dolls.

"Yes." I got up from the harpsichord bench. "Mamma never sends for the midwife until the time is near." Mamma'd said it wouldn't be long until the baby's birth, but I hadn't expected it this soon.

I hurried down the hall with Isabella close behind. Just as I was about to knock on Mamma's door, Nina came out with a basket of bloody linens. She quickly shut the door behind her. "You mustn't go in, Miss."

"Is Mamma all right?" I asked.

"I can't say. All I know is the midwife wants more linens." Nina waved us away. "Now off with the both of you."

Nina obviously knew more than she was letting on. Before I could question her further, a horrible scream came from Mamma's room. "Jesus, Joseph, and Mary," Nina said, making the sign of the cross with her free hand. I did the same.

Isabella buried her face in my shoulder. "Mamma's going to die," she muttered into my sleeve.

"Hush, Isabella! Don't even say such a thing. Come." I took her hand and led her away. "We must go to the chapel."

Our family chapel was brighter than I expected. Despite the pounding rain, orange- and gold-tinted light still filtered in through the stained-glass windows. But the main source of light came from the corner of the room, where six votive candles burned before the alabaster statue of the Blessed Mother. To my surprise, Maria was kneeling in the pew in front of the statue, her forehead resting on her folded hands.

Seeing my older sister calmed me. But as Isabella and I walked toward her, I realized Maria must have learned of the midwife, too, yet she'd said nothing to me. If not for Isabella, I would have been left completely unaware. For a moment, resentment made me forget my fear.

Isabella tugged on Maria's arm and asked in a loud whisper. "What's going to happen to Mamma?"

Maria raised her head. She blinked for a moment, as though coming out of a trance. Then she hugged Isabella. "We must pray for her. And for the baby, too." She slid over so Isabella and I could kneel beside her. Maria pulled out her rosary. With the crucifix in her hand, she made the sign of the cross and began leading us in prayer, "In the name of the Father, and the Son, and the Holy Ghost."

Even as my lips recited the *Ave Marias*, my mind imagined horrible possibilities. I thought of how difficult Vincenzo's birth had been for Mamma. What if she died this time? How would we manage without her? Heaven forgive me, I gave little thought to the baby she carried.

To add to my distraction, Isabella kept fidgeting. She shifted from kneeling to sitting to standing then back to kneeling. It was hard to believe Isabella was only fifteen months younger than I. Despite being nearly twelve, she often behaved more like a five-year-old.

When we finally came to the end of the rosary, Isabella announced, "I'm going to see what Paola is doing."

"That's fine," Maria said, "as long as you don't tell her about Mamma."

Isabella frowned. "Why not?"

"We don't want to worry her, too." Still on her knees, Maria put an arm around Isabella's shoulders. "She's not as grown up as you."

Isabella? Grown up? If I hadn't been so worried about Mamma, I would have laughed out loud.

Isabella put on a serious face. "You're right," she said. "Paola's just a baby. I won't tell her."

"*Brava.*" Maria patted Isabella's shoulder.

As soon as the chapel door had closed behind Isabella, I stood and faced Maria. "Why didn't you tell me?"

Maria's brow wrinkled in confusion. "Tell you what?"

"When you found out about the midwife, why didn't you come and tell me?"

"I'm sorry." Maria's voice was hushed. "I thought only of praying." She gestured toward the statue of the Blessed Mother.

"Why?" I asked, but the word stuck in my throat. I coughed then tried again. "What do you know?"

Maria half-stood then slid back to sit in the pew. "I was in my study," she explained, "preparing for my lesson, when I realized I'd left one of my books in our room. On my way to get it, I heard Mamma cry out in pain. I ran into her room."

Maria stared down at the wooden rosary beads in her hands. "There was blood everywhere." She gripped the beads tighter. "Nina came in soon after. She tried to reassure me, saying the midwife was on her way. But when the midwife arrived…"

"Tell me, Maria. What happened?"

Maria looked up. Tears filled her eyes. "The midwife told Nina to send for a priest."

"A priest?" My legs went weak. I sat down beside Maria. Priests were only summoned to a birth if death was imminent. He would baptize the baby or administer last rites to the mother.

Or to both.

"Why, exactly, did the midwife call for the priest?"

"I don't know." Maria swiped at her tears. "The midwife said only that there was little she could do. It is up to God now. That's why, when Padre Gilberto arrived and sent me from the room, I came directly here. I didn't think to look for you."

I nodded, dazed. *Dear God, not Mamma.*

"Come," Maria said. "Let's keep praying."

We knelt again and began reciting another rosary. I tried to keep hope. I thought of how, even though Vincenzo's birth had been difficult, both he and Mamma had survived. I prayed with all my heart that would happen this time, too.

By the end of the rosary, my knees ached. I shifted my weight, but it didn't help. Maria, on the other hand, showed no signs of discomfort. I think she could have remained on her knees all day and night. She began a third rosary. I prayed with her awhile longer, trying to ignore my discomfort. When I couldn't bear it anymore, I stood. Pain shot up from my knees into my thighs. I offered up the pain as a prayer for Mamma as I waited for the strength to return to my legs.

The rain had stopped. Except for the murmur of Maria's prayers, all was silent. I wondered what was going on upstairs. Would anyone come fetch us if there was news? Perhaps I should go and see what I could learn. In a moment, I thought. When my knees feel better.

I sat again and gazed up at the alabaster statue of the Blessed Mother. Her white face glowed softly in the light of the votive candles. Yet the Madonna's downcast eyes seemed sadder than usual.

Suddenly the air stirred. I glanced at the door, but it was still shut. Maria must have sensed it, too, for she stopped praying. When I turned again to the statue, the face was shrouded in flickering shadows. The votive flames that had burned brightly a moment ago quivered violently now, as though someone had brushed past them.

The hair rose on my arms. Sitting there, watching the quivering flames, I knew. It was Mamma, come to say goodbye.

"No!" I cried out. "You can't leave us."

My voice echoed through the chapel. Then all was quiet.

The candle flames righted themselves, again bathing the Madonna's face in light. The flickering shadows were gone. And so was Mamma.

Second Movement

February 1737 -

October 1737

Chapter Nine
Cerulean Madonna

My new baby sister lived only a few hours. We buried her and Mamma together. Giovanni and Alessandro came home for the funeral, but they returned to boarding school the next day. They seemed relieved to go. I didn't blame them. The pall hanging over our palazzo felt heavier than the black mourning drapes on the windows. Even the little ones were quieter than usual.

Father locked himself in his study and suspended all our lessons. But that didn't keep Maria from burying herself in her books.

I, on the other hand, couldn't even enter the harpsichord salon. I don't know why. Perhaps I thought if I punished myself enough God would have pity and bring Mamma back.

Heaven knows how long I would have gone on that way if not for Maestro Tomassini. About a month after Mamma's death, he sent sheet music for several new pieces along with a letter admonishing me not to let my fingers grow lazy. At the end of the letter, he repeated his condolences on Mamma's passing then added with uncharacteristic kindness, "I commend you to find solace in music—it is the best medicine for sorrow."

The maestro's words blurred as I fought tears. Could he be right? Could music chip away the frozen blackness surrounding my heart?

Before I could try the new pieces, I had to tune the harpsichord. That took longer than usual because I'd left it idle for so long.

When I finally sat down to play, I began with something familiar, Pachelbel's Canon in D. My fingers remembered the keys well enough, but the music gave me no comfort. Instead, the iciness in my chest seemed to expand.

I played one piece after another. None of them expressed the depth of my sorrow. Finally, I began composing a sonata of my own. The maestro had taught me a little music theory, and I'd tinkered with writing music before. But this was different. My life suddenly depended on this work. If I failed, I feared my heart would remain frozen forever.

Day after day, I sat at the harpsichord trying out various combinations of chords, keys, and tempos. Nothing felt right.

Weeks passed. Then, late one evening, I closed my eyes and played without thinking. By shutting out all light and focusing on the darkness within me, I began to find my way. Gradually, over the course of many days, I worked out an opening movement that at least hinted at my profound sadness. Only then did I transcribe the notes to paper.

For the second movement, I again closed my eyes and let my fingers lead me. The music that came out this time was not so somber. As I played, images of Mamma appeared in my mind—singing me to sleep with a lullaby, holding me when I was sick, standing behind me brushing my hair. I translated those images into music as best I could.

In between my sessions at the harpsichord, life limped on. The month of March brought heavy snow and the Lenten fast. Neither was of consequence to me. I never went outside, and I ate only enough to sustain my strength for the long hours at the keyboard.

I began working on the third movement of my sonata in early April. More glimpses of light seeped into the music as I recalled Mamma's soft smiles, her patience with the little ones, her approval of my needlework. Then one day anger flared up within me. With Mamma gone, who would cherish me now? Certainly not Father.

I struck the keyboard with both hands. A harsh dissonance filled the room. My fingers trembled from the fierceness of my feelings.

I clasped my hands together. "I need you, Mamma," I cried out. "Where are you?"

A shadow crossed the salon. Naldo had come in at dusk to light the candles. They still burned brightly, but the light in the room seemed somehow different.

I thought of Mamma's words on the night of Epiphany, when she'd told me of her disturbing dream. She must have foreseen her own death, yet she'd promised, "I will help you in any way I am able." Could she be trying to help me now, from beyond the grave?

I glanced about the salon. "Mamma, are you here?"

There it was again, an almost imperceptible shifting of the light. A log cracked in the fireplace. As I turned toward the sound, my eyes fell on the painting to the right of the mantle—a portrait of the Madonna and infant Jesus surrounded by four angels. The Madonna was covered from head to foot in cloth of deep cerulean blue, the same color Mamma had been wearing when I last saw her alive.

"Oh, Mamma," I cried. "How am I to manage without you?"

There was no answer. I stared at the painting. The Madonna held baby Jesus in a protective embrace, gazing down on him with love.

I closed my eyes. A warmth enveloped me. That's when I knew—Mamma *was* here. I leaned into her embrace. All the anger drained from me.

My hands went to the keyboard. With my eyes still closed, I finished the sonata. The final movement contained moments of both joy and anger, but it ended with the calm I'd felt in Mamma's embrace.

After transcribing the notes to paper, I looked back at the painting of the cerulean Madonna. I pointed the feather of my quill at the music I'd just written. "This is for you, Mamma." I wrote at the top of the first sheet, *Mamma's Sonata*. As I played it again from beginning to end, my tears fell onto the keyboard.

I dried the keys with my handkerchief then wiped my face. The candles on the fireplace mantle flickered. A gentle breeze stirred the air, as though Mamma was brushing past me. Then I was again alone.

Not even death could stop Mamma from keeping her promise. My heart warmed at the thought. At the same time, I recalled my own promise—I'd told Mamma I would do whatever I could to help Maria when she needed me. Yet I had barely spoken to my sister in ages. Had I already failed her?

I got up immediately and went to our room. There, I found Nina helping Maria out of her gown. I was shocked to see how much thinner my sister had grown in the three months since Mamma's death. How could I have not noticed?

After helping me undress, too, Nina left. Maria and I knelt to say our prayers. I silently begged God's forgiveness for failing Mamma and vowed to do better.

Maria, however, did not make it easy. The next day, on our way to the midday meal, I told her of my concern. "You must eat more. You're wasting away."

"I'm fasting for Lent."

"Your fasting is too extreme," I said. "I fear for your health."

Maria gave me a weak smile. "Do not fret, Emmi. I am eating enough to maintain my strength."

The evidence, however, was to the contrary. At table, Maria took only a crust of bread and a tiny sliver of cheese. She finished both, but that was all. My meager portion seemed gluttonous in comparison.

Day after day, my sister ignored my pleas to eat more. I had to find another way.

I thought of Father locked away in his study. He was, no doubt, as unaware of Maria's condition as I had been. If he commanded Maria to eat, she would surely obey.

I mustered my courage and knocked on the door of Father's study.

"Who's there?" Father's voice sounded tired.

"It is I, Emilia. May I have a word, Signor Padre?"

"Enter."

Father, who always sat so straight and tall, was slumped in a chair before the fireplace, staring at the dying embers. I shivered at the cold.

"What is it, Daughter?" The quietness of his voice surprised me, as did the paleness of his face. Wrinkles I'd never noticed before now rimmed his eyes.

"It's about Maria, Signor Padre. I am worried for her health."

"Maria?" Father rubbed his eyes as though I'd wakened him from a deep sleep. "Is she ill?"

"No," I said, "but I fear she soon will be. She has grown even thinner since ..." I couldn't bring myself to say "since Mamma's death."

I began again. "Maria has grown terribly thin. She says she's fasting for Lent, but I believe the true reason runs deeper. She eats almost nothing." My eyes fell on the table beside Father's chair. The stuffed trout on his plate appeared untouched. Maria wasn't the only one who wasn't eating.

"Is that so?" Sorrow lurked behind the fatigue in Father's eyes. Mamma's death had left him as bereft as the rest of us. Until that moment, I hadn't realized how much he'd loved her. I swallowed the sadness that rose in my throat.

Father turned back to the dying fire. "I'm afraid I've been too preoccupied to notice any change in your sister. I had charged Mademoiselle Duval with supervising all of you, not only the little ones. Obviously, she has failed in her duties."

I hadn't expected Father to blame our governess for Maria's lack of appetite. In addition to watching over us, Mademoiselle Duval had taken over management of the household. "Perhaps Mademoiselle Duval has too many duties now." The words slipped out without my thinking. I cringed in anticipation of Father's anger.

But there was only sadness in his voice. "Yes, it is a great deal of responsibility for one person." He straightened in his chair. "It is time I find a remedy for the situation."

Father stood, walked to the fireplace, and took the iron poker from its stand. He stirred the dying embers until the fire sparked back to life. "Meanwhile, I shall take a more active role in household affairs." He returned the poker to its stand. "Tell your sister I wish to speak with her." His voice grew stronger as he added, "Then have Nina send Mademoiselle Duval to me."

"*Sì*, Signor Padre." Relieved, I curtsied and ran off to find Maria. Yet, despite my relief, my heart flapped about like a wounded bird. I couldn't help wondering: Would Father have acted as quickly if *I* had been the one starving myself and not Maria?

I clenched my fist to my bodice at the thought. How could I still envy Maria after all we'd been through? I vowed to confess my sin to Padre Gilberto as soon as possible.

In the following weeks, I watched closely to make sure Maria ate well and took fresh air and exercise. To my great relief, she gradually filled out. A spring glow bloomed on her cheeks.

I believed I'd succeeded in keeping my promise to Mamma. I had no idea then of the perils that yet lay ahead for both of us.

Chapter Ten
New Lessons

After I completed *Mamma's Sonata*, my head began bursting with music—music that required the voices of several instruments, not only the harpsichord. I couldn't properly compose such pieces without more knowledge of music theory. When Father announced our lessons would resume the first week of May, I saw my chance. I would convince Maestro Tomassini I was worthy of such knowledge.

My plan was to be playing *Mamma's Sonata* when the maestro arrived for our next lesson. By God's grace, Maestro Tomassini would find enough good in my composition to want to teach me more.

The morning of my lesson, I sat waiting at the harpsichord, my sheet music propped before me even though the sonata was already engraved on my heart. The balcony doors stood open to the warm spring air. A pair of sparrows happily *creep-chreeped* in the garden.

I glanced at the portrait of the cerulean Madonna embracing baby Jesus and whispered, "Mamma, give me strength."

At the first *bing-bong* of the basilica bells chiming the hour, I began to play.

Bing-bong, bing-bong, …

I put the sound out of my mind and focused on the music, *my* music.

"What's this?"

I started at the maestro's voice. My hand slipped and struck a wrong note. The bells must have drowned out his footsteps.

I played on as Maestro Tomassini set his satchel on a chair and came over to stand beside me. "This isn't one of the pieces I sent you," he said in an accusing tone.

I shook my head. I couldn't speak. Playing the first movement had rekindled my sorrow. I closed my eyes. *I will not cry*, I told myself. *I will let my fingers express my feelings.*

As I played the transition into the second movement, the emotions welling up within me poured into the music—anger, sorrow, and loss blended with peace, joy, and love. But now I wondered if I'd broken the rules of music composition by merging together such discordant feelings. I pushed the worries aside. Instead, I imagined Mamma sitting nearby in her cerulean blue gown, listening with an open heart.

In the middle of the third and final movement, I felt the air stir, not from the balcony, but from behind me. *Mamma.* My eyes still closed, I leaned into her loving embrace. As I played the ending *coda*, a profound sense of peace filled me.

I let my hands fall to my lap. *Thank you, Mamma.*

The maestro cleared his throat. I opened my eyes to see him wiping his nose with a handkerchief. Were those tears in his eyes?

"How did you come by this piece?" he asked.

"I wrote it."

The maestro's eyes widened. Before he could say anything more, I quickly added, "I know I have much to learn about music theory. Please, will you teach me, Maestro?"

"You? Wrote this?" He took my sheet music from the harpsichord and read the title aloud, *"Mamma's Sonata."* He studied the composition, nodding his head slightly at different parts. When he reached the end, the maestro said again, *"You* wrote *this?"* He fixed his eyes on mine. "On your own? With no one's help?"

"Sì, Maestro. I know it needs work, but I really want to learn. Will you teach me? *Per favore."*

"Well ..." He looked back down at my music. "Of course it needs work ..." He frowned. "I would never ..."

My heart tightened. He would never what? Teach me?

The maestro seemed shaken. The pages trembled in his hands. He moved away from the harpsichord and sat down.

Was he angry? I thought not. I'd seen him angry before, and he'd never acted like this. Perhaps he was unwell. That had to be it.

I got up from the bench. "Are you ill, Maestro? Would you like a glass of water?"

He nodded. "*Sì*, water would be good."

I filled a goblet from the pitcher Naldo had left on a side table then handed it to the maestro.

"*Grazie*." The maestro laid my music in his lap and took a long drink. I stood by, still waiting for the answer to my question.

He handed the goblet back. "I have been a fool!"

His words startled me.

Maestro Tomassini rose to his feet, taking my music in hand again. "You proved yourself to me over and over, yet I stubbornly refused to acknowledge it. Simply because you were, you are, a girl!" He paced the room now, his long, violin-bow arms gesturing as he spoke. "I expected you to regress while I was in Venice, but instead your musical abilities advanced by leaps and bounds. Even so, rather than admit your extraordinary talents, I convinced myself you'd show your weakness at the governor's reception, performing before so many important dignitaries. Yet you played better than ever, better than any *male* student of your age. And now, now this ..." He stopped and waved my music at me.

I stared in confusion. What was he saying?

"My stubbornness has cost us precious time. I could have taught you so much by now." His face suddenly brightened. "But perhaps it's not too late. Perhaps God will forgive my hardheadedness. I must speak with your father immediately. If he consents, we'll begin your new lessons this very day." The maestro hurried from the room, still clutching my music.

His words swirled in my mind. All this time, the maestro had been impressed with my abilities but wouldn't admit it. Just because I was a girl.

I'd thought it was because I wasn't good enough. In truth, I was *better than good enough*. Maestro Tomassini had said so himself—I had "extraordinary talents." The very words Father had used to describe Maria's abilities. And, at this moment, the maestro was seeking Father's permission to begin my new lessons in music theory!

I danced about the harpsichord salon, hugging myself for joy. When I ended up on the balcony, I leaned against the railing to catch my breath. The breeze carried the sweet scent of magnolia blossoms from below. Again I heard the happy *chreep-chreep* of sparrows. Oh, what a glorious day!

I didn't blame Maestro Tomassini for dismissing my talents. How could I, when most people, men and women alike, believed a woman's mind inferior to a man's? I only wished God had opened his eyes sooner. Then I wouldn't have spent so much time doubting my abilities. I would have understood that Count Riccardi wasn't simply being polite when he said I played beautifully and that Abbot Zanetti wasn't trying to be rid of me when he called my talent stupendous.

The maestro and Father had been the only two who never complimented my playing. Had my gender blinded Father the way it had my teacher? Even though Father was now considered one of the most enlightened men in Milan, he had doubted girls could learn the same subjects as boys—until Maria had proved it so.

It all started when she was six or seven. Unbeknownst to Father, Maria had listened in on Giovanni's Latin lessons with Abbot Zanetti. She soon knew Latin better than our older brother did.

Somehow, Father found out. Instead of being angry, he let Maria study Latin, too. She did so well Father kept Abbot Zanetti on after Giovanni went away to boarding school. Mamma protested, saying Latin was not a suitable subject for a girl and that Maria should be schooled in a convent. But Father would not be swayed.

Thinking back on it now, I realized Maria's gift for languages may have been what inspired Father to start hosting his academic meetings. I gazed down at the paved *terrazzo* in the garden below, the site of Maria's speaking debut. If not for Maria's success that day and her intervention on my behalf, Father would never have hired Maestro Tomassini to teach me to sing and play.

The joy suddenly drained from my heart. During these months of terrible sadness, I'd forgotten about the possibility of Father sending me off to a convent. Now that life was returning to normal, the threat seemed suddenly real again.

But if I became a successful composer, surely Father would keep me here, to help impress the guests of his academic meetings when they resumed.

Father's voice interrupted my thoughts. "What are you doing out there, Daughter?"

I turned to see Father and Maestro Tomassini standing beside the harpsichord. The maestro still held my music in his hand, but the excitement was gone from his face.

Chapter Eleven
A Fellow Student

I hurried into the harpsichord salon. "Just getting a breath of air, Signor Padre."

"Let us not waste the maestro's time. He has asked my permission to extend your studies." Father pointed at the harpsichord. "First I want to hear this piece you have composed."

"*Sì*, Signor Padre." I looked away to hide my surprise. It was unlike Father to question Maestro Tomassini's opinion when it came to music.

I sat down at the keyboard and took a calming breath. I reminded myself of how impressed the maestro had been with *Mamma's Sonata*. Surely Father would be, too.

But how would he react to the music's feelings? In the weeks since I'd spoken to Father of Maria, he'd gradually returned to his former self. Yet sadness still lingered in his eyes. I feared my tribute to Mamma would rekindle his sorrow. At the same time, I hoped the music might help heal some of that sorrow, as it had my own.

The maestro set my sheet music before me on the harpsichord then took a seat. Father sat down beside him. He gestured for me to begin.

As I played the opening chords, I shut my eyes and focused again on expressing my feelings through my fingers.

Partway through the second movement, I heard a rustling and footsteps, but I kept my eyes shut. I didn't open them again until after I'd played the ending *coda*.

The last notes of the sonata faded away. Then all was silent. Even the sparrows had stopped twittering.

Father stood at the fireplace with his back to me, his left hand on the mantle. The portrait of the cerulean Madonna hung just above his head, to his right. He seemed unaware of it. His eyes were fixed on the empty hearth.

What was Father thinking? Had my music hurt him, or helped?

He dropped his hand from the mantle and slowly turned around. His face showed no emotion. It was as though he wore a mask.

Father's lips parted. I sat straighter, waiting for what he might say to me, but he addressed Maestro Tomassini instead. "You have my permission to teach my daughter music theory, as well as any other lessons she requires to compose properly." He bowed to the maestro.

Maestro Tomassini bowed in return. "*Grazie*, Signor Salvini."

My heart sang with joy—I was to study music theory with the maestro!

But when Father left without saying anything of my sonata, my shoulders sagged. Had he liked it? Had it touched him? I feared I'd never know.

"Come," the maestro said. "You have much to learn, Signorina."

My eyes widened in surprise. He'd never called me anything but "girl" before.

～

Spring brought new life in the flowers and the trees, but that didn't keep me from missing Mamma. I was grateful to have new lessons to distract me.

Corresponding with Gabriella Riccardi provided another pleasant diversion. Gabriella had returned to her convent school soon after we'd met. The first time she'd written, it had been to express her condolences for Mamma's death. Since then, a steady stream of letters had flowed back and forth between her school and our palazzo.

One warm, sunny morning, I took a break from my studies to read her latest letter. I carried it with me out to the garden and sat on my favorite bench under the shade of two tall cypress trees.

May 3, 1737

My Dearest Friend,

Do not blush at being addressed as my "dearest friend," Emilia, for that is what you now are. The few friends I had here have either returned to their families or been married off. Father, however, insists I stay until the end of September when I turn sixteen. He says it is the best way to ensure my virtue, which is vital to attracting a suitable husband. (Why must I alone have such a cruel father?)

I do have some cause for hope, though. Father has formally announced the betrothal of my brother to Count Sormani's eldest daughter. They will wed within the year. That means Father can now focus on my betrothal.

Mother has suggested to him the very match I mentioned to you on the Feast of Epiphany. I pray to Our Lady daily for her intercession that Father will consent. Dreaming of such a future is the only thing that makes my time here tolerable. How happy I will be to have a husband of noble birth who is both rich and handsome. What more could a girl want? ...

Gabriella's question gave me pause. Sorrow had so consumed me these past months that I'd given little thought to my future. From what I could tell, neither had Father. But it was only a matter of time before he did.

No doubt Father would wait until the formal mourning period had ended before resuming his academic meetings. I'd vowed to be an accomplished composer by then. I'd make myself such an excellent marriage match Father would never consider sending me to the convent.

I skimmed the rest of Gabriella's letter then hurried back to the harpsichord salon.

—

I'd composed my first sonata to give vent to my feelings of loss and sadness. Now, under the maestro's guidance, I studied counterpoint. I learned the finer nuances of figured bass and the rules of voice leading in formal composition—knowledge I needed to refine my craft.

In between my lessons, I spent every spare moment writing, studying, and creating music. By June, I was working on a sonata for three instruments: the harpsichord and two violins.

"It is time to hear your composition performed in full," the maestro said one day. "I shall arrange for my nephew to join us at our next session."

I nodded without answering. Antonio Bellini here, in our palazzo? For some reason, the thought unnerved me. I hadn't seen him since January, when he'd surprised me by accompanying the maestro to Mamma's funeral.

Later that day, my surprise increased when Bellini expressed his condolences to me, for he exhibited none of the stiffness or formality of our first meeting. In truth, his words of sympathy struck me as sincerer than anyone else's. I later wrote of it to Gabriella. In her response, she wondered at his motives, saying Bellini had no social responsibility to attend Mamma's funeral, given the lack of connection between our families. Gabriella suggested a personal reason for Bellini's behavior—he was smitten with me.

I told her then, and still believed now, that the idea was ridiculous. Bellini's disappearance after my performance for Governor von Traun was all the proof I needed. If Bellini felt anything toward me, it was jealousy.

—

The day Antonio Bellini joined us, I was so absorbed in rehearsing my new sonata I didn't hear him arrive. When I finally glanced up, I was startled to see him standing at the foot of the harpsichord.

His appearance had changed greatly since our first meeting. He now stood nearly as tall as his uncle. And, like the maestro, Bellini was wigless, with his brown hair tied back in a queue. The black suit he had on today was much more becoming than the dated one he'd worn for the governor's reception. At the time, I'd guessed we were close in age. Since then I'd learned Bellini was three years my senior, which meant he was now sixteen.

He bowed and said only, "Signorina Salvini."

"Signor Bellini," I said. "Thank you for joining us. I am anxious to hear my composition played in full."

Bellini gave me a somber look before averting his gaze. His eyes were as blue, or perhaps even bluer, than I remembered. And their effect just as powerful.

Gabriella's suggestion came to mind. I felt my cheeks flush. *He's* not *smitten with me*, I told myself. *It's obvious he doesn't even want to be here.* I tried to collect myself while Bellini and the maestro tuned their violins.

Still, I couldn't keep from peeking over at Bellini as we played. Although my music sat on the stand before him, he didn't need it. He played his part perfectly without it. I felt honored he'd taken time to memorize the piece.

Of course, that didn't begin to match my thrill at hearing my composition performed in its entirety. The interplay between the harmony and melody sounded even better than I'd imagined. My sonata was by no means perfect—there were some places where the counterpoint lacked balance. But overall, I was quite pleased.

The maestro must have been as well, for he said only, "The second movement still needs work."

"*Sì*, Maestro," I replied, though I couldn't keep from smiling.

Maestro Tomassini suggested several improvements for the troublesome measures. By the end of our session, I had worked out the changes, and we had played the revised sonata several times.

"A good day's work," the maestro said as he packed up his violin.

"Yes, Maestro." To Bellini I said, "Thank you again for joining us."

"I should thank *you*, Signorina," Bellini said. "My uncle has been teaching me music theory also, but my compositions are naive compared to yours." Despite his flattering words, Bellini kept his gaze averted. I wondered again if he might be jealous of my talent.

"Signorina," the maestro said, "I have been thinking. Perhaps my nephew could join in your lessons. He would benefit from the regular exposure to your work. At the same time, he could provide assistance by accompanying us on the violin or the violoncello. He is quite adept at that instrument as well."

Bellini's posture stiffened ever so slightly. Wounded pride flickered in his eyes.

I suppressed a smile. He *was* jealous.

I said to the maestro, "I would welcome his assistance."

"*Eccellente*," Maestro said. "I will speak to your father."

And thus began my rivalry with Antonio Bellini.

Chapter Twelve
Viola d'Amore

The rivalry kept us both sharp. Before Bellini joined my lessons, I'd been so focused on learning music theory that I'd grown careless at the keyboard. After realizing how much Bellini's skill on the violin exceeded mine on the harpsichord, I put in extra practice time. Soon, my proficiency matched his. I could tell because Maestro Tomassini showed no partiality when he criticized our playing.

That was not the case with our composing. The maestro actually praised my work at times, but he only reproached Bellini's. The rebukes obviously rankled my fellow student—he'd clench his jaw in a way that made the cleft in his chin even more pronounced.

I might have felt sorry for Bellini, if not for his pride. And his continued coldness. After playing together for several weeks, he still barely spoke to me. No doubt he thought himself socially superior because of his kinship to Marquis don Vittore Bellini. Well, I'd show Antonio Bellini! I'd prove myself *his* superior when it came to music.

I spent long hours studying our lessons and applying them to my compositions. My efforts were rewarded, for my work showed steady progress. Bellini's, on the other hand, continued to disappoint. He was competent enough as a composer, but his music lacked feeling.

One sweltering summer afternoon, Maestro Tomassini was particularly vexed with his nephew. Beads of perspiration dotted the maestro's brow as he said, "How many times must I tell you, Boy? If you wish to touch the hearts of your listeners, you must be willing to express your deepest emotions in your music, to expose *your* heart." The maestro pointed a long finger at Bellini, as though aiming a pistol to his chest.

Sitting beside me at our work table, Bellini remained silent, his noble chin tilted upward as usual. I wanted to shake him and say, *You have nothing to be proud of!*

The maestro pulled out his handkerchief and mopped his brow. "Perhaps it was a mistake to have you join in Signorina Salvini's lessons. You showed such promise before. Now all the pieces you produce consist of plodding melodies underscored with trite chord progressions."

"Please, Maestro," Bellini said. "Give me another chance. I know I can do better."

"Bah! I know it, too," Maestro said, waving his handkerchief at Bellini, "or I wouldn't be wasting my time on you."

Maestro Tomassini tucked his handkerchief back into his pocket and began rummaging through the papers in his satchel. "Here it is!" He pulled out some sheet music. "I want you to study this piece as an example." He handed the score to Bellini. My throat tightened when I saw the title, written in my own hand—*Mamma's Sonata.*

Except for Father and Maestro Tomassini, no one else had ever seen or heard the piece. It was too personal, too revealing, to share. But now Bellini, of all people, held it in his hands.

Maestro nodded toward me. "Signorina Salvini composed this sonata with minimal training in music theory, yet she manages to exquisitely express a wide range of human emotions." The maestro punctuated his next words by waving his right arm up and down as though conducting. "Study it. Play it. Imitate it. Do whatever you must to learn how to replicate what she has accomplished."

"*Sì*, Maestro."

"And remember, Boy." The maestro bent his lanky body so far over his long, thin nose practically touched his nephew's. "This is your *last* chance. If you fail again, your lessons with me will end."

Bellini's chin lowered almost imperceptibly. The sheet music trembled in his hands. "I will not fail."

Heaven forgive me, but I hoped he *would* fail. Then I could be rid of him and his haughty attitude.

That evening, I wrote to Gabriella:

July 2, 1737

Dearest Gabriella,

My fellow student's compositions continue to disappoint our teacher. The maestro is giving him one last chance. I confess, I hope Bellini fails. I am tired of his arrogance. He thinks himself superior simply because his great-uncle is a marquis. Well, he is definitely not superior to me when it comes to composing music.

Of course, his presence is useful for testing out my compositions. I must admit he is an excellent musician. But perhaps the maestro can find someone a bit more modest to take Bellini's place.

Enough of Bellini. Have you had any word regarding your father's marriage plans for you? Is there any chance you'll be coming home sooner than September? I would so love to be able to speak with you in person again.

Your dearest friend,
Emilia Teresa Salvini

When Gabriella's reply arrived, I read it in the garden, sitting on my favorite bench between the cypress trees.

July 9, 1737

My Dearest Emilia,

When I read your letter, I felt compelled to respond immediately. You must be mistaken, my friend, in your belief that your fellow student is haughty. I recently wrote my mother to ask about him

*(using the excuse of sharing a bit of gossip about how he'd
become your fellow student). She informed me that, despite his
great-uncle's status, your young violinist is himself quite poor.
He regularly hires himself out as a paid musician, as he did for
the reception in honor of Governor von Traun. Did you not
notice Bellini's dated attire that evening? He must have
borrowed or rented the suit for the occasion.*

*So, my friend, what you perceive as haughtiness must be a mask
for some other emotion, perhaps shyness, or, as I have said all
along, affection! I believe he is indeed smitten with you.*

*Hah, I can see you shaking your head as you read this. Before
you take up your quill to deny it, ponder this: Could it be that
Bellini's aloofness is a shield to keep you from guessing his true
feelings? I believe the answer is a resounding yes! And no
wonder, given your callousness toward him. You are too cruel,
my friend. But perhaps your cruelty hides your own feelings. I
cannot believe your heart so impervious to his azure eyes and
handsome countenance. Come, you can tell me the truth…*

I stopped and re-read the first paragraph. I could hardly
believe it—Bellini was *poor*? I'd never imagined he might have
been paid to perform. I'd assumed he'd played as a favor to
Count Riccardi, as I had.

I'd mistaken Bellini's shyness for snobbery.

Or was it shyness? Could Gabriella be right, that Bellini's
apparent aloofness was, in truth, a disguise to hide his affection?

Feeling suddenly warm, I stood and fanned myself with the
letter, but that only made me hotter still.

—

After the maestro's ultimatum, Bellini's attitude seemed
changed. Or was *I* the one who'd changed?

Bellini now greeted me at the beginning of every lesson
with a pleasant, *"Buon giorno*, Signorina." He no longer stiffened when the maestro complimented me. And, surprisingly,
Bellini actually praised my work himself at times.

But my greatest surprise came in late July, on the day of our final lesson before the August holidays. While most everyone had already fled to the countryside or seashore to escape the summer heat, our family was staying in the city this year. Father didn't say why, but I guessed he couldn't bear returning to our country house without Mamma. She so enjoyed spending time there.

Bellini arrived for our lesson carrying his violin case and a second case I didn't recognize. The contents of that case remained a mystery until it came time for us to play his newest composition. Bellini handed the score to the maestro.

"What's this?" Maestro said as he scanned the music. "A sonata in D minor for harpsichord and viola d'amore?"

"*Sì*, Maestro." Bellini's hand trembled ever so slightly as he handed a copy of the score to me. This was his last chance. If this composition didn't live up to the maestro's expectations, Bellini would no longer be my fellow student. My chest tightened. I wanted him to stay after all.

"*Grazie*," I said, taking the music from Bellini. He gave me a nervous smile, his blue eyes clouded with worry. I smiled in encouragement.

The maestro sniffed once, twice, as he studied the score but said nothing.

Instead of reading my part, I watched Bellini. He opened the second case he'd brought and carefully took out a viola d'amore. The instrument looks much like a violin, except for the carving of the blindfolded Cupid's head where the scroll would be. But unlike its cousin, the viola d'amore has a second set of strings beneath those played with the bow. These secondary strings vibrate in response to the movement of the upper strings, extending their sound.

"Interesting," Maestro Tomassini said at last, looking up from the sheet music in his hand. "I can't say I agree with your choice of instrument, Bellini. However, I am pleased you've finally had an original idea. We shall see how well you've executed it."

As Bellini tuned the viola d'amore, I practiced my part. For the entire first movement and much of the second, the harpsichord provided only the *basso continuo*, the bass harmony. At the end of the second, slower, movement I had a long rest while Bellini played a solo cadenza on the viola d'amore. Only in the third and final movement would we play a true duet.

When Bellini had finally tuned the viola d'amore to his satisfaction, he stood and dried his forehead with his handkerchief. The room *was* warm, but it seemed to be affecting him much more than the maestro or me.

"Ready?" Maestro asked.

"*Sì*, Maestro." Bellini raised the viola d'amore to his shoulder. I brought my hands to the harpsichord keys.

Maestro Tomassini counted out the tempo of the moderately *allegro* first movement then signaled for us to begin.

I was immediately struck by the energy of the opening. It was so unlike Bellini's other compositions.

As we played, I was entranced by the viola d'amore's sweet sound, sweeter than a violin's. The instrument's secondary strings added depth to the music. How challenging it must have been for Bellini to allow for their resonance in his composition.

The sonata slowed to an *andante* tempo for the second movement. During Bellini's closing cadenza, I dropped my hands and watched him. The touch of his bow on the viola d'amore's upper strings was gentle, like a caress. Yet, it produced an intense, rich tone.

The sound resonated within me, just as it did in the secondary strings. A quivering sensation began in my fingertips, flowed like a river up my arms, into my chest, and through my body. I fought the urge to shut my eyes and submerge myself in the music.

I regained my composure just in time to resume playing the *basso continuo*. The tempo quickened again when we began our duet. At first, our two instruments played in turns, the harpsichord echoing the viola d'amore, but in a lower register. Then the music changed. The instruments' two voices melded together into a sequence of sweet, beautiful chords. I found myself smiling.

The feeling of water flowing through me returned, more powerful this time, threatening to sweep me away.

Finally, the duet ended, and the music changed once more, back to separate strands of melody and harmony, as in the first movement. And then the sonata was over.

Not until I dropped my hands to my lap did I realize how profusely I'd been perspiring. I glanced up to see Bellini watching me. His forehead glistened with sweat. Beneath his brow, a look of expectation, or perhaps hope, shone in his brilliant blue eyes.

Feeling suddenly shy, I lowered my gaze and found myself staring at the face of the blindfolded Cupid.

"At last," the maestro said. "You've written something with true heart, Bellini."

And in doing so, he'd captured mine.

Chapter Thirteen
Change in Season

To my great relief, Maestro Tomassini decided Bellini's sonata was good enough for him to continue as my fellow student. At the end of our session, the maestro assigned us enough work to fill the break in our lessons. But in the weeks that followed, every time I sat down at the keyboard, my first thought was of Bellini's sonata.

I couldn't resist practicing the harpsichord part every day. Each time I came to the extended rest for the viola d'amore cadenza, I shut my eyes and remembered how Bellini had played it—the caressing touch of his bow on the upper strings, the rich, resonant tones of the secondary strings. Just thinking of it set my fingertips to quivering.

I put off responding to Gabriella's last letter. I wasn't ready to tell anyone of my feelings for Bellini. First, I had to find out if he really did have similar feelings toward me. But with our lessons suspended, I couldn't think of any way to do so.

When I finally wrote to Gabriella, I conceded I'd been wrong about Bellini—what I'd perceived as aloofness really must have been shyness. I told her, too, how his shyness seemed to be wearing off a bit. But that was all.

She replied:

August 12, 1737

My Dearest Emilia,

Your letter took so long in arriving that I'd begun to fear you were angry with me for scolding you regarding your treatment of your fellow student. I'm glad you admit misjudging him. But you say little more. Surely with your music lessons suspended for the month you have plenty of time to write your poor, imprisoned friend.

I'll forgive your brevity this time for I have some delicious news. In just over a month I will finally quit this place for good. Thanks be to God! I will spend my sixteenth birthday in my own home. And what a wonderful homecoming I shall have— Mother and Father are planning a ball in my honor shortly after my return. Of course, you will be invited, as will a certain rich and handsome don. I hope Father will share an announcement about my future that evening. If so, it will be an answer to my prayers.

I am counting the days until then!

Your dearest friend,
Lady Gabriella Maria Angiola Riccardi

I smiled, not only at Gabriella's good news but also at her continued resolve regarding Lord Lodovico Volpi, "the rich and handsome *don*" of her letter. Perhaps I would finally meet him at her ball.

And perhaps I could persuade Gabriella to invite Bellini, too.

———

Like Gabriella, I counted the days as well. Not to her homecoming but to my next music lesson.

When the day finally arrived, I rose early. Nina helped me dress then I pressed her into assisting with my hair. We used my favorite tortoiseshell combs to pull my hair back in a way that would draw attention to my eyes—Mamma had often said they were my best feature. A sudden pang of sadness stabbed my heart. I raised a hand to my bodice. How I wished Mamma was here at this moment.

"Is something wrong, Miss?" Nina asked.

"No, Nina. I'm fine." I quickly stood. "Thank you for your help."

Maria paused at the door of our room before heading off to her study. "You're looking especially lovely this morning, Emmi. Do you have an engagement?"

My face flushed. I mumbled something about wanting to keep my hair out of my eyes.

Despite the extra time I took dressing, I was still early for my lesson. I practiced for a while but soon grew restless. I went to the balcony and gazed up at the gray September sky. The breeze carried a hint of autumn. The absence of birdsong was another sign of the coming change in season.

"*Buon giorno*, Signorina Salvini."

I turned and curtsied. "*Buon giorno*, Signor Bellini." Bellini's smile seemed wider than usual, revealing a dimple in his left cheek. How had I not noticed it before?

"You are looking well today, Signorina."

"*Grazie.*" I hurried to the harpsichord so he wouldn't see me blush. An awkward silence followed. Bellini took his violin out of its case. Before I could think of anything to say, the maestro arrived.

While Maestro Tomassini introduced our lesson for the day, I stole glances at Bellini. Once, I caught him watching me. I turned away quickly, shame-faced but exhilarated by his attention. Was it attention? Or was it happenstance? I had no way of knowing.

As our lessons resumed their normal pattern, I was no closer to discovering Bellini's feelings toward me. But I did grow surer of my own toward him.

~

When the day of Gabriella's ball arrived, I looked forward to not only being reunited with my friend but also to the possibility of seeing Bellini outside of our lessons.

"I don't understand why Father won't let me come, too," Isabella said. She was sitting in a chair near the window, watching as Nina helped Maria dress. "I love to dance."

Maria replied, "I wish he'd take you in my place."

"You need to hold still, Miss," Nina said to Maria, "or I won't be able to finish lacing these stays." Maria had been agitated all day. I had no idea why.

"Yes, Maria, you need to calm yourself," I said. "Come, hold the bedpost here." I took Maria's hands and placed them on the bedpost just above her head. Then I kept my hands over hers while Nina tightened the gown's bone stays.

Nina gave a tug, and Maria cried out, "Ouch!"

"Sorry, Miss," Nina said. "Almost finished now."

Maria frowned. She tried to pull her hands free from mine, but I held tight. "I don't see why we have to dress in these ridiculous gowns," she said. "The panniers are so wide as to make walking awkward, and yet I can barely breathe."

"I think your gowns are magnificent," Isabella said. "Mademoiselle Duval says wide panniers are all the rage in Paris."

"Isabella, you're not helping," I said. "Why don't you go see if the hairdresser's here yet."

"Oh, very well."

"There, Miss," Nina said, patting Maria's back. "All done."

Maria said, "At last!"

"Thank you, Nina," I said. "Would you go downstairs and make sure Isabella hasn't trapped the hairdresser in the parlor?"

"Yes, Miss."

As soon as the door closed behind Nina, Maria said, "And that's another thing. Why did Father insist on a professional hairdresser? Mademoiselle Duval could have done our hair."

"Mademoiselle Duval has enough on her mind running the household and caring for the little ones," I said. "Besides, I think it will be wonderful to have our hair done by a professional."

I pulled out the dressing table chair and sat down carefully so as not to rumple my skirts. "I don't understand why you're upset, Maria. Aren't you looking forward to all the music and dancing this evening?"

"You know I like music, especially when you play, Emmi." Maria gave me a small smile. "It's the dancing I don't care for."

"Not care for dancing? But why? You dance better than I do." I wasn't flattering Maria. Father had kept his long-ago promise to Mamma regarding Maria's health—he'd required her to follow a strict regimen of dance lessons. As a result, Maria was much more practiced than I, and it showed.

"Oh, I can perform the steps well enough, I suppose." Maria eased herself onto the settee opposite me. "But what do I do if a man I barely know asks me to dance?"

"Well, that's simple enough." I stood and demonstrated. "You curtsy like this and say, 'Thank you. I would be honored.' Then you take his hand."

"But I don't want to take any man's hand."

Maria looked so forlorn, I couldn't help laughing. "It's only a ball. No one is going to propose marriage."

She jumped up, her face suddenly flushed. "Don't jest about such things."

"What is it, Maria? Has Father said something to you? Something about arranging your marriage?"

"Not to me." She placed a hand on the wooden bedpost as though to steady herself. "I overheard Father speaking with Mademoiselle Duval the day he told her about accepting the invitation to Lady Gabriella's ball." With her free hand, Maria grasped the gold cross she always wore and began running it back and forth along its chain. "After giving Mademoiselle Duval instructions about ordering new gowns for us, Father mentioned that Count Riccardi was inviting several possible suitors for Lady Gabriella to the ball. Father said it would only be a matter of time before the count announced her betrothal. Then Mademoiselle Duval commented on how Lady Gabriella was just one year older than I."

"Well, that's true enough." I sat down again. "That doesn't mean—"

"Wait. There's more." Maria let go of her cross and clutched the bedpost with both hands. "Mademoiselle Duval then said to Father, 'Perhaps you will be announcing a betrothal soon, too.' To which he replied, 'I certainly hope so.'"

"A betrothal?" I said. "*Whose?*"

Maria leaned against the bed. The color drained from her face. "Whose can it be but mine?"

"Yours? I think not. After all, Giovanni is eldest."

Maria shook her head. "Giovanni has years to go to finish his schooling. I, on the other hand, am already more educated than any nobleman's daughter, and we aren't even nobility."

Maria tugged at her skirts. "Besides, why else would Father have insisted on these ridiculous gowns and a professional hairdresser? He is putting us on exhibition this evening, Emmi. To attract suitors for us."

I couldn't argue with her reasoning—I still recalled the argument Mamma and Father had had on the subject, an argument I'd never mentioned to Maria.

"I must confess," I said. "I once overheard Mamma and Father discuss our betrothals. Mamma said it was time to plan for your future, and mine, too. That was nearly a year ago, just after you turned fourteen, and now *my* fourteenth birthday is barely a week away. It would make sense for Father to seek suitors for both of us at the same time." An image sprang to mind of Antonio Bellini playing the viola d'amore. I blushed. Fortunately, Maria was preoccupied with settling into the chair Isabella had vacated.

I hid my face behind my fan. If Maria was right, I needn't worry ever again about being sent to the convent. But now I wanted something more than simply avoiding the convent—I wanted to wed Antonio Bellini.

"I wonder if Father has any particular suitors in mind," I said, trying to sound nonchalant. "I've been praying he'll choose a husband for me who loves music as I do."

"I don't want a husband, Emmi." Worry filled Maria's eyes. "*I've* been praying Father will allow me to take the veil."

"I can't say that I'm surprised, but are you sure?"

She squared her shoulders. "I made up my mind years ago."

"How could you decide something like that as a child?"

"It's my calling," Maria said. "God told me so in a vision."

"A vision? I don't understand."

"Do you remember when I had the terrible throat illness?" Maria said. "You and Isabella had it first."

"How could I forget? You were so sick with fever I feared the doctor would bleed you the way Nonna Marianna had been bled."

Our grandmother had died shortly after being treated with leeches. Nonno Giuseppe blamed the doctors for Nonna's death, calling them *ciarlatani*—quacks. He said they should never have bled Nonna when she was already weak.

"The vision came during that fever," Maria said. "But it was so clear it felt real. You and I were riding side by side in our best carriage. Outside the window, I saw ahead of us a blind woman begging at the side of the road. She stood leaning on a staff, for one of her legs was shriveled. Suddenly, she began hobbling into the road. I knew she wouldn't be able to cross in time. I screamed, 'Stop! For the love of God, stop the carriage!' Our driver pulled up sharply and we all fell to the floor of the carriage. Father was with us, and another woman, too. I didn't see her face, but she wasn't Mamma. Father cursed in anger as he helped the woman up. When the driver opened the door to make sure we were unharmed, I ran outside to the beggar. She lay face down in a puddle in front of the carriage." Maria pointed at the floor before her, as though the beggar lay there, in the room with us.

Maria went on, "I was about to kneel to help her, but you stopped me. I was wearing an especially fine gown, and it would have been ruined. So I called to our footman and he turned the beggar onto her back. She groaned, and her eyes fluttered open. My heart filled with joy. I silently thanked God for sparing the beggar's life. And that's when God spoke to me."

"You heard God's voice?"

Maria nodded, closing her eyes. Her worried brow smoothed as she said, "God told me, 'This is your calling, my child. To help the poor.'"

Sitting there with her eyes shut and her chin raised, Maria smiled. Her expression reminded me of the peaceful look on Santa Clara's face in the painting in Mamma's sitting room.

I hated to plant seeds of doubt, but I recalled all too clearly how confused Maria had been during her illness. "Are you sure it was a vision from God and not the fever? You were so delirious at the time you thought Mamma was me."

Maria opened her eyes. "Well, I *was* sure. Until I heard what Father said to Mademoiselle Duval. If my calling is to help the poor, why would God allow Father to arrange my betrothal?"

"You don't have to be a nun to help the poor, Maria. Father gives alms to confraternities that do charitable work. Perhaps that's what God means for you to do, too."

"That's not enough." She held out her hands. "I want to be God's hands on earth—to feed the hungry, nurse the sick, clothe the naked, as Jesus instructed his disciples to do."

I stared at my own hands. "I can't imagine touching a beggar, let alone nursing one." The words sounded heartless, even to me.

"You're already living your calling, Emmi."

"I am?" I looked up at my sister. "What is it?"

"I'm surprised you don't know," Maria answered. "It's music, of course."

I laughed. "Music-making is pure joy for me. How can it be my calling?"

"Don't you see, Emmi? God blessed you with a gift for music so that you could glorify him and bring joy not only to yourself but to others, too."

"By your logic, learning must be your calling then, for it is surely your gift."

"I used to think so," Maria said. "I've always liked learning and never minded when Father kept expanding my studies. But these last few years I've come to believe God intends my studies for a greater purpose, perhaps to help the poor somehow. Learning has never given me the kind of joy I felt helping the beggar in my vision."

Could it be as simple as Maria believed: Our calling was to use our gifts to give and receive joy?

We were both quiet for a moment. Finally, I said, "Have you told anyone else of your desire to take the veil?"

"Only Padre Gilberto. He thinks it's a wonderful idea."

Of course our family confessor would approve. He didn't know Father's feelings on the matter. I did. But I couldn't bring myself to tell Maria the rest of what I'd overheard between

our parents. How Mamma, in her great foresight, had anticipated Maria's desire to be a nun. And how Father had said he'd
never allow Maria to hide her "extraordinary talents" in a convent.

"What should I do?" Maria asked.

"Perhaps it's best to leave things in God's hands. If it really
is your calling to take the veil, then God will find a way to make
it happen."

Maria's face brightened. "Yes, of course," she said. "You're
so wise, Emmi."

It was not wisdom that prompted my words. I simply
wished to ease her anxiety. I had little hope Maria could avoid
a betrothal if Father had already set his mind on one.

I could only pray he hadn't. For Maria or me.

Chapter Fourteen
Chantilly Lace

When Father saw us in our new gowns with our hair all done up, he said, "Ah, Daughters, you both look lovely."

A compliment from Father? I didn't know what to say. Maria glanced at me, then said to him, "*Grazie*, Signor Padre."

I cleared my throat and thanked him too.

"*Andiamo*," Father said. "Let us depart."

Seated in our carriage, Father again surprised me by humming. I recognized the piece immediately as one of my own compositions. Even though Father had not yet resumed his academic meetings, he sometimes asked me to play for small groups of his friends. Could my music have helped inspire Father's transformation? The thought warmed my heart.

When we arrived at Palazzo Riccardi, a servant led us to the same large salon where Maria and I had performed for the governor. Chamber music filled the hallway as we approached. It occurred to me then that Bellini might be one of the performers. Gabriella had never mentioned if she'd invited him as a guest.

My eyes went immediately to the harpsichord, which today stood in the far corner. The man playing it now wore a white bag wig and black suit. Beside him, a much older man sat hunched over his violoncello. The two violinists seemed young in comparison, though they had to be at least Father's age. I sighed in disappointment.

"There you are." I heard Gabriella's voice before I saw her. "I thought you'd never arrive." Gabriella smiled widely as Father, Maria, and I exchanged greetings with her and her family.

As soon as Father turned to ask Lord Raffaele about his recent travels, Gabriella grabbed my arm and pulled me away. "We have much to discuss before the dancing begins. But first, let me have a good look at you." Gabriella stepped back and put her hands on my shoulders. "You're taller," she declared. Then she leaned over and whispered in my ear, "and more *womanly*." Heat flushed my face. Gabriella laughed.

Her crimson and turquoise gown exposed her own womanly attributes, which were ampler than I recalled. At least the fringe of white Chantilly lace edging her bodice protected her modesty. "You're looking well," I said. "Perhaps convent life suits you."

Gabriella pretended to be horrified. "You must never say such a thing! If my father should hear he might send me to that awful place again." The gleam in her eyes made it clear she spoke in jest.

"So," I said, "any word on your betrothal?"

"Not yet," Gabriella answered. "But last night I overheard my brother talking to Father about some information he'd gathered in Austria. I suspect Raffaele was investigating the character of my potential suitors."

"Suitors? You mean there's more than one?"

"Of course." She laughed, and the sound reminded me of a bell tinkling. "At least two of them will be here this evening. We invited *your* suitor as well, but unfortunately, he had a prior engagement."

My heart sank. I tried to keep my tone light as I said, "If you mean Antonio Bellini, he's not my suitor. We're just studying music with the same tutor."

"If he is only a fellow student," Gabriella said, "why do you blush at the mention of his name?"

"I'm not blushing. It's warm in here." The room had indeed grown warm with the arrival of more guests.

"In that case, perhaps this will help." Gabriella opened her fan and fluttered it at me. The fan, which matched her gown, was trimmed in the same white lace as her bodice. Gabriella beat the air so vigorously I laughed out loud. Just then, Marquis Volpi entered the salon accompanied by a man I'd never seen before.

I reached out and stopped Gabriella's fan. "I believe one of your suitors has arrived."

Gabriella turned. "Lord Lodovico," she whispered. "I do hope he *is* one of my suitors."

We watched as Gabriella's parents greeted Marquis Volpi and his son. This evening, the marquis's walking stick was of a light-colored wood. Between his fingers, the jewel-encrusted handle reflected the light of the chandeliers. The marquis held his shoulders back stiffly, as though he were a wealthy prince. His rich-looking purple suit only added to his regal bearing.

Lodovico Volpi was much more flamboyantly attired. He had on a brocade waistcoat in bright shades of red, blue, and gold. The same brocade covered the upturned cuffs of his charcoal gray coat. Beneath the cuffs, white Chantilly lace extended from his wrists to his fingertips. More lace adorned the silk cravat at his neck. Although the younger Volpi bore a strong resemblance to his father, he lacked the marquis's haughty air.

Gabriella raised her fan to her face. I noticed then that the lace trimming her fan was very like that of Lord Lodovico's shirt. He and Gabriella apparently shared a taste for Chantilly lace.

From behind her fan Gabriella whispered, "Isn't he impeccably dressed? And handsome, too."

Actually, he struck me as a bit of a fop. He even wore a black beauty patch on his left cheek. To tease Gabriella, I pretended to misunderstand. "Don't you think the marquis is rather old for you?"

"You know of whom I speak." Gabriella pinched my arm. "Ouch!"

Lord Lodovico must have heard my cry, for he turned toward us. He bowed in our direction.

"Look what you've done," Gabriella said. "What shall I say if he comes over here?"

"It's your fault for pinching me."

Countess Riccardi frowned then waved us to her.

Marquis Volpi had moved to one side, where he was deep in conversation with Gabriella's brother. Lord Lodovico, however, still stood beside Gabriella's parents. As we approached, Count Riccardi said to him, "Lord Lodovico, allow me to present my daughter, Lady Gabriella."

Lord Lodovico looked Gabriella over from head to toe as though appraising her. Then he smiled. I had to admit that despite the silly beauty spot, he really was handsome. He stood quite tall, taller than father, and his eyes were the darkest brown I'd ever seen. But he appeared to be at least thirty years old.

He bowed to Gabriella and said, "It is my great pleasure to finally make your acquaintance."

Gabriella curtsied. "And I, yours."

"And this is Signorina Emilia Salvini," Count Riccardi said, "Milan's musical prodigy."

"You are too kind, my lord." I lowered my gaze to hide my pleasure at the compliment.

"And you are too modest," Lord Lodovico said. "Many have praised your musical skills as well as your sister's intellectual abilities. Is your sister here, perchance?"

"Indeed," Count Riccardi answered before I could. "She's there, by the fireplace, with her father." The count nodded toward them. Maria stood between Father and a monk wearing a dark brown cassock. She appeared calm enough talking to the monk, but she no doubt still dreaded the prospect of dancing with any man Father might consider a suitor.

"Come, then," the count said to Lord Lodovico. "I shall introduce them to you. Salvini will surely want to invite you to his next meeting. Then you can witness the young ladies' abilities for yourself."

"Excellent," Lord Lodovico said.

As Countess Riccardi greeted the next guests, Gabriella pulled me aside again. "Well, what say you, Emilia? Don't you think he'd make the perfect husband?"

"He's handsome enough," I said, "though he's older than I expected."

"At least he's never been married," Gabriella said, "unlike some of his rivals."

"Are any of them here?" I asked.

"Only Count Giorgio Cavalieri."

"Count Cavalieri? The Senator?"

"Old Bulldog himself." Gabriella gestured toward a stocky man standing near the refreshment table. I wondered if the nickname was a reflection of his character or his appearance—his round face and heavy cheeks did give Count Cavalieri a certain resemblance to a bulldog.

"He's younger than I imagined, given his reputation as a diplomat."

Gabriella opened her fan to conceal her face. "Even so, he's older than Lord Lodovico. And, as a widower with two daughters, the count is anxious to remarry to produce a male heir." She shook her head behind her fan. "Not only are his looks no match for Lord Lodovico's, the Cavalieri estate isn't worth nearly as much as what Lord Lodovico will inherit."

"But Cavalieri is one of the most respected statesmen in all of Lombardy," I said. "Surely that counts for something."

"Not as much as a pleasing face and a fine fortune."

I disagreed, but I didn't tell Gabriella so. I couldn't help thinking of what Maria had said about Father seeking suitors for us, too. Glancing about, I wondered if any of the bachelors present could meet *my* expectations.

"Are you looking for someone?" Gabriella asked.

"Can you keep a secret?"

"Is Charles VI emperor?"

I told Gabriella about Maria's suspicions—that Father was using the ball to exhibit us to possible suitors.

"It's an interesting theory," Gabriella said, "but it's unlikely your father wants to betroth either of you anytime soon."

"Why?"

"He still expects to be granted a title, does he not?"

"Yes."

"Well, as daughters of a nobleman, your prospects would be entirely different from what they are now. You and your sister are still young, and your father is no fool. He'll surely want to postpone any marriage arrangements until his title is granted."

"I hadn't thought of that."

Gabriella smiled. "I may not know much about music or mathematics," she said. "But I do know how the nobility think." She tapped her fan to her forehead. We both laughed.

"We must tell Maria right away," I said. "She'll be so relieved."

Maria had somehow escaped the company of Lord Lodovico and Count Riccardi and was seated in a chair near the musicians. When I told her what Gabriella had said about Father, she wasn't convinced.

"Then whose betrothal could he have been speaking of to Mademoiselle Duval?"

"I don't know," I said.

"I think I do." Gabriella gestured with her fan toward the far end of the room, where Father stood talking to a tiny young woman wearing an emerald green gown.

"I don't understand," I said. "Who is she?"

"Adriana Grilli," Gabriella said. "Daughter of Alfonso Grilli, a wealthy silk merchant."

"I've met him," Maria said. "He's attended several of father's academic meetings." She stood and glanced around the room. "Signor Grilli is there, on the other side of the harpsichord. The short man in the blue silk suit."

The musicians were taking a break, so, despite Alfonso Grilli's short stature, I had a clear view of him. He stood alone.

"Where's his wife?" I asked.

"He's a widower like Father," Maria said.

Alfonso Grilli was obviously watching his daughter as she talked with Father.

"I still don't understand," I said.

"I should think it's obvious," Gabriella said. "The betrothal your father spoke of is his own."

"*What?*" Maria and I said at the same time.

"It's to be expected," Gabriella said, "especially with a household as large as yours. Your father needs help raising your siblings."

I couldn't believe it. Father remarry? What of his love for Mamma?

Then I remembered—the day I'd warned him of Maria's health, Father spoke of finding "a remedy for the situation" of managing our household. A new wife could indeed be that remedy. A small "Oh," escaped my lips.

Maria's gasp was much louder. "It can't be. Not so soon."

"I'm afraid it can," I said, putting a hand on Maria's arm. "Father spoke to me last spring of finding a way to ease the burden on Mademoiselle Duval."

"There, you see," Gabriella said.

"But why her?" Maria nodded toward Adriana Grilli. "She can't be any older than I am."

"She's at least twenty or maybe even twenty-one," Gabriella said. "Now that I think of it, I'm surprised she isn't already married, or at least betrothed. Her father has done quite well. As his only child, her dowry will be substantial."

The musicians returned and took up their instruments. "You'll have to excuse me," Gabriella said. "The dancing is about to begin."

Maria looked pale. "I need to sit down."

As she took her seat again, I realized a ray of sunshine might hide behind this cloud. "Console yourself, Maria. This means Father isn't planning to marry off either of us right now."

She tried to smile. "Thank heaven for small favors."

—

To my relief, no one asked me for the first dance. Despite what I'd said to Maria, my head still spun at the thought of Father's possible betrothal. I knew the truth of Gabriella's words. Widowers with young children were indeed expected to remarry, but I hadn't anticipated Father doing so, at least not this soon. And definitely not to someone so young. Perhaps Gabriella was mistaken. Even if Father *was* planning to remarry, it might not be to Adriana Grilli.

As the musicians began the prelude to an allemande, I sat up and scanned the dancers—the ladies were lined up in a row facing their partners, with their backs to me. Finally, I spotted the one emerald green gown. The music started. Adriana Grilli stepped forward, raising her arm as high as she could to meet her partner. She was so small, I saw him easily, even from across the room. *Father.*

I slumped into my chair. Of course. This explained Father's strange behavior earlier—the compliment he'd paid to Maria and me, his humming in the carriage. He'd been excited about seeing Adriana Grilli. Now, as he met her in the dance, he was smiling wider than he had in a long time.

I shook my head. Could Father have forgotten Mamma already?

Maria must have been watching Father, too, for she said, "I suppose we must resign ourselves to God's will."

"But how do we know it *is* God's will?"

Maria didn't answer.

Chapter Fifteen
Adriana Grilli

The next dance started with a promenade. To put Father out of my mind, I watched Gabriella. She looked uncharacteristically serious as she danced with a fair-haired young man I didn't recognize. Perhaps he was another of her suitors.

The dance turned out to be a *saltarello*. I couldn't help tapping my foot to the lively music.

"Really, Emmi," Maria scolded. "It's quite unladylike for you to fidget so."

I crossed my ankles to keep from tapping. "Doesn't the music make you want to dance?"

"No," she said. "I'm content to simply listen and watch."

"Well, you may not have much choice," I said as the *saltarello* ended. "Gabriella's brother is headed this way."

I sat up straighter. He would no doubt ask Maria to dance first, since she was older, but I hoped he might come back for me afterward.

Lord Raffaele bowed to Maria. "I am surprised to find you without a dance partner, Signorina." He reached out his hand. "Would you do me the honor of the next dance?"

Maria blushed. "You are most kind, Lord Raffaele. But I beg you to take my sister as your partner instead. She can barely sit still for want of dancing."

"Maria, how could you!"

Lord Raffaele laughed. Unlike his sister, he had a deep baritone of a laugh. "Do not be embarrassed," he said to me. "I have no doubt you were merely keeping time to the music." He bowed and extended his hand again. "You must not refuse me as your sister has, or I will be thoroughly crestfallen."

"Rest assured, Lord Raffaele," I said, placing my hand on his, "I have better manners than my sister."

Dancing the minuet with Gabriella's brother at a crowded ball felt quite different from practicing at home with our dance instructor, Monsieur LeClaire. Fortunately, all that practice meant my feet knew what to do even as my mind struggled to produce appropriate small talk.

"I must congratulate you on your betrothal, Lord Raffaele." We'd reached the point in the dance where I had to circle around him. "Is your future bride here this evening?"

"*Grazie*, Signorina," Lord Raffaele said. "Unfortunately, my fiancé is in Rome attending a family wedding."

"That is indeed unfortunate for me," I said. "I do hope to meet her soon."

"I am certain it will be only a matter of time, given your friendship with my sister. And may I add, I am most pleased a young woman as accomplished as you has befriended Gabriella. She could use your sobering influence. My sister can be a veritable flibbertigibbet."

I stood still, as it was now his turn to dance around me. "I hope I'm not *too* sobering an influence. Lady Gabriella has a gift for making me laugh."

"Yes, laughter *is* a gift." He took my left hand in his right, and we began dancing side by side. "But there is a time for jest and a time for seriousness."

Just then, I heard Gabriella's tinkling laugh. I followed the sound across the room to where she was dancing with Lord Lodovico.

When I glanced at Lord Raffaele, he was staring after his sister with a troubled expression. "Is something wrong?" I asked.

We had dropped hands for the next step, which required us to dance across each other again. In his distraction, Lord Raffaele stepped forward instead of back. I couldn't stop myself and ended up tripping over his feet.

"Oh, I'm dreadfully sorry!" Lord Raffaele grabbed my arm to keep me from falling. "Are you hurt?"

"Not at all." I'd taken much worse spills dancing with Monsieur LeClaire.

The music came to an end before we could resume dancing. Lord Raffaele bowed and said, "Please forgive my clumsiness."

"Certainly." I knew something other than clumsiness had caused him to stumble.

"May I get you something to drink?" he asked.

"That would be lovely."

I followed Lord Raffaele to the refreshment table. He handed me a glass. As I took a sip, he grabbed a goblet of wine for himself and swallowed a large gulp. His mood had changed so abruptly I wondered if he was upset with Gabriella for laughing too loudly, or perhaps for showing her preference for Lord Lodovico.

Lord Raffaele watched his sister over the edge of his glass. She now stood at the far end of the room talking with Lord Lodovico.

"Gabriella seems rather taken with Lodovico Volpi," I said. "Do you know him well?"

"I've had little personal contact with the man," Lord Raffaele said, his eyes still on Gabriella. "However, I did hear much about him on my recent trip to Austria. He was, in fact, the source of a great deal of gossip at court." Lord Raffaele drank the last of his wine and set his empty glass on the table.

"You can't put much stock in gossip."

"Aha, you are wise as well as talented." Lord Raffaele's expression softened. "I am investigating the matter further. I am confident the truth will be known in the end."

"Lady Gabriella is blessed to have such a conscientious brother," I said.

Lord Raffaele finally smiled. "Then she is doubly blessed since she also has you for a friend."

The musicians were ready to play again. Lord Raffaele held out his hand. "Will you give me a chance to make amends for my clumsiness?

"It would be my pleasure."

As we moved onto the floor, Lord Raffaele glanced over at his sister. She was partnered with Count Cavalieri this time. Lord Raffaele took a spot beside the count, and the two men exchanged friendly nods. Clearly, Lord Raffaele would prefer the count over Lord Lodovico as his future brother-in-law.

I lined myself up across from Lord Raffaele, which meant I now stood next to Gabriella.

"*Two* dances with my brother?" Gabriella arched an eyebrow. "If his betrothed were here, she'd be jealous."

I laughed. "She has nothing to fear. Lord Raffaele is a most honorable gentleman."

Count Cavalieri struck me as a gentleman, too. Throughout the dance, he focused his attentions on Gabriella. I don't think he ever took his eyes from her.

When the dance came to an end, I thanked Lord Raffaele and went off to find Maria.

She was not where I'd left her. I eventually found her sitting in a quiet corner of the adjacent parlor. "Here you are," I said. "I've been looking all over for you."

"I'm sorry, Emmi," Maria said. "I've been trying to sort out my feelings. I thank heaven Father hasn't been arranging my betrothal. At the same time, though, it feels strange to think someone so young may soon be our stepmother."

I sat down across from Maria. "Don't you feel a little hurt, too, that Father never told us about her and that she'd be here?"

"Perhaps he didn't know she'd be here?"

"Of course he knew," I said. "Why else would he have been so excited earlier? He should have told us about her, prepared us. Then we wouldn't have been so, so ... stunned."

Maria's gaze drifted toward the door. She stiffened. "Brace yourself, Emmi."

"What is it?"

"Adriana Grilli is headed this way. With her father."

"Oh, no." I sat up straighter. Despite my unmannerly thoughts, I was determined to act the perfect lady.

"Here they are, Adriana," Alfonso Grilli said as they approached. His voice was surprisingly deep coming from someone of his short stature. "The two most accomplished young women in all of Milan." He bowed to Maria. "*Buonasera*, Signorina Salvini. I trust you are enjoying this splendid ball, eh?"

"*Buonasera*, Signor Grilli." Maria nodded. "I must say, I can't recall ever having spent such an evening as this." She gestured to me. "I don't believe you know my sister. Allow me to present Emilia."

"My pleasure, Signorina." Grilli bowed to me.

I said only, "Signor Grilli."

He introduced us to his daughter.

Adriana Grilli curtsied then clapped her hands together like a little girl. "I've been *so* looking forward to meeting both of you. Papà has told me much about you."

As she spoke, I noticed the bodice of her emerald green gown was embroidered with gold thread and edged in gold piping. The overall effect was to draw the beholder's eye upward toward her face. The tailoring created an illusion of height, while the colors brought out the green in her hazel eyes. I had to admit she had a pleasing countenance.

Alfonso Grilli pulled up a chair for his daughter. "I shall leave you to get acquainted, eh?" He winked as though we all shared a wonderful secret.

Once seated, Adriana chattered away without stopping. She held a handkerchief in her right hand, which she waved about as she spoke. The handkerchief must have been soaked in violet water, for the scent of violets soon filled the air.

Adriana gushed about the elegance of Gabriella's gown, expressed her gratitude for the count and countess's hospitality, and marveled at the grandeur of the palazzo. Her incessant, high-pitched prattle put me in mind of a cricket chirping on a hot summer night. When she finally paused, Maria and I were caught off guard. Neither of us said a word.

"Oh!" Adriana covered her mouth with her handkerchief as if to silence herself. But she removed the handkerchief all too soon. "I'm sorry. I tend to chatter when I'm nervous."

"What could you have to be nervous about?" I asked in the sweetest voice I could muster. Maria glared at me. I pretended not to notice.

"Your father hasn't said anything to you then?" Adriana asked.

I continued to feign innocence. "About what?"

"Well, you see ..." She twisted her handkerchief in her hands. "*Your* father has asked *my* father for my hand in marriage."

"Really? How interesting. Father hasn't mentioned anything to me. Has he said anything to you, Maria?"

Maria again scolded me with her eyes. Then she said to Adriana, "No, he hasn't. However, I should think it's a subject a man would not care to broach with his daughters."

"Of course," Adriana replied. "And you're both so grown. I didn't expect ..." Adriana's voice trailed off. She squeezed her handkerchief into a ball.

"And what, pray tell, was your father's response?" I asked.

Adriana blinked at me. "To what?"

Heaven help us, I thought. The cricket is empty-headed. "To my father's request for your hand."

"Oh, Father didn't give an answer. He said it was up to me."

"He did?" I couldn't keep the surprise from my voice.

Maria gave me a hopeful look. I said to Adriana, "How kind of him. It's a rare father who allows his daughter to make such a decision for herself."

Adriana smiled. "Father says he's in no hurry for me to marry." She leaned over and whispered. "I think he's afraid he'll miss me too much."

Miss her? The man must loathe peace and quiet.

Maria asked Adriana. "Have you made your decision then?"

"Not yet," Adriana said. "though I was sorely tempted to give my consent right away. Father tells me you live in a grand palazzo and that your father is highly regarded among the aristocracy. I've no doubt he'll soon accomplish his goal of gaining a title. Then, as his wife, I would be a real lady."

She sat up as tall as she could and waved her handkerchief with a flick of her wrist. "Wouldn't that be marvelous?" She reminded me of my little sister Paola when she played at being a princess. I couldn't imagine Adriana Grilli as my stepmother.

Adriana went on. "And your father is so handsome and charming."

Father? She was worse than empty-headed; she believed her own fancies.

"We do have a large household to manage," Maria said. "And our youngest siblings are only four and six years of age."

"Oh, I *adore* children," Adriana said. "I play with my young cousins at every opportunity. I can't wait to have children of my own." She blushed and covered her mouth again.

My stomach felt queasy.

Adriana soon found her voice again. "Really, the two of you were the only reason I didn't give my consent immediately. I worried over how you'd take to my being your stepmother, given the closeness of our ages. And now that we've met ... Well, you're even more mature than I'd imagined."

"We have an older brother, too," I added.

"Yes, your father told me. But Giovanni's away at school so I'll see little of him. No, it's the need to win *your* affection that made me anxious." Adriana held out her arms. "I know what it is to lose a mother—I was only nine when my mother died, may she rest in peace." Adriana made the sign of the cross before going on. "I would have resented any woman who tried to take her place." Her expression turned solemn.

All her talk was making my head spin. Was she going to marry Father or not?

Adriana was quiet for several moments. Then her face lit up as though she'd just had a brilliant idea. "Perhaps the close-ness of our ages is an advantage. Instead of trying to act like your mother, I can be your friend!" She reached out one hand to me and the other to Maria. "You'll be like the sisters I never had. Won't it be marvelous?"

I saw nothing "marvelous" about having another sister—I already had three.

"You mustn't make any hasty decisions," Maria said. "You said yourself your father is in no hurry for you to marry."

"But there is no need to procrastinate any longer," Adriana said. "Now that we've met, I just know we'll get on marvelously!"

I gritted my teeth. I was beginning to hate the word "marvelous."

Adriana stood and clapped her hands together. "I must find Father and tell him I've made up my mind." She kissed Maria's cheek then mine. "Thank you so much!"

As soon as she was out of earshot, I groaned. "How can this be happening, Maria? She not only looks like a child, she acts and talks like one, too."

"She seems to have a good heart," Maria said. "I'm certain Father could have done worse."

I was not so certain.

Third Movement

January 1738 -

July 1739

Chapter Sixteen
Charms

Father married Adriana Grilli at the end of January, barely a year after Mamma's death. From the moment Adriana entered our household, she showered attention on the little ones. Father's new wife was so childlike herself, it was no surprise Vincenzo and Paola took to her right away. She won Isabella over easily enough, too.

What did surprise me was that our young stepmother turned out to be quite capable at managing the household. She told us she'd had practice helping her father, not only at home, but with his business, too. No wonder Signor Grilli hadn't married her off sooner.

With the influx of funds from Adriana's dowry, Father began shopping for a feudal estate. Such property would bring with it the title he'd sought for years, assuming Emperor Charles VI approved the purchase. Then Father would finally become a *don*, and his new wife, a *donna*. Mamma had shown little interest in gaining noble status. Adriana, on the other hand, encouraged Father's efforts at every opportunity.

She also influenced Father in other ways. He smiled often now. In my mind, *too* often.

Adriana must have bewitched him. Otherwise, how could Father have forgotten Mamma so quickly?

⌒

Adriana's energy seemed boundless. In addition to managing the household and tending to the little ones, she began helping Father plan the return of his academic meetings. The news spurred me out of the lethargy that had set in when Adriana became my stepmother. I rededicated myself to my music. I was as determined as ever to avoid being forced to take the veil.

One evening in early spring, while Maria, Isabella, and I worked on our embroidery, Adriana began telling us of the plans for Father's next meeting. We were all seated together in our stepmother's sitting room. The room bore little resemblance to when Mamma was here. Adriana had brought in all new furniture and changed the wall coverings. Even the portrait of the peaceful Santa Clara was gone. I resented our stepmother for taking away so many mementos of Mamma.

From her seat near the window, Adriana announced, "I've finally convinced your father to allow women guests at his meetings."

"How did you ever manage that?" Maria asked.

"It was easy," Adriana said. "When he showed me the guest list, I simply asked why none of the gentlemen's wives were included. Your father said, 'Well, I've never invited them before.'" Adriana mimicked Father's voice, making Maria and Isabella laugh. I didn't find it at all funny.

Adriana went on. "So then I replied, 'Why would *you*, an advocate for women's education, ban women from witnessing the talents of the two most accomplished young women in all Milan, especially when they happen to be your own daughters?' For a moment, your father was dumbstruck. Then he said, 'Well, I suppose you have a point.'" Adriana smiled, pleased with herself. "And that was that."

It was my turn to be dumbstruck. Beneath her petite appearance and childlike demeanor, our stepmother was a cunning woman.

Of course, Maria didn't see it. She said, "How generous of you, Signora Madre."

"I'm ashamed to confess that it's not generosity, but self-ishness, that inspired me," Adriana said. "I want to attend the meeting myself, to witness your performances."

"May I come, too?" Isabella asked.

"I don't see why not," Adriana said. She chattered on as she resumed working on her embroidery project, a pillow cover in the greens and golds of her bedroom, which she'd also redecorated.

She suddenly cried, "Ouch!"

Startled, I looked up to see Adriana sucking her finger. She must have pricked herself. I covered my mouth and coughed to hide my smile.

"Perhaps I've been too ambitious in choosing this piece," Adriana said. "I'm rather inept at needlework. How is it you girls are so proficient?"

Maria laughed. "I doubt anyone is clumsier at needlework than I. Emilia can attest to how often Mamma scolded me about it."

"Yes," I said, "in this very room." But Mamma had praised *my* needlework here and my musical talent, too. The memory brought unexpected tears. I squeezed my eyes shut to keep the tears from falling onto my embroidery.

My sadness turned to anger. Adriana wasn't going to be satisfied with simply ridding Mamma's mementos from these rooms. She intended to chase Mamma herself from our hearts. Well, Maria and the others might give in to our stepmother's charms, but I never would.

"Excuse me." I stood and gathered my things.

"Is something wrong?" Adriana asked.

"Nothing rest won't help," I answered as I left the room.

I recounted the scene to Gabriella the next time I saw her. We were strolling through the gardens of Palazzo Riccardi. Delicate white blossoms covered the pear trees, their sweet scent perfuming the air. The hum of bees flitting among the flowers provided the *basso continuo* to our conversation.

"It's natural to dislike your stepmother," Gabriella said as we walked. "What is *unnatural* is how the rest of your family has so readily accepted her. I don't imagine to be as fortunate if I should marry Count Cavalieri."

"Has your father made a decision yet?"

"He has eliminated all the suitors save two," Gabriella said. "Count Cavalieri and Lord Lodovico. Father and my brother both favor the count. Mother is convinced either would make a suitable match, but she has agreed, for my sake, to entreat Father to choose Lord Lodovico."

"Have your brother's inquiries revealed anything about Lord Lodovico?"

"Only that he's partial to wine, women, and gambling," Gabriella said with a laugh.

"Doesn't that trouble you?"

"I'd be more worried if a rich, handsome nobleman like him had no such vices," Gabriella said. "I'm confident marriage will reform him."

As we walked on, the breeze stirred the tree branches. White pear blossoms drifted down like snow. Several landed on our hair and shoulders.

"When will your father decide?" I asked.

"I don't know." Gabriella brushed the blossoms from her shoulder. "He can't wait much longer. Count Cavalieri keeps pressing for an answer."

"Do you think the count will tire of waiting and find someone else?"

Gabriella smiled. "That is my hope."

"And what of Lord Lodovico? Is he anxious for an answer, too?"

"If he is, Father hasn't mentioned it," Gabriella said. "But I have a plan to spur Lord Lodovico to action."

"You do?"

"Yes, and it involves you, my dear friend."

"Me?" I said. "How?"

Gabriella took my arm in hers. "Lord Lodovico is attending your father's next academic meeting, is he not? And Count Cavalieri, too?

"They're both invited."

"Well, thanks to your *marvelous* stepmother, I will be there as well," Gabriella said. "And I intend to use the evening as an opportunity to make Lord Lodovico jealous. I will feign favoritism toward the count. Your task will be to urge Lord Lodovico to press his own case with my father so as not to lose me for himself."

"Isn't that risky, Gabriella? What if Lord Lodovico doesn't rise to the challenge?"

Gabriella let go of my arm. "Well, then he would not be worthy of me."

I did not relish the role Gabriella was asking me to play. But I had no choice.

Chapter Seventeen
Father's Meeting

In the months following Father's marriage to Adriana, the maestro received several new commissions. That meant our lessons together—and my opportunities to see Bellini—became less frequent.

I continued to watch for signs of Bellini's feelings toward me. Some days, I'd look up from the harpsichord to find him staring at me. He'd blush and turn away immediately, convincing me he was indeed smitten with me, as Gabriella would say. But later, when I thought back on how little we actually said to each other, the idea that he cared for me seemed a foolish daydream.

Of one thing I was certain—Bellini's music had blossomed like the flowers that now filled our garden. His compositions were no longer boring or trite. The energy he'd first expressed in his sonata for the harpsichord and viola d'amore had become his signature. But underneath that energy, his music was often imbued was a sense of tenderness and vulnerability that spoke directly to my heart. I wondered if my music ever touched him in the same way.

As the end of May drew near, new concerns distracted me from thoughts of Bellini. I had to prepare to perform at Father's next meeting—the first since Mamma's death. I'd never played my own compositions in public before, but that wasn't all that worried me. Over a year had passed since I'd confessed my envy of Maria to Padre Gilberto. As part of my penance, I'd resolved not to repeat my sin. Until now, that resolve had been easy to keep, for I'd had little temptation. Father had been too preoccupied—first by his sorrow, then his remarriage, and finally his pursuit of a title—to take much notice of Maria or me. Now, with both of us performing at his meeting, I feared my envy would be rekindled.

At the last rehearsal before Father's meeting, Maestro Tomassini said, "Forgive me, Signorina, but I must leave early today for an appointment." The maestro quickly packed his things. "I will see you tomorrow evening. Rest easy tonight— your performance will surely be well-received."

"*Grazie*, Maestro."

To my surprise, Bellini didn't hurry out after his uncle. Instead, he came over to where I sat at the harpsichord. "Is something wrong, Signorina? You seem troubled."

He'd noticed. I stared at my hands in my lap. "I confess, I'm anxious about tomorrow evening. There will be many important dignitaries at the meeting, people my father especially wants to impress."

"You've no need to worry," Bellini said. "I have no doubt they'll be awed by both your playing and your music."

"You are too kind."

"It isn't kindness," he said. "I speak only the truth."

Something in his voice made me look up.

"And, in truth," he went on, "I must say it has been a privilege and an honor to be your fellow student. I've learned much from you." He smiled and I caught sight of his elusive dimple. "I'll be sad when our lessons together end."

My heart quickened. "Why must they end? Has something happened?"

"Not yet," he said. "But it's inevitable. I'll soon turn eighteen. I must think of the future." His gaze met mine. The deep blue of his eyes reminded me again of Lake Como on a summer day. Today something new lay in their azure depths.

Surely, he was about to confess his feelings for me. I smiled my encouragement.

But when Bellini finally spoke, he said only, "I must be going, too. I'll see you tomorrow evening."

My disappointment stuck in my throat. I nodded without speaking.

After he left, I realized my hands were trembling. I pressed them to my bodice.

Bellini had spoken so calmly of quitting our lessons. Perhaps I'd misread his feelings. Perhaps Bellini didn't care for me after all, or at least not in the way I'd hoped.

I looked at the portrait of the cerulean Madonna. Swallowing the lump in my throat, I raised my hands to the keyboard and began playing *Mamma's Sonata*.

———

Adriana had ordered the harpsichord salon decorated with violets for Father's meeting. Pots of the dainty purple flowers—Adriana's favorite—stood scattered about the room. Their soft scent filled the air. Adriana even wore several sprigs in her black hair. Her hairdresser had arranged them in a way that made my tiny stepmother appear taller. And it was no coincidence that the color of Adriana's silk gown matched the purple flowers.

Isabella, Maria, and I stood beside Adriana and Father to greet the guests. My stepmother had insisted my sisters and I dress in pale colors. Now I understood why. As the guests entered the salon, their eyes were immediately drawn to Adriana. How clever of her.

Maestro Tomassini and Antonio Bellini arrived before anyone else. While the maestro was dressed in formal attire, Bellini had on the same black suit he always wore to our lessons. But that didn't keep my heart from leaping at the sight of him. His gaze held mine for a long moment as we exchanged greetings. Then he excused himself to tune his violin.

When the Riccardis arrived, Gabriella hurried past her parents to embrace me. "Is Lord Lodovico here yet?" she whispered.

"No, I'm not anxious at all," I said to tease her. "How kind of you to ask."

"Oh, I suppose that *was* rather thoughtless. Forgive me." She pulled me aside. "I've been thinking of my plans so much I forgot about tonight being your debut as a composer. How do you feel, really?"

"Like a flock of butterflies are trapped in my belly."

"I don't understand why," she said. "I have no doubt everyone will be awed by both your playing and your music."

"Funny, those were Bellini's exact words to me at our last rehearsal."

"Well then, it must be true." A familiar gleam appeared in her eyes as she said, "So tell me, how is your suitor? Is he here?"

"He's there, tuning his violin." I gestured toward Bellini, adding quickly, "And he's *not* my suitor. He's a fellow musician who will be performing with me this evening." Bellini glanced up just as I spoke. He smiled, then went back to tuning his instrument.

"Ah, he's grown taller and handsomer since I last saw him," Gabriella said. "But if he is only a 'fellow musician,' why does he have eyes for you and no one else."

Oh, if only her words were true. "Stop being silly, Gabriella." I scanned the room for something to distract her. "Oh, look. The man of your dreams has arrived."

Gabriella watched with me as Lodovico Volpi entered the salon, alone.

"I wonder where his father is?" I said.

"The marquis is incredibly pompous," Gabriella said. "He likely thinks this meeting is beneath him."

"Beneath him? Why?"

"On account of your father not having a title. But I, for one, am glad the marquis isn't here. His absence will make it easier to attract Lord Lodovico's attention." Gabriella glanced around the room. "Has Count Cavalieri arrived?"

"Yes. He's there, by the fireplace." I nodded toward him. "Your father appears to be headed in his direction."

"*Perfetto*," Gabriella said. "Let's join them."

"You go ahead," I said. "I need to continue greeting the guests."

"Oh, that's even better," Gabriella said. "When you speak to Lord Lodovico, make sure he notices where I am." She strode toward the fireplace before I could ask how, exactly, she expected me to do that nonchalantly.

I returned to my post beside Maria just as Adriana said to Lodovico Volpi, "Welcome to our humble home. We're so happy you could join us. But the marquis isn't with you?"

"I am afraid not, Signora." Volpi bowed. "He instructed me to express his deepest regrets."

Father's brow furrowed, but he kept his lips pressed together.

Volpi said to Maria, "*I* wouldn't have missed your presentation for the world, Signorina. I understand you will be discussing the theories of that Englishman, Sir Isaac Newton?"

"I fear my talk will only bore you, Sir," Maria said. "The real treat tonight will be my sister's music." She put her hand on my arm.

Lord Lodovico tilted his head and smiled. "I doubt you could ever bore me, Signorina. However, I trust I will enjoy your sister's performance as well." Lord Lodovico bowed to me.

I curtsied. "I hope not to disappoint you, Lord Lodovico."

"And whom have we here?" Upon seeing Isabella, Volpi began stroking the black beauty patch on his left cheek.

"Forgive my poor manners," I said. "May I present my younger sister, Isabella."

"How enchanting." Volpi bowed. "Will you be performing as well this evening, Signorina Isabella?"

"No, Lord Lodovico," Isabella replied. "I am not as talented as my sisters."

"Whatever you may lack in talent, Signorina, you more than make up for in beauty."

Isabella blushed, covering her face with her fan. Was he flirting with my little sister?

I had to steer Volpi's attention to Gabriella. "I hope you'll enjoy visiting with the other guests until it's time for Maria's performance, Sir. Count Riccardi and Lady Gabriella are there, by the fireplace." I gestured toward them.

"Yes," Lord Lodovico said. "I see they're with Old Bull-dog." Gabriella's eyes were fixed on Count Cavalieri, who was speaking directly to her. Gabriella laughed, but the sound lacked its usual bell-like tinkle, a sure sign it was forced. Apparently, Count Cavalieri couldn't tell, for he smiled broadly at her.

"Lady Gabriella is obviously enjoying herself." Lord Lodovico seemed unperturbed. Gabriella's plan to make him jealous wasn't working.

Before I could say anything more, Father said, "Excuse me, Daughters." He motioned to two guests who had just arrived. "I would like to present you to Duke von Hildebrandt and his daughter, Lady Elizabeth. They are visiting from Vienna."

The duke was an extraordinarily large man—taller than the maestro and almost as round as Count Riccardi. In compari-son, his golden-haired daughter seemed slender. She too was tall, but that didn't keep her from wearing her hair piled high atop her head. The green and red jewels studded throughout her coiffure twinkled in the candlelight as she nodded toward us. Lady Elizabeth quite overshadowed my tiny stepmother. Perhaps that was why Adriana remained uncharacteristically si-lent.

Maria and I curtsied deeply as we exchanged greetings with the duke and his daughter.

Then Father said, "Your Excellency, do you know Lord Lodovico?"

"Yes, indeed," Duke von Hildebrandt said. "We met during his visit to Austria last fall." The duke spoke perfect Italian, though with a heavy German accent.

Lord Lodovico bowed to Duke von Hildebrandt. "What a pleasant surprise to see you and your lovely daughter here in Milan."

The duke said, "As I recall, Volpi, you were embarking on a hunting trip the day after I last saw you. How did the hunt go?"

"You have an extraordinary memory, Your Excellency. Yes, I did go on the hunt. However, it was a most disappointing outing. I let my prey slip away."

Lord Lodovico fixed his eyes on Lady Elizabeth. "I hope to have better fortune here in my homeland." He tilted his head at the duke's daughter and smiled.

Father said, "My lady, is this your first trip to Lombardy?"

"Yes, it is," Lady Elizabeth answered. "And I am pleased to be able to attend your meeting this evening." Her accent was much less pronounced than the duke's. "I have heard remarkable things about your two daughters. I hope to learn much from them."

"You will excuse us, then," Father said. "It is time to make our preparations. I will leave you in my wife's care." Father gestured to Adriana. Then he signaled for Maria and me to follow him.

As we left the room, I glanced over at Gabriella. She'd moved away from Count Cavalieri and was watching Lord Lodovico. His attention was entirely focused on Lady Elizabeth.

If anyone was jealous, it wasn't Lord Lodovico.

Chapter Eighteen
Colors of the Rainbow

The presence of women in the audience wasn't the only thing that made this meeting unusual. It was also the first time I'd be performing after Maria. I'd suggested the change to Father for Maria's sake. She was even more anxious than usual because her presentation tonight included a demonstration. And afterward, she'd be tested in her first public debate.

Maria took her place beside the harpsichord and forced a smile as Father described the evening's program to his guests. Maria would be discussing Sir Isaac Newton's theories on Optics—the study of the nature of light. She would speak in Italian instead of Latin, for the benefit of the women present.

Maria began hesitantly but was soon swept up in her passion for the topic. Her enthusiasm was contagious. The audience sat in rapt attention, especially the women. Newton's theories were all the rage, thanks to the popularity of Francesco Algarotti's book *Newtonianism for the Ladies*.

At the end of her talk, Maria said, "I will now demonstrate one of the experiments that led Sir Isaac Newton to his conclusions. Please come with me."

Maria signaled to Naldo, who stood in a corner. He picked up a candelabrum bearing five lit candles and led us into the adjacent parlor. The drapes had been drawn tight so the room was completely dark except for the light of the candelabrum. Naldo set the candelabrum on a table in the center of the parlor.

When she reached the table, Maria said, "Come close, everyone." She waved the guests toward her. "So you will have a clear view."

Maria reached into her pocket and pulled out a large triangular crystal. "I have here a prism." She lifted the crystal prism above her head for everyone to see. A murmur went through the guests. "Now, observe."

Maria signaled to Naldo to raise the candelabrum. She then held the prism before the lit candles. Suddenly, a rainbow appeared high on the far wall.

The guests gasped in astonishment. Someone said, "Amazing."

Next to me, Gabriella said, "How pretty."

"What magic is this?" someone asked.

"It's not magic." The prism trembled slightly in Maria's hand as she spoke, making the rainbow dance on the wall. "Newton deduced the crystal separates the light into its constituent colors. What the human eye sees as white light is actually made up of all the colors of the rainbow."

"May I try?" Count Riccardi asked.

"Of course," Maria said.

The count and several other guests took turns with the crystal. All produced the same results. "Fascinating," Lord Lodovico said.

When the demonstration was over, we returned to the harpsichord salon. There Maria debated some of Newton's other ideas with her tutor. As they argued away, my thoughts wandered to Gabriella. She was now seated between Lord Lodovico and Count Cavalieri. She showed little interest in either the debate or the count. Instead, she kept trying to catch Lord Lodovico's attention. But he was focused on Lady Elizabeth, who was seated on his other side. At first, Lady Elizabeth waved him away and tried to listen to the debate. Eventually, though, he said something that made her cover her mouth to keep from laughing. They were soon deep in conversation.

Gabriella's back stiffened. She raised her chin and rested a hand on Count Cavalieri's forearm. When he looked at her, she smiled sweetly. His face beamed.

The debate came to a close. Everyone applauded enthusiastically. Maria sighed, obviously relieved. Father said something in her ear, no doubt a compliment. I averted my eyes to avoid the sin of envy.

I had to prepare for my own performance now. Watching Gabriella had distracted me from my anxiety. As I made my way to the harpsichord, the butterflies in my stomach resumed their fluttering with full force. I worried at how the guests would respond to my music. Would they consider it impudent for a woman (in truth, a girl, for I was not yet fifteen) to consider herself a composer?

When I reached the harpsichord, Bellini bent down and whispered, "You have nothing to fear, Signorina. Everyone will be touched by the beauty of your music." The reassurance in his eyes melted my anxiety.

I settled myself at the keyboard. After a brief introduction by Father, I began with one of my most recent compositions—a cheerful sonata in C major. Next, I accompanied myself while singing a hymn in honor of the Blessed Mother. Finally, the maestro and Bellini joined me in performing a pair of sonatas I'd written for the harpsichord and two violins.

As usual, I lost myself in the music and completely forgot I was playing for an audience. At the sound of applause, I looked up. Everyone was on their feet. My heart thrilled at their shouts of "*Brava! Brava*, Signorina!" Even so, I wondered—were they impressed by my music or by the fact it had been composed by a female?

The maestro signaled for me to stand. I got up and curtsied then gestured toward the maestro and Bellini. The applause grew even louder. Bellini smiled at me. I smiled back. All sound faded away. It was as though we were the only two people in the room.

Someone tapped my shoulder. "My compliments, Signorina!" I turned to Count Riccardi and his wife. "What a most wonderful performance!" the count said. "Your playing was phenomenal, as always. And your compositions—"

The countess finished his sentence, "are simply splendid!"

Adriana and Father joined us. Adriana said to Countess Riccardi, "I agree!"

I waited for Father to say something, but Gabriella appeared then. "That was fantastic," she said. "I wish I were but half as talented!"

Lady Elizabeth approached with Lord Lodovico at her elbow. Gabriella squeezed my arm.

"I must confess," Lady Elizabeth said to me. "I truly did not expect your performance to live up to all the praise I had heard. Yet your skill actually exceeds your reputation. You are a most gifted musician and composer."

I wanted to dislike Lady Elizabeth for Gabriella's sake. But the lady's smile seemed so genuine that I couldn't. I curtsied and said, "*Grazie*, Lady Elizabeth."

Gabriella addressed Lord Lodovico. "And what say you, Lord Lodovico? What do *you* think of my friend's performance?" If Gabriella was upset about his attentions to Lady Elizabeth, she hid it well.

"I fear I, too, underestimated her abilities." He said to me. "I hope you will forgive me as well." I sensed his words were more for Lady Elizabeth's sake than mine.

"Come, Emilia," Gabriella said, tugging my arm. "You must be in need of refreshment after your hard work."

"Excuse us." I curtsied again and followed Gabriella to the adjacent parlor. The previously darkened room was now ablaze in candlelight. Refreshments had also been laid out.

"Do you believe that woman?" Gabriella said when we were ensconced in a corner. "Openly flirting with him. Why she's nothing but a—"

"Hush, Gabriella. Do not say something you may regret later." I glanced around to make sure no one was in earshot. "From what I saw, *he* was the one doing the flirting."

"Oh, you are too innocent, my friend. You have not *my* experience in high society." Gabriella pulled back her shoulders as though to remind me of her superior station. "I have witnessed how a woman can entrap a man in a snare so fine he doesn't even see it."

"And how, pray tell, are *you* able to see it, Gabriella?"

"Mother has taught me what to watch for—the tilt of a head, the curl of a smile, the turn of a fan." Gabriella turned her own fan in front of her face to demonstrate.

With the exception of the fan, I had witnessed Lord Lodovico employ the very same gestures this evening, not only with Lady Elizabeth, but with Isabella, too. "You noticed no such clues in the gentleman's behavior then?"

"Why, of course not," Gabriella said.

How could she be so blind? Rather than argue, I said, "Even if you're right about Lady Elizabeth, a loyal suitor would not have allowed himself to fall prey to her charms. Look at Count Cavalieri." I nodded toward the food table, where the count stood talking with Maestro Tomassini. "The count is taking care to act above reproach."

Before Gabriella could answer, Lord Lodovico entered the parlor with Lady Elizabeth on his arm. Naldo held a tray of wine glasses out toward them. Lord Lodovico took two of the glasses and, with a tilt of his head and a curl of a smile, he offered one to Lady Elizabeth. She smiled modestly as she accepted the wine.

"Ha!" Gabriella said. "She thinks that as the next Duchess von Hildebrandt she can have any man she sets her sights on. But I won't let her win that easily." Gabriella hurried over to Lord Lodovico.

Poor Gabriella. She saw only what she wished to see. I thought of Maria's demonstration, how the light passing through her crystal wasn't really white but a multitude of colors. Gabriella perceived only the white light, and not the rainbow—Lord Lodovico had set *his* sights on Lady Elizabeth.

Chapter Nineteen
Godsend

After the last of the guests had left, Adriana said to Father, "We should toast our marvelous success this evening, Husband!" She reached for two glasses of wine from the refreshment table. Maria was sitting on a sofa nearby. I collapsed beside her, exhausted.

"Our meeting will be the talk of Milan for days," Adriana went on, "and not just because our daughters performed brilliantly."

I cringed when she said, "our daughters." I was not Adriana's daughter and never would be.

My stepmother raised one of the glasses toward Father. "The presence of Duke von Hildebrandt and Lady Elizabeth will certainly be lauded."

Father pushed the wine away. Why was there anger in his eyes? The meeting had gone exceptionally well.

He crossed his arms over his chest. "The gossipers will also note the *absence* of Marquis don Cesare Volpi."

"Of what consequence is that?" Adriana said. She set both wine glasses back on the table. "His son was here, and he expressed his father's regrets."

"The only thing the marquis regrets is that Lord Lodovico accepted our invitation."

"But why?" Adriana asked.

"Isn't it obvious?" Father replied. "Marquis don Cesare Volpi believes his title makes him too good to associate with the likes of us."

Interesting. Gabriella had said the same to me earlier.

"Don't let it perturb you, Husband," Adriana said. "There are plenty of noblemen who disagree with him." She began numbering them on her fingers. "Duke von Hildebrandt, Senator Cavalieri, Count Riccardi—"

"Enough!" Father slammed his hand on the table, giving us all a start. The wine glasses trembled momentarily. "I tell you, the list of unenlightened aristocrats is much longer. However, I will show them all. After I am granted a title, not even Marquis don Cesare Volpi himself will have the audacity to slight me!"

Father turned to Maria and me. "Meanwhile, I expect you both to work harder than ever so that when I *am* named a nobleman, my daughters will be the two most accomplished noblewomen in all of Italy. Understood?"

Maria and I answered in unison, "*Sì*, Signor Padre."

Father stormed from the room.

For a moment, Adriana stood speechless. Then she took a deep breath and said, "Girls, we must do all we can to help your father secure that title."

<hr />

The day of my next music lesson, I was surprised to find Antonio Bellini already in the harpsichord salon when I walked in. He sat beside the harpsichord, his shoulders hunched and his back to me. He seemed busy with something, but his violin case rested unopened on a nearby chair.

Curious, I crept closer without speaking. I soon saw that Bellini was working on a long piece of flax-colored twine tied together at the ends. He had looped the twine between his palms and was now weaving it back and forth.

"What are you doing, Signor Bellini?"

"*Signorina!*" Bellini rose from his chair. "I didn't hear you come in." His cheeks flushed pink as he held out his hands. Suspended between them, the twine had taken the shape of a basket. "It's a game, for flexibility."

"I've never heard of using string to improve flexibility."

"It was my mother's idea," Bellini said. "When I was five years old, I begged my uncle to teach me to play the violin. I was determined to be a great violinist. But even with a child-size violin, I had difficulty with the fingerings." As he spoke, Bellini undid his string basket and began reweaving the twine. I was intrigued, not only by his movements, but by the mention of his mother. Bellini had never spoken of her before.

He continued working the twine. "Seeing my tears of frustration one day, Mamma started teaching me string games. She said they would make my fingers nimbler, and stronger, too." Bellini turned his hands outward, palms facing me, with only his index fingers and thumbs pointed upward. Two strands of twine now ran horizontally from one hand to the other, with three rhomboid shapes stretched vertically between them. "This one's called 'The Three Diamonds.'"

"How clever," I said. "But what makes it a game? You've simply woven the twine into an interesting pattern."

"There's a bit more to it," he said. "Slide your hand through the center diamond, if you will." He extended his hands toward me.

"Very well." I did as he instructed.

Bellini let go of the twine in his left hand and tugged with his right.

"Oh!" To my surprise, my wrist was now ensnared by the string.

He laughed. "You're my prisoner now." Bellini pulled the twine, and my arm rose like a marionette's, completely under his control.

"So I see." I laughed, too. "And what will you do with me?"

"Well, if you were my little sister, I'd make you promise to stop snitching figs from the pantry." He smiled, exposing his elusive dimple. My heart fluttered. I suddenly realized we were standing quite close together, probably closer than decorum allowed.

"However," Bellini went on, "I was hoping to extract a different promise from you. I confess, that's why I'm here early. I wish to have a word before the maestro arrives."

Our proximity made it difficult to concentrate. Had he said promise?

"Of course," he said, "I have no intention of employing coercion." His face grew serious as he lowered my arm and reached down to remove the twine. The touch of his fingers on my wrist sent a shiver up my arm, across my chest, and down into my legs until every part of me hummed like the secondary strings on his viola d'amore.

He snatched away his hand. Had he felt it, too?

Bellini stepped back. "Forgive me, Signorina. I shouldn't have ..." He was blushing again. "I think it best you remove the twine yourself."

I nodded. As I fumbled to free my wrist, the wild thumping of my heart pounded beneath my fingers. What could he have to say that he wouldn't want Maestro Tomassini to hear?

I tried to keep my voice light as I asked, "Pray tell, what would you have me promise?"

Bellini seemed at a loss for words. He stared at my wrist. After I finally managed to slide off the twine he said, "I spoke to you once of how our lessons together would one day come to an end."

"Yes, I remember."

"Well, that day has arrived." Bellini raised his eyes and fixed his gaze on me. "I've accepted a commission in the orchestra at the Royal Ducal Theatre."

"The orchestra? Aren't you young for such a commission?"

"Yes, I thought so, too. However, the maestro assured me I'm as skilled as many of the older violinists. With his encouragement, I dared apply for an audition." He raised his chin ever so slightly. "I was most honored to be offered the position of second violin."

I squeezed the twine in my hand into a ball. "But ... but ... why?" I took a breath to compose myself. "I mean, I'm not surprised they hired you. You play beautifully. But why do you want to perform with the orchestra?"

"I'm afraid my family needs the income."

"Oh, forgive me. I shouldn't have pried." My legs trembled. I leaned against the harpsichord for support.

"No, I want you to know. I wouldn't quit our lessons together if there were any other way." Bellini came to stand beside me, though he kept a careful distance between us now. He ran his fingers over the waves carved into the harpsichord's side panels. "You see, my father doesn't have much of a head for business. My mother always ran the shop. Ever since she died …" His blue eyes filled with sadness.

"I'm sorry. When you spoke of your mother earlier, I had no idea she was dead."

"It's been over two years, yet sometimes it seems only two weeks."

I understood all too well. I still had sudden flashes of longing for Mamma even though nearly a year and a half had passed since her death.

Bellini sighed. He stared at the painting inside the harpsichord's lid. A small white ship sailed across a blue-green expanse. At that moment, I felt as though we were standing together on that ship, surrounded by a sea of sorrow.

Finally, he said, "The orchestra commission will be a great help to my family. My sister will soon need a dowry. She's nearly fifteen."

Like me. I thought of my own dowry. For years, I'd been praying Father wouldn't force me to become a nun, but even that required a donation to the convent, though much less than a marriage dowry. Whatever Father's plans, he had no doubt set aside the money to carry them out. My brothers would never have to concern themselves with such matters.

How unselfish of Bellini to want to provide for his sister. Yet what a shame he should have to end our studies together to do so.

"I hope you won't mind my asking," I said, "but isn't your uncle Marquis don Vittore Bellini? Surely he could help."

"Actually, he's my father's uncle." Bellini tightened his jaw, making the cleft in his chin stand out. "And Father would sooner die of hunger than ask *his* assistance." Anger flashed in Bellini's eyes. "You see, the marquis refused to acknowledge my parents' betrothal because my mother was from a merchant family. When they wed anyway, he disinherited Father. The two haven't spoken since." Bellini clenched the harpsichord's side panels with both hands as though to steady himself. "I've never met the man myself. He didn't even have the decency to come to my mother's funeral."

"Oh. I see." Marquis Bellini sounded a lot like Marquis Volpi. My heart sank.

What more could I say? That I was happy Bellini had found employment he would enjoy? In truth, I was. But I was also sad for myself.

"Well then." I tried to sound enthusiastic. "I should be congratulating you. What a wonderful opportunity—playing in the orchestra!"

He relaxed his grip on the harpsichord. "Yes, indeed. And I hope to sell some of my compositions, too." He smiled. "By God's grace, I'll soon have more than enough money for my sister's dowry. And then ..." Bellini's face grew serious again as he stepped toward me. "There's something I wish to ask, Signorina."

The promise he'd spoken of earlier? My heart skipped a beat. Could Gabriella be right? Could he really want to be my suitor?

He cleared his throat. "I wish to ask ..." He looked down at his empty hands. "I wonder if—"

"Bellini!" the maestro called from the doorway. "I didn't expect you here today."

Bellini's head jerked up. He said to Maestro Tomassini, "I wanted to give Signorina Salvini the news myself."

"I understand," the maestro said striding toward us. "But you'd better hurry, Boy. You don't want to be late for your first rehearsal."

"Indeed." Bellini said to me, "*Arrivederci*, Signorina." Our eyes met for the briefest of moments. Then he made a quick bow, grabbed his violin case, and hurried from the room.

I wanted to call after him, "Wait! Come back and ask your question." Instead, I said only, "*Buona fortuna!*"

After he'd gone, I realized I still held the strand of twine, now a tangled heap.

"The orchestra commission is a true godsend for his family," the maestro said. "And a tremendous opportunity for the boy."

I nodded, only half listening. I stared down at the flax-colored mass in my hand. Such dreadful timing on the maestro's part. A moment more and Bellini would have asked his question. Now I could only guess what it might have been.

I told Maria all about my conversation with Bellini as we prepared for bed. She sat at the dressing table. I stood behind her brushing her long brown hair.

She met my eyes in the mirror. "What do you think he was going to ask?"

"Lady Gabriella believes he's smitten with me," I said. "So I can't help wondering if he wanted to ask to court me or for me to promise to allow him to do so when he'd proven himself a worthy suitor."

"Have you been encouraging his attentions?"

"No. Of course not." I set the brush on the table. "I've always treated him as a fellow musician, nothing more."

"But you'd like him to be more, wouldn't you?"

"In truth, I would." I thought of how his touch on my wrist had sent a shiver through my whole body. I didn't tell Maria of the string game, or of the flax-colored twine that now sat in my desk drawer. "I've been hoping all along that Gabriella was right. He is kind and handsome, and he loves music as much as I do."

"He's obviously devoted to his family, too," Maria said, "to put his sister's future ahead of his own. Perhaps that is why God has blessed him with an orchestra position at such a young age. But you seem to have forgotten one thing, Emmi. If Antonio Bellini wishes to court you, he needs Father's permission, not yours."

"Yes, of course, you're right," I said. "I hadn't thought of that. Bellini probably wanted to ask something ordinary. And in that case, I may never know what it was." I took off my dressing gown and climbed into bed.

Maria blew out the candles and came to bed, too.

Staring up into the darkness, I couldn't stop thinking about Bellini. What if he had wanted to know my feelings first, before he approached Father? And what of Father? Would he allow me to wed? If so, would he approve of Bellini?

"Maria," I said, "Father hasn't mentioned anything to you about finding suitors for us, has he?"

"No, thank heaven."

"Is it still your intention to join a convent?"

"Yes, but not as a cloistered nun. I believe it is my calling to help the poor. I must find an order that will allow me to do so."

I thought again of the conversation I'd overheard between our parents. I never told Maria what Father had said about not letting her waste her talents.

"Does Father know?" I asked.

"I have left it in God's hands."

My sister's faith was so much stronger than mine. If only I could have her confidence in God's plans.

For years, I'd prayed Father wouldn't force me to take the veil. As that possibility had grown less likely, my prayers had changed. Now I beseeched God for a kind husband who would truly love me. In my mind, that husband was Antonio Bellini. But I had no way of knowing if God agreed.

Or even if Bellini did.

Chapter Twenty
Playthings

A few weeks after Father's academic meeting, Adriana took ill. She vomited so violently Father sent for the physician immediately. As it turned out, she wasn't ill. She was with child. Father was overjoyed. Of course, Adriana was, too.

She called Maria and me to her room to give us the news. Adriana was sitting up in her huge bed—she'd refused to sleep in the one Mamma had died in and had ordered this one shipped from Florence. Adriana looked like a porcelain doll propped up in a sea of pillows, her skin strangely pale next to the bright pink of her dressing gown.

"Come," she said, waving us over. "Sit." She patted the bed.

Maria and I sat on either side of her.

"Isn't it wonderful, girls?" Adriana said. "I'll finally have a child of my own." She caressed her belly. Then she must have realized what she'd said, because she quickly added, "Of course, I already love Paola and Vincenzo as my own. It's just not exactly the same."

Maria smiled and said, "We understand."

We understand all too well. Once this baby was born, it would become the center of Adriana's life. I cared not if she ignored *me*, but I did worry about the little ones, especially Vincenzo. My five-year-old brother barely remembered Mamma, and he had already grown quite attached to our stepmother. I prayed to the Blessed Virgin that no matter what happened, Adriana would not abandon Vincenzo or Paola.

———

A few days later, Nina announced an unexpected visitor—Gabriella. "Show her to the parlor," I said.

The early summer heat had already made the parlor uncomfortably warm. I opened the balcony doors for some fresh air. On seeing Gabriella, I said, "What a lovely surprise," then paused. The strained expression on my friend's face told me something was wrong.

To Nina, I said, "Please bring us some cold refreshments."

"Yes, Miss."

"Gabriella, won't you sit down?" She moved to the high-backed chair near the balcony doors but didn't sit. As soon as Nina shut the parlor door, Gabriella exclaimed, "The nerve of that woman!"

"What woman?"

"Lady Elizabeth." Gabriella stiffened her posture and feigned a haughty air. "The future Duchess von Hildebrandt."

"What has she done?"

"She's gone back to Austria."

I still didn't understand why Gabriella was upset. "Isn't that good news?"

"It would be if Lodovico Volpi hadn't gone after her."

"What?" I sat down on the sofa across from Gabriella. "Why would he do that? I thought he was one of your suitors."

"I thought so, too, until today." Gabriella clutched the top of the chair. "This morning my brother heard a rumor that Volpi was planning to pursue Lady Elizabeth instead. Rather than bother Father with what might be idle gossip, Raffaele went to see Volpi himself. Well, when Raffaele arrived, Volpi was climbing into his carriage. The scoundrel admitted to my brother that he was headed for Austria. Raffaele asked him what his intentions were regarding me. And Volpi said he had none!" Gabriella slapped the top of the chair. "Can you believe it?"

Unfortunately, I could. But I didn't want to remind Gabriella of how she'd ignored my warnings at Father's meeting. Instead, I said only, "Oh."

"My life is in ruin, and all you can say is, 'oh'?" Gabriella slapped the chair again then whipped around and stormed out onto the balcony.

As I stood to follow her, Nina arrived. She set a tray containing two glasses of iced lemon water on a table. "Anything else, Miss?"

"No, thank you, Nina."

I carried the glasses to the balcony. Gabriella was leaning over the railing, looking onto the courtyard below.

The day was unusually warm, even for June. "Here, drink this. It will help calm you." I handed her a glass.

She took a sip then gazed back down at the courtyard.

"I'm sorry, Gabriella. I can imagine how devastating this must be for you. But after the way Volpi behaved at Father's meeting, I can't say I'm surprised."

"I suppose I shouldn't be either," Gabriella said. "I underestimated that woman. She must be toying with him. She can't seriously be thinking of marrying him."

I sat down on one of the balcony chairs. "And why not?" I sipped some water. The coolness eased my parched throat.

"Because she could marry an archduke or even a prince if she wanted." Gabriella sat down in the other chair. "Why would she want Lodovico Volpi?"

"Isn't it possible she cares for him?"

"I don't know." Gabriella's shoulders sagged. "All I know is *I* care for him." She took a large swallow of water then clutched the glass in both her hands. "And now I shall never marry him." Gabriella blinked quickly as though fighting tears.

I set my glass down on the little table between us and dried the condensation from my glass on my handkerchief. "Doesn't this prove what you said yourself, Gabriella?" I patted her arm. "He isn't worthy of you."

She didn't answer.

Finally, Gabriella sighed. "I suppose I must resign myself to marrying Old Bulldog. He is the most acceptable alternative."

"Count Cavalieri is a respected statesman," I said. "You will be the envy of many."

"Yes, I suppose there is some consolation in being the wife of a senator. I just wish he wasn't so old."

"At least his daughters are young. They may come to love you as much as Vincenzo and Paola love Adriana."

"Oh, forgive me." Gabriella straightened her shoulders. "I forgot to ask. How *is* your stepmother?"

"Not well at all," I said. "She can barely eat. The slightest smell makes her feel ill. She has confined herself to her room. Mamma never did that when she was with child."

Gabriella shook her head. "I am in no hurry to be in your stepmother's position. I will postpone my marriage as long as possible."

~

Adriana's nausea lasted weeks. The only sustenance she could tolerate was a light soup containing bits of bread in broth. Instead of gaining weight, she grew thinner. Still, the midwife assured her the stomach upset would eventually pass.

Finally, around mid-July it did. Adriana began to tolerate more solid food, and her strength gradually returned. By the end of the month, she was taking her meals with the rest of us again.

"Oh, how I've missed dining with all of you," she said the first time she joined us. We weren't "all" present, though. Father was away on business.

"We've missed you, too, Signora Madre," Paola said.

"Me, too," Vincenzo said.

Adriana smiled. "Really, my little puppet?" She stroked his cheek. "Tell me, how did you spend the morning?"

Vincenzo told of how he and Paola had played hide-and-go-seek in the garden. "I hid so well the last time," he said with a grin, "she almost didn't find me."

"I knew where you were," Paola said. "I just wanted to make the game last longer."

Adriana laughed her high-pitched cricket laugh. "You two are lucky to have each other. When I was your age, I had only my dolls." She prattled on about her five dolls, describing each of their outfits in detail, right down to the hair ribbons.

"Did you give them names?" Paola asked.

"Now, Paola," I said, hoping to cut short some of Adriana's chatter. "We don't want to overtire our stepmother on her first day out of bed."

"Oh, I don't mind," Adriana said. She not only told us the dolls' names, she went on to tell us of the various other childhood toys she'd owned.

"I just thought of something!" Adriana clapped her hands together. "My father must still have my playthings packed away somewhere. We'll have to send for them."

"For us to play with?" Vincenzo asked.

I held my breath. This was the first test. Would she allow Vincenzo and Paola to play with the toys, or would she lock them away for the baby?

Adriana grinned at Vincenzo. "Well, of course," she said. "But you'll have to share them." She paused for a moment, then added, "with me." She laughed.

Vincenzo and Paola laughed, too. I couldn't help smiling at their joy. Yet I still worried. Would Adriana abandon them after the baby arrived, just as she had discarded her old playthings?

Chapter Twenty-One
Puppets on a String

Father had originally planned for us to spend the summer at our country house in Masciago. He changed those plans when the midwife advised Adriana against travel, at least until after her nausea ceased.

I was glad. Staying home meant I could continue my lessons with Maestro Tomassini. The lessons weren't the same without Bellini, but they were a welcome distraction from my thoughts of him.

Then one day at the end of July the maestro announced, "I'm afraid I must suspend our lessons after all, Signorina. The preparations for the opening of my opera are not going well."

"I understand, Maestro." His announcement did not come as a surprise. He'd told me of his difficulties with the singers. I couldn't resist asking, "Is Bellini playing for the opera?"

"Indeed," the maestro said. "He already knows his part well. If the singers had one-tenth his dedication, we could open next week."

"I'm sure that under your direction all will be ready in time." I tried to sound nonchalant as I added, "Perhaps I'll be allowed to attend." In truth, I could hardly wait to see Bellini again. I'd hoped he might send a letter, or even call on me, to ask the question the maestro had interrupted two months ago, but I'd had no word. With each passing day, my hope diminished. If Bellini had intended to ask permission to court me, he would surely have done so by now.

"I will suggest your father bring you to the opera," the maestro said, "as part of your music education."

"*Grazie*, Maestro."

The sweltering heat of August made us all short-tempered. When the midwife announced Adriana fit to travel (with caution), Father renewed his plans for our retreat to the country. He sent word to Nonno Giuseppe that we would be arriving soon. My grandfather had taken to living in our family's country house year-round after Nonna's death. He still visited Milan occasionally, but I hadn't seen him in ages.

We left for Masciago early in the morning. It took two carriages to transport all of us—Father, Adriana, Maria, and me in one, and Isabella, Paola, Vincenzo, Mademoiselle Duval, and Nina in the other. With the windows screened to shield us from dust, the air in the carriage was stifling. I was soon drenched in perspiration. Thankfully, clouds blocked out the sun's fierce rays for much of the journey.

As we climbed higher into the countryside, our carriage passed vineyards, orchards, and fields of grain. I dozed awhile. When I opened my eyes again, we were crossing the bridge over the Seveso River, which bordered the southern end of our property.

By the time the horses clip-clopped through the gates of the estate, the air felt markedly cooler. The green, earthy scent of the breeze contrasted sharply with the sour, dusty odors we'd left behind in Milan.

Tall poplars lined the road leading to the house, their triangular leaves clattering a greeting. Our carriage stopped in front of the house.

Nonno came out to meet us. "Welcome, welcome," he said. "I thought you'd never get here."

"Neither did I," Adriana said. "But I can tell already it was worth the trip. It's so much cooler here." She inhaled deeply. "I can finally breathe again!"

For once, I agreed with my stepmother.

"Isn't the country air wonderful?" Nonno smiled. He was shorter and thinner than Father, but they had the same dark eyes. Nonno gestured toward the house. "Come, come inside. I've had the servants prepare a magnificent meal."

~

The next morning, Adriana wanted to visit the village for the annual summer fair. Paola and Vincenzo were eager to go along. Father had no interest in the fair, nor did Maria.

"You'll join us, Emilia, won't you?" Adriana said.

"Yes, do come with us," Paola said. "Please."

I had no desire for Adriana's company, but I couldn't resist Paola. Besides, there would no doubt be music at the fair.

Naldo took us in the carriage—Adriana, Isabella, Paola, Vincenzo, Mademoiselle Duval, and me. Nina rode outside with Naldo.

As soon as we'd stepped from the carriage, Nina insisted Adriana open her parasol against the sun. "You must take every precaution, Mistress," Nina said. "We don't want you overheating." Then Nina said to me, "You should open yours, too, Miss, to protect your complexion." The morning sun was still low in the sky, but I acquiesced, as did Isabella.

Paola ignored the parasol Nina extended toward her. She ran off with Vincenzo instead. Mademoiselle Duval hurried after them. "Careful, children. You'll get lost in these crowds." The "crowd" consisted of thirty to forty people strolling among the vendor booths. Masciago was tiny compared to Milan.

Adriana laughed. "They'll be fine."

Our skirts stirred the dust as Adriana, Isabella, and I walked from booth to booth. Nina followed close behind with a basket ready to carry any purchases we might make.

We sampled cheeses, nuts, and sweetmeats. "*Delizioso*," Adriana said after tasting a peach *sorbetto*. "And so refreshing." She asked the vendor, "How do you keep it cold?"

"We pack it in ice from the mountains, Signora," the vendor said.

Adriana paid an extravagant price for a tiny cup of the *sorbetto*. At least she let me have a taste.

The *sorbetto* was indeed cold and sweet but not very creamy. "Nonno's cook makes an even better version," I said.

"She makes this, too? I'll have to request some as soon as we return."

"Signora Madre," Paola called as she and Vincenzo hurried toward us. "There's to be a marionette show in the square. Mademoiselle Duval says we need your permission to watch."

"A marionette show?" Adriana said. "How marvelous!" She clapped her hands together. "Of course you may watch."

Mademoiselle Duval walked up behind them. "It may be a story of war, Madame," she said. "I was not sure if you would approve."

"But there are important lessons to be learned in stories of battle," Adriana said. "And it may well turn out to be a fairy tale or a religious story in honor of Our Lady's Feast Day this week." She asked Paola. "Where is it?"

"This way," Vincenzo replied before Paola could. He took Adriana by the hand. Isabella and I followed.

Vincenzo led us to the far end of the piazza where someone had set up a puppet stage. A tall, thin man in a harlequin costume of red, green, and blue patches climbed onto the stage. He called out, "Ladies and gentlemen, boys and girls, come witness the most talented marionette troupe to ever visit the Duchy."

We joined the gathering crowd. The harlequin stood center stage, in front of a large black velvet curtain. "Today's tale is 'Filadora and the Prince,'" he said. "A story that proves again the Latin maxim *Amor vincit omnia*—Love conquers all."

"Oh, how romantic," Isabella said.

"It's not a battle story," Vincenzo said, disappointed.

"But it *is* about a prince," Paola said. "That's even better."

The harlequin took off his hat and bowed. "I, Arlecchino, will be your narrator."

Arlecchino moved to the far end of the stage. He motioned for us to direct our attention back to center stage. We stared at the black velvet curtain. Suddenly, a small slit opened about halfway up the curtain, and a marionette dressed in a suit of dark purple descended onto the stage.

We all applauded his entrance. The puppet, which stood about two feet tall, bowed gracefully, his strings invisible against the black backdrop.

"Ahh!" a cry went up from the audience. Adriana clapped her hands in delight, as did Paola and Vincenzo.

Arlecchino's voice boomed out, "One day, our fine prince was out hunting with his friends. He somehow lost his way and ended up alone in the woods." Two large planks cut and painted to represent trees were lowered onto the ends of the stage. The prince marionette walked from one tree to the other, shaking his head in confusion. His movements were surprisingly lifelike.

"Unbeknownst to the prince," Arlecchino went on, "the woods belonged to a mean ogress who despised trespassers. But Heaven was smiling down on him this day, for instead of the ogress, he encountered her lovely daughter, Filadora."

A female marionette appeared dressed in a gown of rose-colored silk. Someone in the audience called out, "*Bellissima*!" With her long blond hair and sky-blue eyes, the puppet really did look "beautiful."

Arlecchino continued, "Immediately upon seeing Filadora, the prince fell in love. And she, in turn, fell in love with him." I couldn't help thinking of my feelings for Antonio Bellini. But I still didn't know if he felt the same toward me.

I watched, enthralled, as the marionettes acted out the story. An ugly ogress puppet appeared. She threatened to eat the prince, but Filadora begged her mother the ogress to show mercy. The ogress relented, saying she would grant the prince his freedom if he could perform three tasks: splitting six huge stacks of wood, clearing and planting a garden, and digging a new well. Filadora used magic to help the prince complete the tasks. Then they escaped together.

When the ogress realized they'd run away, she cast a spell from afar separating Filadora and the prince. They suffered many trials as they searched for each other. In the end, though, they were reunited.

Arlecchino concluded by saying, "And this tale proves once again that true love conquers all."

The story filled me with hope. If love conquers all, then perhaps Bellini and I would one day marry and live happily ever after, too. I applauded along with the rest of the audience.

"Marvelous, simply marvelous," Adriana said. "I almost forgot the puppets weren't real people."

"It was well done," I said.

A man dressed in black began making his way through the crowd, collecting donations in a small black sack. Adriana drew a few coins from her purse and dropped them in his bag.

"*Grazie*, Signora," the man said. His voice sounded like that of the prince in the play.

"Are you one of the puppeteers?" I asked.

"Yes, Miss."

"The marionettes seemed so real," I said. "How do you keep their strings from tangling together?"

"It requires practice, and much skill, which I learned from my father," he said. "He is a master puppeteer." The man bowed and moved on.

"I want to be a puppeteer," Vincenzo said.

"Me, too," Paola said.

Adriana laughed and tousled Vincenzo's hair. "But you're my little puppet, Vincenzo."

"Please, Signora Madre. May we have puppets of our own?" Vincenzo said. "Then Paola and I can put on shows for you."

"How can I resist this face?" Adriana squeezed Vincenzo's cheeks between her fingers.

We soon came upon a vendor selling simple wooden marionettes. Adriana bought a girl puppet for Paola and a boy one for Vincenzo. Paola immediately named hers Filadora. Vincenzo, on the other hand, said, "My marionette's name will depend on the story."

"Ah, you're wise beyond your years, my little puppet," Adriana said. "Now let's head for home before the sun gets any hotter."

On the carriage ride back to the house, Paola and Vincenzo sat on either side of Adriana. They made their puppets dance across our stepmother's lap.

"Oh, my." Adriana suddenly clutched her abdomen with both hands. "The baby just kicked. He must be enjoying your show."

Paola and Vincenzo laughed. Adriana giggled along with them. I wondered if she'd still be so childlike after the baby's birth.

Chapter Twenty-Two
Country Air

Even in Masciago, Maria got up early every morning to go to Mass. The ancient church of San Martino stood just around the corner from our country house. Yet Father still insisted one of the servants accompany Maria, as etiquette required. Nina usually volunteered.

While Maria was off at church, Isabella and I usually slept in. Adriana was not an early riser either. It was one of the few things I had in common with my stepmother, though she often lingered in bed much longer, sometimes until midday. By then, I was usually at the harpsichord in the front parlor, working on my music lessons. That is, when I wasn't staring out the window dreaming of Antonio Bellini. I wondered if he ever thought of me.

I'd hoped to return to Milan for the opening of the maestro's opera and see Bellini perform in the Royal Ducal Theatre. But Adriana was in no hurry to leave Masciago. She enjoyed the country air too much. As the days passed, I worried we might miss the opera altogether.

When I wasn't playing, Maria and I sometimes went horseback riding. We'd taken lessons years earlier upon our family doctor's orders. He'd said the physical exercise would do us all good following the throat-and-fever illness. For once, Nonno Giuseppe had agreed with the physician. Our grandfather was an avid horseman himself. He made sure our family's horses were always well tended.

Maria favored an old brown mare named Castagna. I preferred Allegra, a spunky gray Arabian. Both her name and personality suited me well. Isabella disliked riding, so she rarely joined us.

One day Maria and I arrived at the stable to find Nonno Giuseppe already there. *"Buon giorno,"* he said with a wide smile. *"Buon giorno."* He took off his hat and bowed to us, exposing his thick head of white hair. He had no use for wigs. Today he wore his hair tied back in a black ribbon that matched his riding clothes. "I'm glad to see you taking advantage of the fine weather," he said. "May I join you?"

"Of course," Maria said.

Nonno Giuseppe put his hat on and called for a groom. "I'll ride Diavolo today," Nonno told the groom. "He can use the exercise."

As we waited for the horses, Nonno said, "Poor old Diavolo. He earned his name in his younger days, when he was full of the devil. But like me, age has slowed him down."

"You don't seem slow to me, Nonno," I said.

"Or aged," Maria added.

Nonno Giuseppe's smile made his wrinkles deepen, but his sparkling eyes belied his age. "You girls certainly know how to flatter an old man."

We were soon ambling along the countryside. Maria and I rode side by side behind Nonno Giuseppe.

When we reached the meadow, Nonno Giuseppe fell back to ride between us. "So, Girls," he said, "I hear your father left Masciago this morning. What was so urgent that it couldn't wait until your return to Milan?"

"He didn't go to Milan," I said.

"No? Then where did he go?"

"I don't know," I said. "Father told Adriana he was going to look at a feudal estate that's for sale, but he didn't say where it is."

"He's still set on acquiring a title then?" Nonno said.

"Oh, yes," I replied, recalling the scene after Father's last meeting. I didn't say anything about Father's determination to earn Marquis Volpi's respect.

"It's been your father's goal from a young age," Nonno said. "Carlo was a mere boy when he learned he could never become a nobleman if he worked as a merchant. From then on, he refused to have anything to do with the family business. After your grandmother died, I didn't have it in me to keep it going. I let my cousin take over. It nearly broke my heart, it did, that your father wouldn't." Nonno patted old Diavolo's neck. "I've never understood this ambition of his. Having a title doesn't make a man any better than one who does not."

"We are all equal in God's eyes," Maria said.

"So true, so true," Nonno said. "My father used to say, 'At the end of the game, the king and the pawn go back into the same box.'" Nonno chuckled. "Unfortunately, few noblemen see it that way. As I recall, my rudest customers were always noblemen. For some reason, they think their titles give them the right to be insolent."

I thought of the time I'd seen Marquis Volpi at Gabriella's ball. She'd called him "conceited." He'd certainly seemed so, wielding his fancy walking stick. Did Father really want to be like him?

"I hear the stream," Nonno said. "Let's water the horses." Nonno Giuseppe took the lead again and led us to the right, where the ground sloped down toward the gurgling stream.

Nonno dismounted and walked all three horses to the water. Maria and I remained in our saddles. She stroked Castagna's neck as the horse drank. "Not all nobility are rude," she said. "Count Riccardi and his family are most kind and honorable."

"That may be true," Nonno said. "But in my experience, a count or marquis is much more likely to be an arrogant scoundrel than a tradesman or merchant is. And those noble ladies,

why, they're even haughtier than their husbands, they are."
Nonno waved a finger at us. "I won't tolerate such behavior
from either of you, should your father's plans succeed."

Maria said, "You needn't worry about us, Nonno."

"I hope not!"

Nonno took off his hat and inhaled deeply. "Ahh," he said.
"This country air gives me such an appetite." He patted his
belly. "I think it's time we head back."

~

Adriana was sitting in the parlor, listening to me practice the
harpsichord, when Father returned from his trip a few days
later. He came in and handed a bottle to Adriana. "For you,
my dear," he said. "Some wine from our estate."

"Our estate?"

I stopped playing mid-measure.

"Well, it's not ours *yet*, but by God's grace it soon will be."
Father smiled. "In addition to the vineyards, the property includes a spring-fed lake full of trout, and some prime hunting
land."

"What about the house?" Adriana asked.

"The house? It's not a house, it's a villa!" Father swept his
hand through the air. "It sits high atop a hill overlooking the
lake. Inside, the grand staircase has a wrought-iron balustrade
sculpted with figures of angels. There's also a lovely little
chapel dedicated to Sant'Anna. And behind the house is a magnificent marble fountain leading out to the gardens."

I couldn't recall the last time I'd seen Father so animated.

Adriana clapped her hands together. "It sounds marvelous," she said. "Where is it?"

"In Montevecchia, a day's ride northeast of our home in
the city," Father answered. "Tomorrow we must return to Milan. I've sent word to my attorney to enter into negotiations
right away."

"Well, I shall miss the fine country air," Adriana said, "but
it'll be good to see Papà again."

I got up from the harpsichord. "Can we attend Maestro
Tomassini's opera when we get back? It opened last week."

"I have already reserved a box," Father said. He reached down and grabbed Adriana's hands, pulling her to her feet. "After the purchase of the estate is finalized and I am granted a title, I will be able to buy a permanent box at the theatre. Until then, a rented one will have to do."

"Papà loves opera," Adriana said. "May I invite him to join us?"

"Of course," Father said.

"I'll tell Nina and Naldo to start packing." I hurried from the room. I could hardly contain my excitement. Finally, I would see Antonio Bellini again.

Chapter Twenty-Three
Royal Ducal Theatre

"I feel like Paola's puppet," Maria said as we waited in the front hall for Father and Adriana.

"Why?"

"Look at me," Maria said. "My hair's been curled, my face powdered, my stays laced so tight I can barely breathe. Father should take Isabella to the opera in my place. She would love all this." Maria held out her arms. "I want only to stay home and study."

"Aren't you excited about seeing the opera and hearing the wonderful singers?"

"I suppose so," Maria said. "But I'm *not* excited about being crushed by the crowds, especially in this, this, … costume."

"I think you look elegant. We both do." I gazed at my reflection in the hall mirror, pleased Adriana had insisted on the curls and face powder. I hoped to dazzle Antonio Bellini tonight. That is, if I managed to have a word with him.

"I'd rather look natural," Maria said. "The way God made me."

Father finally came down the stairs with Adriana on his arm.

"Sorry to keep you waiting," Adriana said. "My hair took longer than I expected." My stepmother's black hair was piled ridiculously high, higher than she'd ever worn it before. And it was adorned with yellow bird figures. "What do you think?" She twirled around to give us the full effect. It looked as though a flock of miniature orioles had nested on her head, but I couldn't tell her that.

Maria was quiet. She, too, seemed at a loss for words. Finally, she said, "The birds match your gown perfectly."

"Yes, they do. Aren't they marvelous?" Adriana giggled.

Naldo spared us any further discussion of Adriana's hair by announcing, "The carriage is ready, Master."

"*Grazie*, Naldo," Father said. "Come, ladies. Let's be going."

~

As we passed the *Duomo*, the road became increasingly crowded with carriages of opera-goers. Dirty beggars in tattered clothes lined the streets asking for alms. I watched a pair of nuns in turquoise-colored habits walk among them, distributing bread. A one-legged beggar grabbed a nun's hands and kissed them in gratitude. I cringed. How could she stand to be touched by him?

Our carriage came to a stop near the Royal Ducal Theatre. Naldo opened the door and helped us out. Then he took a basket and lantern from the back of the carriage and led the way to the theatre entrance. Ahead of me, Father's powdered wig shimmered in the lantern light.

The Ducal theatre occupied a wing of the Royal Palace, where Governor von Traun lived. Four soldiers dressed in Austrian uniforms stood guard at the building's entrance. Maria clung to my arm as we joined the crowd making their way through the door. The scent of violet water, wig powder, and fine perfumes couldn't completely mask the smells of lantern oil and body odors that assaulted us in such a confined space.

Maria and I stayed close behind as Father guided Adriana up the steps to the third level. We walked down a long hallway until we reached our box's anteroom. Naldo hung the lantern on the wall, then waited while Father, Adriana, Maria, and I stepped inside.

A lit candelabrum sat on a small table in the anteroom. No doubt, this is where Naldo would serve the refreshments he carried. I could hardly wait to slip through into the box itself. I tried to be patient while Adriana and Father led the way.

"Oh, this is quite lovely," Adriana said as I joined them. The box was lined in red velvet. The same red velvet covered the six seats—three on each side, facing each other. Of course, my stepmother picked the best spot, the seat nearest the railing, looking toward the stage. Father sat down beside her.

I took the seat across from Adriana and immediately turned to face the stage. The orchestra was warming up, but I could barely hear them over the din of the people walking to and fro in the gallery below. There appeared to be about 40 musicians in all. Most of their instruments were stringed, with the exception of the oboes, trumpets, and bassoons. The violins were divided into two sections. Our seats were so far away the violinists all looked the same in their powdered wigs. One man on the far side was thinner than the others. Could he be Bellini?

"After I am named Count of Montevecchia, my dear," Father said to Adriana. "We shall acquire a box in the row reserved for nobility."

"How marvelous that will be." Adriana pointed her fan at the lowest row on the opposite side of the gallery. "Look, there's Governor von Traun," she said. "His box is the largest of all."

The governor sat in the very first box, with what had to be the best view of the stage. I wished I could join him.

"Oh, and there's Count Riccardi with his wife and daughter," Adriana said. Gabriella's family's box was on the noble level, too. I waved to get Gabriella's attention, but she was too busy talking with her mother.

Father said, "I will have to go over and pay my respects."

"*Buonasera*," a deep voice said from behind us.

"Papà!" Adriana said.

Alfonso Grilli kissed Adriana's hand. "You're lovely as ever, dear daughter." His deep bass voice always struck me as odd coming from someone so short.

Grilli bowed to Father. "Thank you for allowing me to join you, Salvini. It should be a marvelous evening, eh?" Grilli sat down beside Father. "Everyone's been saying wonderful things about Maestro Tomassini's opera."

"You haven't seen it yet?" Father asked.

"No, I've been away on business." Grilli proceeded to tell Father and Adriana the details of his trip.

I turned back to the orchestra. The maestro raised his baton and began directing the musicians in the opening *sinfonia*. Most people in the audience were too busy talking and laughing to even notice. They seemed more interested in socializing than in watching the performance. They'd probably already seen the opera several times by now—many came night after night. I wished I could shush them all.

The thin violinist on the far side seemed more focused than the other violinists. He put his whole body into his playing, the same way Antonio Bellini did. It had to be him. My heart skipped a beat. This was the closest I'd been to him in three months. Yet I wanted to be closer. I longed to speak with him, to finally learn what he'd meant to ask the last time we were together.

The crowd quieted when the famous *prima donna* Vittoria Tesi took the stage. As she sang the first aria, chills went down my spine. Her voice had such power and range! Of course, the maestro deserved credit as well, for creating music that took full advantage of her abilities. How I wished I could compose for such a voice.

Next came a duet between Tesi and the male lead. The beautifully melodic song spoke of the characters' love for each other. They executed it perfectly! Maestro Tomassini must have worked out whatever problems he'd had with his singers. The audience applauded enthusiastically. But as soon as it was over, they returned to their diversions.

During the comic intermezzo, Father excused himself to call on the Riccardis. At the same time, Adriana and her father went to the anteroom of our box to share the refreshments Naldo had laid out.

I said to Maria, "Isn't the opera wonderful?"

"I confess I am enjoying it," Maria said. "The music is amazing, the singers have beautiful voices, and the set is a work of art."

I moved to Adriana's seat for a better view of the stage. "I only wish we could sit closer."

"Aha, I've found you!" a familiar voice said.

"Lady Gabriella!" I said. "What a lovely surprise."

Gabriella sat down beside me. "So how was your sojourn in the country?"

"Too long." I pointed toward the stage. "I missed the first week of performances."

"And a certain young man's debut at second violin?" Gabriella nudged my elbow.

I raised my fan to hide my suddenly hot cheeks.

Gabriella leaned across me to look down at the orchestra. "Why, you can barely see him from here." She grabbed my hand. "Come, you must sit in our box."

"But my father—"

"If we hurry, your father will still be talking to my parents. I'm certain he'll give you permission to sit with us if *I* do the asking."

I followed Gabriella. We found Father in the anteroom of her parents' box, drinking champagne with the count and countess. Of course, Gabriella was right—Father granted permission for me to stay as soon as she asked.

After Father left, Gabriella's parents went to the gaming room to play faro. Gabriella and I had the box all to ourselves. She insisted I take the seat nearest the railing, facing the stage. She sat down beside me.

"What a wonderful view," I said as the second act began. "I can see the expressions on the singers' faces." I was also close enough to confirm that the violinist I'd been watching earlier was indeed Bellini, although his back was to me now.

"Of which view do you speak my friend," Gabriella said. "The stage or the orchestra?" Gabriella laughed her tinkling laugh. I couldn't help laughing with her.

"So tell me," Gabriella whispered in my ear. "Do you miss your fellow student?"

Just then, the soprano began a new aria. Her character's father, the king, did not approve of her suitor and had banished him. The aria expressed her sorrow at losing the man she loved. Keeping my eyes on the soprano, I answered Gabriella. "I miss him more than I care to admit."

"I knew it!" Gabriella said. She lowered her voice again. "And are your feelings reciprocated?"

I raised my finger to my lips for quiet. Finally, after the soprano had finished her aria, I answered Gabriella. "I don't know how he feels. The last time we spoke, he'd been just about to ask a question when the maestro interrupted."

"How exciting," Gabriella said. "Surely he was about to ask to court you."

"If you're right, why haven't I had any word since then? He could have written or even called on me."

"Well, it wouldn't be proper for him to write or call without your father's consent."

"Then how will I learn what he intended to ask?"

"Hmm." Gabriella was quiet for a moment, then she said, "We'll just have to find a way to get the two of you together. Perhaps at my wedding reception."

"Has your marriage date been set?"

"Father won't let me put it off any longer. We will wed on October 19. Just three weeks after my seventeenth birthday." A strange look flickered over Gabriella's face. I wasn't sure if it was sadness or pain. "Have you heard?" she said. "Lord Lodovico is also betrothed."

"No, I hadn't heard. To Lady Elizabeth?"

"Yes," Gabriella said. "Father says Duke von Hildebrandt is planning a lavish celebration at his castle."

"No doubt the food at your reception will be better," I said. "I hear those Austrian chefs don't know how to cook."

Gabriella laughed. "I think the music will be better, too." She nodded toward the orchestra. "Especially if we can enlist the talents of a certain young violinist."

⁓

By the time the opera came to an end, Gabriella's parents had rejoined us in their box. We all applauded together as the final curtain fell. I wanted to go down and congratulate the maestro, but Father had made me promise to stay with the Riccardis until Naldo came for me.

Gabriella and I chatted in the box while the count and countess visited with friends in their anteroom. When the countess called for Gabriella to join them, I remained in the box and watched the musicians pack up their instruments. I stood, hoping Bellini might glance my way. After securing his violin in its case, he did just that. I waved. A smile lit up his face. I smiled back.

I clapped my hands together to show my appreciation for his performance. Bellini bowed. He said something, but in all the noise I couldn't make out his words. I shook my head and cupped my ears to indicate I couldn't hear him.

He gestured toward me and mouthed the word *bellissima*. Then he raised his hands and applauded. Apparently, he was complimenting the way I looked. I curtsied, trying to appear calm while my heart danced at his attentions.

Bellini grinned. He seemed to be enjoying our little pantomime.

"Excuse me, Miss," Naldo's voice said from behind me. "Are you ready to go?"

I hated to leave so soon. "One moment." I gestured to Bellini that I had to go. Then I curtsied again and waved goodbye.

Bellini waved too, his face sad now. Somehow, I knew he was no longer playacting. He was genuinely disappointed at my departure.

We hadn't exchanged a word, yet I felt closer to Antonio Bellini than ever.

Chapter Twenty-Four
Cupid's Arrows

Gabriella looked like a duchess when she and Count Cavalieri opened the dancing at their wedding celebration. She wore a peach-colored satin gown adorned with silver lace and embroidery. As she glided across the floor, tiny jewels on her sleeves reflected the light of the ballroom's chandeliers. Her hair held jewels, too, along with miniature cupids ready to shoot their arrows into the groom's heart. Judging from the groom's countenance, the arrows had already struck their mark. I'd never seen a happier man.

I glanced over at the musicians. Antonio Bellini was not among them. For my sake, Gabriella had invited him as a guest, instead of hiring him to play. But he wasn't here yet. I worried he might not come at all.

I watched from my seat beside Maria as family members and guests joined in the dancing. Because of Count Cavalieri's position, the guests included senators and other dignitaries. Even Governor von Traun was here. I saw no sign of Marquis Volpi, though. I wondered if he'd been invited.

After a while, I grew restless and wandered over to the food table. As I placed a fruit tart on my plate, a familiar voice said, "I expected to find you on the dance floor."

My heart skipped a beat.

I turned to see Antonio Bellini smiling at me. It hardly seemed possible, but he looked handsomer than ever. He'd filled out since I'd last seen him, so he no longer appeared lanky. He wore a chestnut-colored silk suit perfectly tailored to match his new proportions. My heart fluttered at the sight of him. Struggling to keep my voice light, I said, "No one's asked me to dance."

"I find that hard to believe," he said, "for you are even lovelier than the bride."

Heat rose to my face. I didn't know what to say.

"Forgive me," Bellini said, "I didn't mean to embarrass you." He took a step closer. "There's just so much I've been wanting to tell you, so much—."

He was interrupted when a man I recognized as one of the senators reached for a plate from the table. The music had stopped and others were making their way toward us for something to eat.

I noticed then that Bellini carried a brown leather portfolio. "I have something to show you," he said, raising the portfolio toward me. "Perhaps we can find a quiet corner?" He held out his arm.

My pulse quickened as I took his arm. Bellini led the way to two empty chairs near a window. Sitting down, I realized I still had the plate in my hand. The cherry tart stared up at me.

"I hardly know where to begin," he said.

"Perhaps you should begin where you left off," I said, "with the question you were about to ask the day you told me of your position with the orchestra. The question the maestro interrupted."

"Ah, yes." He looked down at the portfolio in his lap. "When the maestro interrupted, I took it as a sign from heaven that the time was not yet right to ask my question."

"Is the time right now?"

"I don't know," he said. "But I do know I cannot go on without confessing my feelings." He swallowed and met my gaze. His eyes were as blue as ever. "I have admired you for a long time, Signorina Salvini, not only as one musician admires another, but as a man admires a woman."

I clenched the plate in my hands to steady them. I thought my heart might burst. These were the words I'd so longed to hear!

Bellini went on, "That day, I'd intended to ask if I might court you, with your father's blessing, of course. After the maestro thwarted my plans, I realized it was too soon to speak of such things. I had yet to prove myself a worthy suitor. To that end, I've been working on this."

He held up the portfolio. "I've been composing a series of violin concertos. I finished the last one just today—that's why I arrived late. If my compositions are a success, I'll be able to use them to supplement my orchestra salary. The combined earnings will provide a comfortable living." He set the portfolio back on his lap. "After I am confident of such success, with your consent, I'd like to approach your father."

My head was spinning now. It could take months, or even years, for his plan to come to fruition. I didn't want to wait that long. "I cannot think of a worthier suitor," I said. "You need not prove yourself to me."

"I can't tell you how happy I am to hear you say so." He smiled wide enough to expose his dimple. My own smile grew to match his.

"However," he went on, "I fear your father might not agree."

"Well, he doesn't know you as I do." I pointed at his portfolio. "May I see?"

"I've made a copy just for you." He held the portfolio out to me. "I'm hoping you'll give me your opinion before I show them to Maestro Tomassini."

"I would be honored." Reaching for the portfolio, I wasn't sure what to do with the plate in my other hand. "Would you like some pastry?"

He laughed. "I've no appetite at the moment, but I'll relieve you of your burden." Bellini's hand touched mine as he reached for the plate. A tingle went through me, an echo of the shiver I'd felt when he'd tried to remove the twine from my wrist so many months ago. This time, he let his fingers linger for a moment before taking the plate away. My heart thumped wildly. Our gazes met. The sorrow I'd always seen in his eyes had disappeared.

Clutching the portfolio with my right hand, I pressed my left hand to my bodice, but it did nothing to slow my heart.

"Ah, there you are, Bellini," Maestro Tomassini said. By heaven, he had a knack for intruding at the worst moments!

The maestro bowed to me. "*Buonasera,* Signorina. Forgive me, but there's someone here I'd very much like my nephew to meet."

"Of course," I said.

Bellini stood and bowed. "I'll be back as soon as I can."

When they were gone, I rubbed the soft leather portfolio in my lap. If the concertos were good enough, perhaps it wouldn't be that long before Bellini approached Father. But what would Father say?

In all the months of waiting and hoping, I'd never allowed myself to truly believe Bellini reciprocated my feelings. I'd feared tempting *il malocchio*—the evil eye that curses those who take happiness for granted. Now that Bellini'd finally declared his intentions, I considered how Father might respond. Although the negotiations for the purchase of the feudal estate in Montevecchia dragged, Father was still confident he would soon be made a *don*. Gabriella had said Father would wait until after he'd acquired his title to arrange betrothals for Maria and me, so he could marry us to noblemen.

Fear clutched my heart. Bellini wasn't nobility. And from what he'd told me, he'd likely never be.

Gabriella's tinkling laughter pulled me from my reverie. She stood beside her new husband in a small group on the other side of the room. She glanced in my direction and waved.

Gabriella whispered something into the groom's ear. A moment later, she was seated before me in the chair Bellini had vacated. "I saw you speaking with your azure-eyed violinist," she said. "So tell me quickly; was I right?"

"Yes." I held up the portfolio. "He's been working to prove himself a worthy suitor. He's written a series of violin concertos he hopes will establish him as a serious composer."

"I knew it!" Gabriella leaned over and grabbed me with both hands. "I told you all along he was smitten with you. I'm so happy for you." She squeezed my forearms. "But you don't look pleased. This is what you wanted, is it not?"

"Oh yes," I said. "I'm just worried about Father."

"Because Bellini doesn't have a title?"

I nodded. "I've just been thinking about what you said at your ball, about Father wanting to marry Maria and me into the nobility. Do you think it's enough that Bellini's great-uncle is a marquis?"

"Not from what I know of your father."

"Then what am I to do?"

"There is hope yet, Emilia." Gabriella released my arms. "Marquis don Vittore Bellini is an old man, and his wife died without leaving him an heir. His quarrel with your suitor's father might actually work in your favor."

"You know about the falling out between the marquis and Bellini's father?"

"I asked my husband about your suitor's family." Gabriella giggled. "It still feels odd to call Count Cavalieri my husband." She shook her head. "Anyway, he happens to be well-acquainted with Marquis Bellini. We even invited the marquis to our wedding celebration."

"He's here then?" I craned my neck to look about the room.

"No, he sent his regrets. He's been ill," Gabriella said. "However, his illness may be a blessing for you. My husband says the marquis has been pondering his situation. As things stand now, his estate will go to a distant cousin in Padua. Marquis Bellini is quite displeased at the prospect. He has no great love for this cousin, and he'd rather his inheritance went to a Milanese."

"What are you saying, Gabriella?"

"I'm saying that, despite the family feud, it wouldn't take much to persuade the old marquis to leave everything to his great-nephew, especially if that nephew plans to marry into a noble family, which yours will soon be."

"So then Father becoming a nobleman would be a good thing?"

"Most definitely," Gabriella said, "especially with a little help from me." The twinkle in her eyes suggested she already had a plan in mind.

"How can you help?"

"As soon as Marquis Bellini is well enough, I'll ask my husband to call on him to speak on your suitor's behalf. Given the count's powers of persuasion, he should have no trouble convincing the marquis to leave everything to his great-nephew."

"*Grazie*, Gabriella." I squeezed her hand. "I don't know how I can repay you."

"My payment will be seeing you married to the man of your dreams."

A hint of sadness flickered in Gabriella's eyes. I wondered if she still wished cupid's arrows had pierced Lodovico Volpi's heart instead of Count Cavalieri's.

Chapter Twenty-Five
Bellini's Portfolio

On the carriage ride home from Gabriella's wedding celebration, I kept the portfolio hidden under my cloak. I didn't want to have to explain how I'd come to have it. Fortunately, Adriana's chatter kept Father distracted.

I'd told Maria of the portfolio and its significance right after speaking with Gabriella. My sister understood, then, why I stayed up late poring over Bellini's music scores.

As I studied the music, I heard the instruments in my mind—the solo violin, the other strings, and the harpsichord playing *basso continuo*. Some of the concertos reminded me of Vivaldi's work. Bellini's music withstood the comparison well. His skill as a composer had continued to blossom in the nearly five months since we'd stopped studying together. His music filled me with pride, and hope, too, especially when I discovered the letter he'd enclosed.

October 19, 1738

Dear Signorina Salvini,

I placed this letter here, behind my music scores, because I did not want its contents to bias your appraisal of my work. By now

*you have seen the three violin concertos. I trust you to give me
your honest reaction to them. I'm hoping you are well-pleased, for
I dedicate these concertos to you. You have been my inspiration.
It was only after studying your touching composition, Mamma's
Sonata, that I dared express my own emotions in my music. I
have learned much from you.*

*With the income from these and other compositions, I hope to
have sufficient funds to provide for my sister's dowry within six
to eight months. Then I can begin saving for our future together,
assuming such a future is agreeable to you. I pray no other suitor
will supplant me in the meantime.*

*For now, I ask your help and advice. Please write to me as soon
as possible regarding how I might improve these compositions.*

*Your faithful servant,
Antonio Carlo Bellini*

I clutched the letter to my chest. I'd been his inspiration.
He was planning for *our* future together. And that future, or at
least our courtship, might begin in little more than six months.
My heart sang for joy at the thought.

I pulled open the desk drawer and took out the twine Bellini had used to ensnare my wrist. I had untangled it so the
twine was now a smooth loop. The knot holding the ends together seemed small, insignificant. I slipped my hands into the
loop, stretching it taut. The tiny knot held tight. I smiled. Up
until now, I'd thought of the twine as a token of my feelings
for Bellini. Now it also represented how we would soon be
bound to each other forever.

The candles had burned low by the time I began writing my
response to Bellini's letter. After listing a few suggestions for
how he might make his wonderful music even better, I wrote:

*Please know that these suggestions are minor. I believe your
concertos are already engaging, innovative works. I feel most
honored that you have dedicated them to me, and I look forward
to hearing them performed one day, with you as the soloist.*

*Meanwhile, know that my heart will be satisfied with no suitor
but you. I can hardly wait for our future together to begin.*

*Your greatest admirer,
Emilia Teresa Salvini*

Once the ink was dry, I folded the sheet and sealed it, pressing my monogram into the hot wax. I placed the letter inside Bellini's portfolio, on top of the one he had addressed to me. I shut the portfolio and stroked the soft leather. I had to hide it somewhere. If Father learned of our relationship too soon, it would ruin all our plans. But I was too tired to think of a good hiding place. I slid the portfolio under my pillow for now. I'd find a better place in the morning.

I blew out the candles and climbed into bed. Despite the late hour, though, sleep would not come. I couldn't stop thinking about Bellini. He was working so hard to shorten the time until we could be together. I wanted to find a way to help him.

~

I must have eventually dozed off because I woke to the sound of someone screaming followed by cries of "No, no. This can't be happening!"

I rubbed the sand from my eyes. "What in the name of heaven?"

Maria was already pulling on her dressing gown. "It sounds like Adriana."

Her words were like a splash of water on my face. I jumped from bed, slipped on my dressing gown, and raced after Maria.

When we reached Adriana's bedroom, Father was coming out. "Stay with her," he said. "I will fetch the midwife myself."

We hurried into the room. Adriana was praying, saying over and over, "Lord in heaven, please help me. Please, please, help me." She lay in the middle of her huge bed clutching her abdomen. She appeared to be in labor, but it was much too soon. The baby wasn't expected for several months.

Adriana screamed again.

"Hush, Signora Madre," Maria said. "Calm yourself." Maria sat down beside Adriana and took her hand. "All this screaming will only make things worse."

"But the pain." Adriana choked down a sob.

Maria said, "Emmi, run and fetch some wine."

I hurried to the parlor. Did Maria mean for me to fill a glass or bring the whole bottle? Adriana screamed again. I grabbed both bottle and goblet and ran to the bedroom.

Mademoiselle Duval was in the room now. "I will keep the little ones away," she said to Maria then left.

I poured wine into the goblet and handed it to Maria. She pressed it to Adriana's lips. "Drink," Maria commanded. "It will calm you."

Adriana took a sip. "*Grazie.*" For a moment, her face relaxed. Then her back arched, and she cried out, "Dear Lord, have mercy."

"More," Maria said, holding the goblet to Adriana's lips again.

Adriana obeyed. She relaxed again but then her forehead broke out in a sweat.

Maria pulled back the bedcovers. I covered my mouth to stifle a gasp. Blood had stained the bottom sheet bright red.

Maria pretended not to notice. "Here, Adriana," she said, "let me slide you closer." After shifting Adriana over, Maria laid the top sheet over the stain.

Nina came in with a tray. "Cook has brewed some valerian tea." Nina set the tray on a table. She poured a cup of the tea and stirred in some honey. As she handed the cup to Maria, I whiffed the tea's horrid aroma. The scent reminded me of the night Mamma told me of her disturbing dream. Only days before she died.

I swallowed hard. I couldn't stay here.

I hurried downstairs to our family chapel. Isabella was already there, praying a rosary.

"How did you know?" I asked as I knelt beside her.

"I ran into Mademoiselle Duval in the hallway when I went to find out what was happening. She wouldn't tell me anything. Is Adriana going to lose the baby?"

"I fear so." I knelt beside her. "Let's pray together."

Partway through the first decade, my mind wandered. Poor Adriana. She'd confessed wanting this baby to be a boy. That way Vincenzo wouldn't feel so outnumbered by all the girls in

the family. I suspected her true motive was to please Father—
he had hoped for another son the last time Mamma was with
child.

Thinking of Mamma made my heart tighten. Could it already be over a year and a half since she left us? *Oh, Mamma, I
wish you were still here.*

I pressed my fist to my bodice in a silent *mea culpa*. I should
be praying for Adriana. Her life was in jeopardy now, along
with her baby's.

—

I have no idea how long we knelt in prayer before Maria finally
came to the chapel to give us the news. Adriana's baby lived
only long enough to be baptized. As soon as our stepmother
learned it was a boy, she began wailing. The midwife tried to
calm her with assurances that she'd be able to have more children in time, but Adriana was inconsolable. She didn't stop
wailing until the midwife gave her a sleeping potion. Poor
Adriana.

"I'll look in on her one more time," Maria said. "Why don't
you two go back to bed?"

We left the chapel in silence. Upon returning to my bedroom, I suddenly recalled Bellini's portfolio. I hurried to the
bed. The portfolio was still under my pillow. Inside, the music
scores sat on top, undisturbed. I breathed a sigh of relief.

I realized then that the scores themselves gave no clue to
my relationship with Bellini. I took them out and placed them
in my desk. Then I hid Bellini's letter in the chest containing
my trousseau—it seemed an appropriate place. Finally, I took
the portfolio, which now contained only my sealed letter to
Bellini, and went in search of Naldo. I asked him to have the
leather case delivered to Bellini right away.

"I shall do it myself, Signorina," Naldo said. He seemed to
welcome an excuse to go out. An eerie silence had settled over
the house in the wake of the baby's death.

Relieved of the burden of the portfolio, I returned to bed.
Despite my concerns for Adriana, exhaustion overcame me
and I soon fell asleep.

Chapter Twenty-Six
A Healing Balm

In the following days, Adriana fell into a deep melancholy. She refused to get out of bed. She ate little. She barely spoke. For the first time since we'd met, I found myself missing her chatter.

Try as he might, Father couldn't coax my stepmother out of bed. Finally, he sent for Adriana's father. Alfonso Grilli left his clerk in charge of the business and came to stay with us. Grilli planted himself beside his daughter's bed early in the morning and chattered away until late at night. He spoke about his business, the weather, the state of the silk industry. Adriana remained listless. After a week, Grilli gave up and went home. I think it pained him to see his daughter so despondent. I know it pained me.

One day, I found myself sitting at the harpsichord playing *Mamma's Sonata*. Adriana's grief had roused my own—I missed Mamma more than ever. I felt as though the scab on my heart had been torn off. The sonata was my healing balm.

When I'd finished playing, I looked up at the portrait of the cerulean Madonna holding the infant Jesus. Today the motherly love in her eyes made me think of Adriana. After carrying her baby boy for so many months, she must have already grown to love him.

Perhaps hearing my sonata might be a balm for her wound, too.

I went to Adriana's room. She lay in bed, staring up at the canopy. Her pale skin and shrunken cheeks put me in mind of a ghost.

"*Buon giorno*, Signora Madre," I said, trying to sound cheerful. "How are you today?"

She didn't answer. But she didn't turn away either.

"I have something I want you to hear." I sat down on the edge of the bed. "It's the first sonata I ever wrote."

Adriana remained silent, but she seemed to be listening. What could I say to get her out of bed? She probably wouldn't believe me if I told her my music would help ease her sadness. In truth, I wasn't sure it would. I knew only how the sonata had helped ease mine.

"If you come with me, I'll tell you something I've never told anyone," I said, "not even Maria."

Adriana looked at me expectantly.

"You have to come hear the music first," I said. "And then I'll tell you my secret."

Adriana gave the slightest nod.

"Good."

Adriana tried to sit up so I could help her into her dressing gown, but she was terribly weak. How would I get her to the harpsichord salon?

"I don't think you're strong enough to walk," I said. "Shall I see if Father will carry you?"

Adriana nodded.

I found Father in his study. "Adriana has agreed to come to the harpsichord salon to hear me play."

He raised his right eyebrow. "How did you manage that?"

"I promised to tell her a secret if she listened to a sonata I wrote—the one I composed in memory of Mamma. I thought the music might help ease her sorrow." As I said the words, I cringed inside. What if Father thought my plan ridiculous?

Father stood. "Well, if nothing else, a change of scenery should do her good." He followed me back to Adriana's room.

He, too, tried to sound cheerful as he said to Adriana, "I understand you'd like to hear some music."

She nodded.

"A splendid idea!" Father lifted Adriana into his arms. I gathered a blanket from the foot of the bed.

When we reached the harpsichord salon, Father set Adriana down on a sofa near the fireplace. I covered her with the blanket while Father stoked the fire.

"I leave you to your private concert," Father said to Adriana. "I'll return in a little while."

After he left, I said, "I had a great deal of difficulty composing the sonata I'm about to play for you. Perhaps you'll be able to guess why." I sat down at the harpsichord and began the first movement, which expressed the depths of my sorrow at losing Mamma. I didn't look at Adriana. I wanted her to feel free to cry unobserved.

The lighter, second, movement was a pleasant interlude. Then came the third movement, with its odd mix of joy and anger. Was that how Adriana's grief felt?

As I neared the end of the piece, I gazed at the painting of the cerulean Madonna. I let myself again feel the embrace of Mamma's love. The calm it brought me flowed through my fingers and into the music.

I played the last chords then let my hands fall to my lap. I paused for a moment before turning to Adriana. She sat hunched over with her knees pulled to her chin, her hands covering her face. Her shoulders shook. Was she sobbing?

I hurried to her side. "Are you all right, Signora Madre?"

Adriana took a handkerchief from the pocket of her dressing gown and swiped at her tears. "You wrote that for your mother, didn't you?" she said, her voice rough. "After her death." Adriana blew her nose into the handkerchief.

"Yes. I call it *Mamma's Sonata*." I pulled up a chair and sat down. "After Mamma died, I couldn't play at all. I didn't think I could ever again enjoy music, or life, without her. Then Maestro Tomassini wrote to console me. In his letter, he called music 'the best medicine for sorrow.' So I made myself play. I tried to find solace in the music, but I couldn't. Nothing I played came close to expressing my grief."

"It's more than grief," Adriana said. "It's anger and guilt, too."

"Yes. I learned that while writing the sonata. Yet even in the midst of the sorrow and anger and guilt, there was light. The light of remembering Mamma's love. I finally came to understand her love will never die."

Fresh tears fell from Adriana's eyes. "But my baby died before I could love him."

"Oh, I don't believe that." I put my hand on her knee. "I believe you loved him from the very beginning, from the moment when you knew you were with child. Isn't that so?"

Adriana nodded, drying her cheeks. "I'd already chosen his name: Alfonso, for my father. In my mind, I called him Alfonsino."

"You can go on loving Alfonsino, just as I have gone on loving Mamma."

Adriana blew her nose again, then said, "Is that your secret? That you still love and miss your mother?"

My throat tightened. My response came out in a whisper. "Yes."

"That's no secret, Emilia. I knew it at our first meeting. I know all of you still miss your mother. I'm not surprised, for I continue to miss my own Mamma, even after all these years. But the others have managed to find room in their hearts for me. You're the only one who has kept me shut out." Adriana put a hand on mine. "You realize, don't you, that letting me into your heart doesn't mean you have to stop loving your mother."

Tears sprang to my eyes. Blinking them back, I said, "I must confess, I *have* missed your chatter."

Adriana smiled. "I suppose that's a start." She curled her legs under her. "I believe Maestro Tomassini is right. Music *is* the best medicine for sorrow. Would you play the sonata for me again?"

From then on, Adriana joined me in the harpsichord salon every day for her dose of "medicine." Her appetite slowly returned as did her strength. But she no longer seemed as child-like as before.

Chapter Twenty-Seven
Gabriella's Sitting Room

Upon learning of the death of Adriana's baby, Antonio Bellini sent a letter to me via Maestro Tomassini to express his condolences. He also wrote:

I revised my violin concertos with your comments in mind. Maestro Tomassini is quite pleased with the new versions. In fact, he has asked me to perform them at a private concert a few weeks from now. I could not have hoped for more. By God's grace, this will lead to lucrative commissions.

I cannot tell you how happy your letter made me. However, I realize it is improper for us to maintain a correspondence, as we are not yet betrothed. That is why I have sent this to you by means of the maestro. From now on, I will save my pen for my work. You continue to inspire me—I have already completed three more violin concertos, and I have begun a concerto grosso. I hope your own work is going well.

Even though I am unable to write to you as I would like, know that you are in my thoughts and prayers daily.

Your faithful and devoted servant,
Antonio Carlo Bellini

I thrilled at Bellini's news about the private concert. How I wished I could be there! And how kind of Bellini to mention my own work. In truth, I'd written no new music since baby Alfonsino's death. Now that Adriana was better, it was time I returned to composing. If only I could use my music to provide for our future, as Bellini was doing. But I couldn't imagine anyone paying for music composed by a woman.

Instead of creating more serious pieces like the ones I'd written for Father's meetings, I began composing lighter, more joyful music. I started writing songs of praise and thanksgiving but soon found myself working on love songs. The words and melodies came easily. I needed only to think of Bellini for inspiration.

Not long after Gabriella returned from her honeymoon, I went to visit her at Count Cavalieri's palazzo. A footman wearing livery in the blue and red of the Cavalieri coat of arms led me into Gabriella's sitting room. The room was larger than our parlor at home and furnished in the Chinese style. A tall, six-paneled screen divided the room. Black and gold geometric designs adorned one side of the screen. The other side bore a painting of tall, exotic-looking birds surrounded by plants and flowers.

Even the tea the maidservant offered me was Chinese, served in fine porcelain cups trimmed with real gold.

"That will be all for now," Gabriella told the maidservant.

"Your home is quite impressive, Gabriella," I said when we were alone. "I've never seen such a large sitting room." I raised my cup toward the paneled screen. "And the furnishings are so intriguing."

"I'm getting rid of it all," Gabriella said, "the furniture, paintings, even the chandelier. My husband has given me permission to redecorate whatever rooms I desire, save for his study and the ballroom."

"Why would you want to part with such lovely things?"

"I feel as though I'm living with a ghost," Gabriella said. "The count's first wife picked out all this." She made a sweeping gesture with her hand. "I want to make the room, and this house, my own."

I wondered if Adriana had felt the same way. I'd never considered how being surrounded by Mamma's furnishings might have made my stepmother uneasy. "As soon as Adriana moved into our home, she redecorated her bedroom and sitting room," I said. "Until then, I'd simply disliked my stepmother. But after she had Mamma's things taken away, I despised her."

"Hmm. I hadn't thought about how my stepdaughters might feel," Gabriella said. "I can't imagine they'd really care. They're only three and five."

"It could mean even more to them," I said, "as they may have little to remember their mother by."

"You do have a point. Perhaps I'll wait awhile longer before I redecorate." Gabriella took another sip of tea. "Heaven knows I have enough other things to occupy my time now that I am the wife of a senator. Which reminds me—a few days ago I had the privilege of attending a private concert at the home of one of my husband's friends." Gabriella gave a sly smile. "And I witnessed a magnificent performance by a certain azure-eyed violinist."

My heart leapt at the mention of Bellini. "You saw him? How did he do?"

"Well, in truth, he seemed rather nervous at first. But he soon settled into the music."

I set down my cup, tapping my foot impatiently, as I waited for more details.

Gabriella drank the last of her tea and set her cup down, too. Finally, she said, "Bellini made a most favorable impression on us all, especially Archbishop Stampa."

"The archbishop was there?"

Gabriella nodded. "He seemed quite enthralled with your young man's music. The archbishop even called Bellini aside to speak with him after the concert."

"Heaven be praised," I said. "This is just what Bellini was hoping for." I told Gabriella of my letter from Bellini, and how he hoped the private concert would lead to lucrative commissions.

"No doubt the archbishop will soon be offering such a commission, if he hasn't already." Gabriella grinned. "So tell me, is your father any closer to becoming a nobleman?"

"His broker called him to Montevecchia again. I expect they may be nearing the end of their negotiations to acquire the feudal estate."

"And then you'll be one step closer to marrying Bellini."

"But what of his lack of title?" I said. "Even if he succeeds in his plans, you said yourself Father won't accept Bellini as my suitor if he isn't a nobleman."

"I told you to leave that to me." Gabriella patted my hand. "A few days ago, I learned Marquis Bellini has finally left his sickbed. My husband has promised to call on the old marquis at the earliest opportunity."

"*Mille grazie*, Gabriella." I wanted to jump up and hug her. But given her new position, I thought it more appropriate to simply squeeze her hand.

In December, word reached Milan that Archduchess Maria Teresa, the eldest daughter of Emperor Charles VI, would soon be visiting Florence with her husband, Francis. Florence was the capital of Tuscany, which lay just south of our region, and the emperor had recently made Francis Grand Duke of Tuscany.

Father was in high spirits the evening he shared the news. He talked about it all through supper. This would be the archduchess's first trip to Italy. Her father, the emperor, had no male heirs and had declared Archduchess Maria Teresa to be his successor. Father hoped that, as our future ruler, the archduchess might want to visit Milan before her return to Austria.

"The archduchess and grand duke should arrive in Florence by mid-January," Father said as the kitchen maid cleared away the dinner plates. "I plan to take advantage of their proximity to send Her Royal Highness a token of our esteem."

To Maria he said, "Daughter, you shall compile a summary of the lectures you have presented at my meetings, as well as a page dedicating the essays to the archduchess. I will have your work published as a booklet and send a copy to the archduchess."

Maria's eyes widened, but she said only, "As you wish, Signor Padre."

Adriana asked, "Is there some greater purpose behind this plan of yours, Husband?"

"Indeed," Father said. "My purchase of the feudal estate at Montevecchia has become mired in bureaucracy. By courting the archduchess's favor, I hope to hasten the process and finally gain the title of 'count.'"

"How clever of you!" Adriana raised her wine goblet.

"We must not toast my strategy until after it proves successful, my dear. And then we will do so with the bottle of Montevecchian wine I've been saving." Father smiled, then said to Maria, "The booklet must be at the printer by January tenth."

That was only a few weeks away. But Maria didn't protest. She simply said, "*Sì*, Signor Padre."

Father said to me, "Archduchess Maria Teresa is known to be a great lover of music. I'm told she especially enjoys singing. Have you written any songs recently?"

My cheeks flushed as I thought of the love songs I'd been working on. "Yes," I said. "A few."

"Good. Gather together your best ones, plus your newest sonatas, and ask Maestro Tomassini which would be most appropriate for a collection dedicated to the archduchess."

"My lessons with the maestro are suspended while he prepares the opera company for *carnevale*," I said.

"Oh, yes, of course," Father said. "This can't wait. Write out copies of your scores and give them to me. I'll bring them to the maestro myself and explain the situation. I'm sure he can make time to look over your work and give us his advice."

"As you wish, Signor Padre."

In the following weeks, I dedicated myself to reworking my songs. This was my chance to contribute to my own future. If my music pleased the archduchess, she could help Father finally become a count. Then, as Gabriella said, I would be one step closer to marrying Antonio Bellini.

I modified several of my best songs to make them hymns of praise—the archduchess was known for her religious devotion. She was also the mother of two young daughters. So I revised my favorite love song into a lullaby Her Royal Highness could sing to her little girls.

When I was done, I carefully wrote out copies of the songs and my newest sonatas, as Father had instructed. There were fourteen scores in all. As I bundled them together, I said a prayer my work would win the archduchess's favor.

I gave the packet to Father on the eve of Epiphany, the same day Maria completed her booklet. On his way to delivering Maria's booklet to the printer's, Father left my music with the maestro for his advice.

Maestro Tomassini returned the scores to me a few days later. In the accompanying letter, he wrote:

I am pleased to see that despite the lapse in our lessons, your composition skills continue to improve. These pieces, while on the surface joyful and pleasing to the ear, also express exquisite feelings of love and devotion. Well done!

Regarding the archduchess: I had the great privilege of meeting her when I was in Vienna several years ago. From what I know of her tastes, she will find all these pieces enchanting. My only suggestion is that you send an even dozen. Then, should the archduchess ask for more of your work, you will have two pieces at the ready.

I relayed the maestro's suggestion to Father. He had me remove one song and one sonata. Then he dictated a letter of dedication for me to pen. When we were done, he said, "The archduchess and grand duke have left Verona and are currently en route to Florence. My messenger will have your music and your sister's booklet there in time for Her Royal Highness's arrival."

"*Sì*, Signor Padre."

As I left Father's study, I couldn't help hoping it would be my music, and not Maria's booklet, that inspired the archduchess to assist Father. That way, I'd help bring about my own happiness.

Chapter Twenty-Eight
Masquerade Ball

In early January, Gabriella and her husband sent an invitation for us to attend a masquerade ball in honor of *carnevale*. Maria, Isabella, and I were in Adriana's sitting room working on our embroidery when our stepmother told us the news.

Adriana was so excited she set down her needlework and paced about. "We are requested to dress as characters from the *commedia dell'arte*."

"I do not wish to attend," Maria said.

Adriana swung around to face Maria. "Why on earth not?"

"I dislike both crowds and costumes," Maria said. "Please don't force me to go."

"Of course I won't force you," Adriana said.

Isabella jumped up. "If Maria's not going, may I take her place?"

"I'll have to consult your father," Adriana said. "What about you, Emilia? Would you like to attend?"

"I wouldn't dream of missing it." I'd still had no word from Gabriella about whether her husband had visited Marquis Bellini.

Adriana clapped her hands together. "Marvelous! What shall we dress as?"

I said, "I should like to go as Cantarina, the singer and musician."

"*Perfetto*," Adriana said. "Too bad there aren't any kindly stepmothers in the *commedia*."

"I think you should dress as La Servetta," I said. "Her costume is simple. You need only borrow a dress and apron from one of the maidservants." I refrained from pointing out how the character matched Adriana's own chatty personality.

"Very well, I will," Adriana said. "Isabella, if your father gives his permission, who would you dress as?"

"I should like to go as the character who bears my name—Isabella." Leave it to my younger sister to pick the role of the leading lady. She would require a fine gown for the part.

"How appropriate," Adriana said with a laugh. "And what of your father? Should he be a servant like me?"

This time, it was our turn to laugh.

Adriana looked puzzled. "Did I say something funny?"

"Father would never humble himself in such a way," Maria said.

Isabella added, "Whenever there's a masquerade, Father simply puts on his best black suit and wears the mask of Il Dottore, the scholar."

"I see," Adriana said. "Hmm. I wonder how he'll feel about my going as a servant then?"

"I'm sure Father will agree with whatever makes you happy," I said. Ever since baby Alfonsino's death, Father'd gone out of his way to please Adriana.

"Then I'll have to tell him it would make me happy for Isabella to attend in Maria's place." She winked at Isabella then sat down and picked up her needlework.

To Isabella's great joy, Father gave his permission. Adriana sent word to Gabriella that the four of us would be attending the event.

The night of the masquerade ball, rows of torches lit the exterior walls of Palazzo Cavalieri. Inside, the light was brighter still. Gabriella and her husband greeted us as we entered the grand ballroom. They were dressed as the *innamorati*—the two lovers, Lidia and Flavio. She wore a stunning royal blue gown with a low neckline that showed off her pearl necklace. Matching pearl earrings dangled from her ears. Count Cavalieri wore a feathered hat and a long cloak of dark blue. Neither of them wore masks, only matching heart-shaped beauty marks just under their left eyes.

"Ah, Cantarina," Gabriella said when she saw me. "I'm glad you brought your lute. I hope you'll play for us this evening."

"My performance will be brief," I said. "for my repertoire is small." I plucked a simple do-re-mi in several different keys.

Count Cavalieri laughed. "Then perhaps it's good we have hired an orchestra." He gestured toward the far end of the ballroom where several musicians were playing a lively sonata. They were all dressed in black, with black masks. "The dancing will commence shortly," the count said. "Until then, please enjoy some refreshments."

Gabriella would be too busy greeting guests to talk for a while, so I followed Father, Adriana, and Isabella into the ballroom.

"Look at all the wonderful costumes," Adriana said. The most conspicuous were the men dressed as Arlecchino. With their costumes of multi-colored, diamond-shaped patches, they reminded me of the narrator of the puppet show we saw in Masciago. At least one man was dressed as Brighella, the conniving shopkeeper, who wore a white suit trimmed with green stripes. A corpulent man in the military uniform and sword of a Capitano bowed to Adriana and said, "*Buonasera*, Signora Salvini." He lifted his hat to me. "Signorina." A mask obscured his face, but I recognized his voice easily enough.

I curtsied and said, "*Buonasera*, Count Riccardi."

"Ah, forgive me, your Lordship," Adriana said as she curtsied. "I didn't know it was you. This will be a fine game, tonight, trying to guess the faces behind all the masks."

"Fortunately for me, you did not choose to hide behind a mask, Signora Salvini," Count Riccardi said.

"It is just like at the *commedia*," Adriana said, "where only the men wear masks. I wonder why that is."

Father said, "Perhaps it is because the men of the *commedia* are embarrassed to appear in the role of buffoons."

"No," Count Riccardi said, "I think it is because the women don't want to hide their beauty. And I am glad for it."

"Come, come, Capitano," Countess Riccardi said as she approached from behind him. From her simple gown and red shawl, I guessed she was Columbina, another servant character. "Are you flirting already?" Countess Riccardi said to her husband.

"Isn't that what *carnevale* is all about," Count Riccardi said, "deception and flirtation?"

"I thought it was about eating and dancing our fill before the season of abstinence begins," Adriana said.

"Let us eat, then," Father said, "for Count Cavalieri has laid out a feast." Father gestured to the food table.

Everything at the banquet table looked delicious, but I was too anxious to eat. "Come, you must try something," Adriana said, holding out her plate.

"Very well." I took a *chiacchiera* from her plate and nibbled the sweet fritter while I watched Gabriella. When the stream of guests finally slowed, I hurried to her side.

"I've been waiting for a chance to speak with you," I said. "Do you have any news for me?"

"Indeed," she said. "Come quickly, before the dancing begins."

Gabriella led me down the hall to a small parlor. "My husband finally saw Marquis Bellini," she said, shutting the door behind us. "The old man is in failing health. He may not be long for this world."

"Oh, my." I leaned against the door.

"Marquis Bellini confessed that his poor health has him worrying about his legacy. He despises the idea of his estate going to someone who is not Milanese. So my husband asked whether the marquis would consider leaving the property to his great-nephew, especially in light of the young man's accomplishments as a musician and composer."

"And what did he say?"

"Marquis Bellini admitted the thought had crossed his mind. But he wanted proof the young man would not repeat his father's mistake. According to my husband, the marquis's exact words were, 'I am willing to leave my estate and title to my great-nephew on one condition. He must first be formally betrothed to a woman of noble rank.'"

My skin broke out in gooseflesh. I stepped away from the door. "He really said that?"

Gabriella grinned and took my hands in hers. "Isn't it wonderful! Once your father acquires his title and gives his consent for your betrothal, Marquis Bellini will change his will. Your handsome violinist will become the next Marquis don Bellini."

My heart rejoiced, but my mind feared the news was too good to be true. "What if the old marquis dies before then? I have no idea how long it will take for Father to finalize his purchase of the Montevecchia property."

"Then we must both pray for the marquis's good health," Gabriella said.

"And for Father to soon obtain his title," I said. "He's had word the archduchess is in possession of our gifts and is hoping they'll please her enough to want to help him."

"We should pray for that too then," Gabriella said.

Chapter Twenty-Nine
The Nivola

L ent seemed to last forever. I kept a strict fast and prayed daily for both Marquis Bellini's health and for Archduchess Maria Teresa to like my music. Father said nothing more of our gifts to the archduchess or of the status of his negotiations for the Montevecchia estate.

I filled the long hours by composing more new music. One afternoon in late April, I was at the keyboard working on my first violin concerto when Adriana rushed into the harpsichord salon. "They're coming to Milan, Emilia!"

"Who's coming?"

"The archduchess and grand duke," Adriana said. "They're stopping here on their way back to Vienna. Isn't it marvelous!"

"Really?" I stood up. "When will they arrive?"

"The first week of May," Adriana said. "Your father's hoping to arrange for an audience with the archduchess while she's here. You and Maria and I are to have new gowns made especially for the occasion, in the Mantua style worn at court." Adriana clapped her hands. "The Montevecchia estate may soon be ours *and* the noble rank associated with it!"

And then, God willing, I would be betrothed to Antonio Bellini.

Unable to contain my joy, I stood and hugged my tiny step-mother.

~

On the second day of May, over 2,000 of the city's soldiers and countless citizens lined the streets of Milan waiting to greet Archduchess Maria Teresa. Father, Adriana, Maria, Isabella, and I sat in our carriage amid the throng near *Porta Romana*—the southern gate that led to Rome. I was filled with nervous excitement. Although I knew there'd be no chance to speak privately to the archduchess today, I couldn't stop thinking about how much my future depended upon her.

As time passed, the sky grew dark with clouds. Thunder rumbled in the distance. The rain, which began with a gentle *ping-pang* against the sides of our carriage, gradually crescendoed to a pounding roar.

Crack. The thunder was so close it made me jump. A burst of lightning lit the murky darkness. Bystanders scattered. Even the troops dispersed.

"The storm must have delayed the archduchess's party," Father said, raising his voice to be heard. "She may not arrive until tomorrow now." Father called out to the carriage driver to take us home.

"Oh, what a shame," Adriana said.

I sighed in disappointment.

"We should pray for their safe travels," Maria said.

I immediately began a silent rosary.

~

The heavy rain continued into the evening. Around ten, a loud boom rang out. At first, I thought the thunder had started again. Then more booms shook our palazzo and I realized it was gunfire—an artillery salute in honor of the archduchess's arrival. Count Visconti, the emperor's majordomo, had planned a grand welcoming ceremony for all to witness on the steps of the Royal Palace. He was to present the archduchess with the keys to the city's gates. *The Gazette* reported later that the unceasing deluge forced the ceremony indoors. Some high-ranking officials were the only onlookers.

My first glimpse of the archduchess came the next day, which happened to be the Feast of the Cross. Our family joined the crowd inside the *Duomo* to participate in the twice-yearly ritual of the Holy Nail, a relic believed to be one of the nails from the cross of Christ. The Nail is stored in a crystal case set in the center of an enormous gold cross suspended high inside the cathedral's dome. The cross can only be reached via the *Nivola*—a mechanical, cloud-shaped lift said to have been designed by Leonardo da Vinci himself. The lift sits behind the *Duomo's* main altar. From where we stood, I could see neither the *Nivola* nor the three cathedral priests who climbed into it.

Bing-bong-bang, bing-bong-bang, bing-bong-bang. The cathedral bells tolled over and over as the *Nivola* floated slowly upward. When it came into view above the altar, I could just make out the statues of the two angels seated atop the man-made cloud. I leaned my head back to watch the *Nivola* continue its ascent. *Bing-bong-bang, bing-bong-bang, bing-bong-bang.* Finally, the *Nivola* came to rest before the gold cross, 120 feet in the air.

The bells stopped.

A majestic chord poured from the cathedral organ, sending shivers down my spine. The choir of monks then led us in singing the litany of saints while one of the priests transferred the gold cross holding the Holy Nail into the *Nivola*.

As the *Nivola* made its slow descent, we sang *ora pro nobis*—pray for us—to one saint after another. The *Nivola* eventually disappeared behind the altar again. I stood on tiptoe to look for it, but a smoky fog obscured my view. I relaxed back onto my feet. The *Nivola* must have come to a stop and the priests were now incensing the cross.

When the litany of saints ended, the choir began singing a sacred motet. The fog of incense grew thicker. Many of the people in the front rows coughed as the acrid scent reached them.

A long line of acolytes and clergymen eventually emerged from the cloud. They processed out to the front of the altar. I stretched up onto my tiptoes again. Finally, I spotted the arch-duchess near the end of the procession. My heart fluttered.

Archduchess Maria Teresa carried the huge cross before her, concealing my view of her face.

The priests cleared a path so she could place the reliquary on the altar. I caught a glimpse of the jeweled diadem in her golden-blonde hair just before she knelt and disappeared from sight. It hadn't occurred to me before that even the emperor's daughter had to submit herself to God.

The rest of us fell to our knees, too. I prayed again for old Marquis Bellini's health, and for the archduchess to help Father.

After the ceremony, Her Royal Highness braved the persistent rain to tour the city in her carriage. As we waited for our own carriage, my tiny stepmother complained, "This infernal rain is ruining everything. I didn't see the archduchess at all."

"You will," Father said. "I promise."

Father was true to his word. He arranged for us to be invited to a reception honoring the archduchess two days later, at Count Visconti's palazzo.

We rode to the reception in our best carriage—Father and Adriana sat facing Maria and me. I kept my hands pressed against my abdomen in a feeble attempt to calm my rising anxiety. I'd never met an archduchess before. I wondered what she was like. I hoped she wasn't as stern as Governor von Traun had been the first time I'd met him. And I prayed the maestro was right about her finding my music "enchanting."

Near the palazzo, the streets seemed even more crowded with beggars than usual. The rain had finally ended, but it had left huge puddles in the road.

Maria suddenly cried out, "Stop! Please! Stop the carriage now!" The driver pulled up sharply. We fell from our seats onto the carriage floor. I bumped heads with Adriana.

Father cursed loudly as he helped Adriana up. He scolded Maria. "Daughter, what in the name of heaven has gotten into you?"

Before Maria could answer, the driver opened the door. "A thousand pardons Signor Salvini," he said. "I heard the Signorina shout just as a beggar was about to step in front of the horses. Is everyone—"

"I must see if she's hurt," Maria said, moving to the door. The driver helped her down. I followed. She ran to the beggar, who lay face down in a puddle before the horses.

My sister was about to kneel on the ground. "Maria, wait!" I called. "Your gown."

She looked down at her elegant new gown and then at the woman in the puddle. Maria motioned to the driver. "Quickly. Come see that she's unharmed."

The driver turned the beggar over. Her face was badly scarred from the pox, and the rags she wore were caked with filth. I stepped back, repulsed.

The woman lay motionless. For a moment, I thought she was dead. Then she groaned. Her eyelids fluttered open. She stared out with glassy eyes as though blind.

I shuddered. The scene seemed oddly familiar.

Father came out of the carriage and said to Maria, "Daughter, what are you doing? You will make us late."

"We can't leave this woman here, Signor Padre. It is our Christian duty to help her."

That's when I remembered—Maria had described this very scene to me the day of Gabriella's ball. I'd thought it had been merely a feverish delusion. Now I understood—Maria had experienced a true vision.

"We also have a duty to Her Royal Highness," Father said. He ordered the footman to carry the beggar to the side of the road. "That's all we can do," Father said to Maria. "We must be on our way."

As I climbed back into the carriage, Maria whispered from behind me. "Do you remember the vision I spoke of?"

I nodded.

"Then you believe me now."

"I do."

"Make haste," Father said. "There's no time to dawdle."

Once we were on our way, Father scolded Maria again. "Ladies of stature don't go about helping beggars in the street.

What could have possessed you to do something so scandalous, today of all days?"

I knew Maria couldn't tell Father the reason, at least not
yet. Fortunately, Adriana spoke up for my sister. "Do not be
too hard on her, my husband. It is because she is too good.
Maria thinks with her heart first and not her head."

"Hmmph." Father opened his mouth to say something
more, but just then we arrived at Count Visconti's palazzo.

Chapter Thirty
The Archduchess

Two servants led us up the grand staircase to the main floor. Count Visconti's palazzo was even more lavish than Count Cavalieri's. The corridor walls were painted in pale hues of pink and blue ornamented with white filigree. Large mirrors in elaborate gold frames covered many of the wall panels. Our reflections greeted us at every turn.

"Look," Adriana whispered as we passed a pair of marble-topped side tables with intricately carved legs. Porcelain figurines depicting scenes from the *commedia dell'arte* sat atop the tables. One featured the character of Ballerina dancing while Cantarina played her lute. The figurine reminded me of my costume for Gabriella's masquerade ball. This was surely a good omen, for it was at the ball that Gabriella had told me Marquis Bellini wanted to leave his estate to his great-nephew. I smiled and hurried after the others.

We finally reached the ballroom—the grandest I'd ever seen. A large red and gold canopy hung from the ceiling at one end of the room. Three throne-like chairs upholstered in red velvet stood beneath it. The chairs were obviously meant for Archduchess Maria Teresa, Grand Duke Francis, and the grand duke's brother, Prince Charles, who was traveling with

them. However, only the two men were seated. The archduchess stood off to one side. A line of guests waited to speak with
her.

Maria and I took our place in line behind Father and Adriana. I soon found myself rubbing the tip of my right index
finger against my thumb, a habit I thought I'd broken long ago.

When Grand Duke Francis joined his wife, Maria gripped
my forearm. She must have felt as anxious as I did. It hadn't
occurred to me that we'd be meeting the grand duke, too. I
tried not to think about that, or about how the archduchess
would one day be empress over us all.

At long last, we reached the head of the line, and Count
Visconti presented us to Archduchess Maria Teresa and her
husband. The golden-haired archduchess wasn't as stern as I'd
expected, though she looked older than her years. She would
soon turn twenty-two, the same age as Adriana.

The royal couple exchanged pleasantries with Father and
Adriana. Then Archduchess Maria Teresa turned to Maria and
me. "How blessed your father is," she said in perfect Italian,
"to have not one, but two such accomplished daughters."

We curtsied and said, "*Grazie*, Your Highness."

The archduchess said something to Maria in German.
From the mischievousness in Her Royal Highness's bright blue
eyes, I guessed she was testing my sister. Maria must have answered satisfactorily, for the archduchess nodded and smiled.
They went on speaking German for several moments. In the
meantime, the grand duke made small talk with Father and
Adriana. My stomach knotted as I waited.

Finally, the archduchess fixed her gaze on me. "And you are
the composer?" she said, speaking Italian again.

"Yes, Your Highness."

"I have been so enjoying the songs you sent me. I'm especially looking forward to singing the lullaby to my little girls
when we return to Vienna." My heart swelled at her praise.
Then she said, "Would you do me the favor of playing it for
me?"

I couldn't believe my ears. "Pardon me, Your Highness?"

"I'd love to hear your own rendition of the lullaby, to know
if I'm doing it justice." She gestured toward the harpsichord

standing before a nearby fireplace. "If you wouldn't mind. The instrument is well-tuned. I tried it out myself earlier."

My hands trembled at the idea of playing here, now, in front of the royal couple and their entourage, and the highest-ranking members of Milanese society. But what could I say?

"As you wish, Your Highness." I clasped my trembling hands together and curtsied low.

Count Visconti stood a few yards away, waiting with the next guests to be introduced to the royal couple. The archduchess said to him, "With your permission, Visconti, I would very much like to hear Signorina Salvini play the harpsichord."

Father's eyes widened at her words.

"Of course, Your Highness," Count Visconti replied, but from the stiffness of his bow, I guessed the archduchess's request was a breach of etiquette. The knot in my stomach grew harder.

The count led me to the harpsichord. To my horror, I saw that the colors of the keys were reversed, in the French fashion—the natural keys were black and the sharps white. I'd only played such an instrument once before, and that was long ago.

My heart raced as I placed my still-trembling hands on the keyboard. I cleared my throat, took a deep breath and prayed silently, *Jesus, Joseph, and Mary, please help me.*

I tried a few chords to get the feel of the keys. Fortunately, the instrument's sound was much like that of the other French harpsichord I'd played. *Thank you, Lord.*

As I began the prelude to my lullaby, the room grew quiet. I glanced over at the archduchess, who was now seated beneath the red and gold canopy. She nodded her encouragement.

I repeated the prelude a second time to ease my nerves. Finally, I sang,

I am so blessed to have you as my own,
my precious, precious one.
I will love you my whole life long.

My love will be the sun that shines on you by day
and the moon that caresses your cheek at night.

For your health and happiness, daily I will pray
and that you'll always walk in God's light.
No matter what pain or hardship life may bring
I'll be ever near, ready to kiss your tears away.
Rest easy now, dear one. For you alone I sing.
Your place in my heart is secure, come what may.

I am so blessed to have you as my own,
my precious, precious one.
I will love you my whole life long.

Calmed by my own words and music, I thought of how this had originally been a love song for Antonio Bellini. I'd changed the lyrics only slightly to make it a lullaby. It would be especially fitting if this song helped secure the archduchess's favor.

After I finished, there was complete silence for a moment. Then everyone broke into vigorous applause. Archduchess Maria Teresa waved me toward her. As I approached, I snuck a peek at Father. Despite his cool expression, excitement, and perhaps even a hint of pride, danced in his dark eyes. My heart thrilled at his approval. He followed me over to the archduchess's throne.

"*Brava*, Signorina," the archduchess said with a clap of her hands. "Please forgive me for putting you to such a test. I wanted to know if what I'd heard about you was true. I'm happy to say it was. You are indeed as gifted a musician as you are a composer. And a lovely singer, too. Thank you so much for indulging me. I admire all the pieces you sent me, but the lullaby is my favorite."

I couldn't keep from smiling. "I am honored you like my compositions, Your Highness."

"And *I* am honored that you have dedicated such superb work to me." The archduchess touched her hand to her chest. "I must say, also, that I am pleased the general prejudice against educating women has not interfered with either your studies or those of your sister." Archduchess Maria Teresa said to Father. "I commend you, Salvini. Few men educate their daughters as you have, especially men outside the nobility."

She seemed to emphasize the phrase "outside the nobility." I wondered if Father noticed it, too.

He bowed low and said, "When I realized what wonderful talents God had bestowed on my daughters, Your Highness, I felt it was my duty to hire the finest tutors for them."

The archduchess gave Father a sly smile. "I am confident God will reward you well for it." Was she saying he would get his feudal estate?

"Thank you, Your Highness." Father bowed even lower this time.

As we stepped away from the archduchess, Father signaled for Adriana and Maria to follow us to the refreshment table. He took two glasses of wine and handed one to Adriana. "We must toast Emilia for her success this evening." Bending low, he whispered, "Thanks to her, I believe we will soon have cause for great celebration."

Adriana grinned. "How marvelous!" She took the wine glass from Father and clinked it against his.

I couldn't help grinning, too. All had gone even better than I'd hoped. By every indication, Father should soon have his title, and I could then be betrothed to Bellini. For the first time in my life, I wasn't the "second sister." My heart felt so light, I could have danced.

Maria was the only one who wore a serious expression. Could she be jealous of the attention showered on me by Father and the archduchess? I didn't think envy was in her character.

"I see the Riccardis are here with their daughter and son-in-law," Father said. "Let us join them."

Countess Riccardi and Gabriella were seated on a fine brocade sofa. Gabriella's father and husband stood talking behind them. We approached and exchanged greetings. Count Cavalieri called a servant to bring chairs for Adriana, Maria, and me. As we stood waiting, Gabriella said, "What a lovely lullaby, Emilia." She placed a hand on her abdomen. "You must teach it to me so I can sing it to my own sweet baby," she said, her face glowing.

"Of course." I smiled at Gabriella. When she'd first learned she was with child, she'd been quite anxious. But the midwife reassured her, saying Gabriella's body was well-suited for child-birth. With a little over two months left, she'd had an easy time thus far. Yet, I still worried for her sake. I prayed daily that all would go well for her and her baby.

The servants brought the chairs and arranged them in a half-circle in front of the sofa. After Adriana, Maria and I were seated, Father took a spot behind the sofa with the other two men. They were soon deep in discussion.

"They're like a gaggle of old gossips." Countess Riccardi tilted her head toward the men. "They scrutinize the archduch-ess's every word and gesture as though she is speaking in code."

But that was how it had seemed—as though the archduch-ess's words had contained a secret message for Father: *You will soon be a nobleman.* Could I have been mistaken?

"From what my husband tells me," Gabriella said, "that is the only way the archduchess can speak right now. Since she is not yet our ruler, she is not in a position to make direct prom-ises. However, Her Royal Highness can still use her influence to benefit those who win her approval."

Gabriella looked right at me as she spoke. I sensed she, too, believed my performance this evening would lead to Father being made a nobleman. I said a silent prayer we were right.

From the corner of my eye, I noticed a man with a walking stick crossing the ballroom. I turned to see Marquis Volpi, of all people, approach Count Visconti. I hadn't seen the marquis in ages.

Countess Riccardi must have noticed him too, for she said, "Well, well, well, speaking of gossip." She lowered her voice. "Have you heard the latest regarding Marquis Volpi's illustri-ous son?"

"No, do tell," Adriana said.

"It seems his bride-to-be had a change of heart," Countess Riccardi said. "No sooner had her father set a wedding date when he announced it was to be postponed. Indefinitely."

I studied Gabriella's face. She smiled as though unper-turbed by the news. Either she'd become adept at hiding her emotions or she no longer had feelings for Lodovico Volpi.

"Oh, my," Adriana said. "I wonder if something happened."

"I imagine we'll find out in time," Countess Riccardi said.

Gabriella nodded toward Marquis Volpi. "I wonder if the broken engagement has anything to do with the marquis's current state of agitation."

Marquis Volpi stood clutching his walking stick by its middle. He waved the stick's jeweled head angrily at Count Visconti. I could not make out what Marquis Volpi was saying, but he was obviously upset.

"Interesting," Father said from behind the sofa. I didn't know he'd been watching, too. "I wonder what has ruffled the old crow's feathers this time."

Gabriella's husband, Count Cavalieri, replied, "I suspect the marquis is feeling snubbed. He wasn't invited to today's private dinner for the archduchess."

Count Visconti kept his demeanor calm as he answered Marquis Volpi. The marquis was apparently dissatisfied with the response, for he struck his walking stick to the marble floor. A loud thump filled the air. Even the archduchess watched as the marquis strode angrily from the room.

"Good riddance," Father said.

A little while later, Count Visconti announced, "This evening we pay tribute to our royal visitors with a fireworks exhibition." The count led the archduchess and grand duke out onto a balcony facing the Royal Palazzo. Father, Adriana, Maria, and I joined Gabriella, her husband, and her parents on another balcony.

A thunderous boom shook the balcony. Green, red, and white lights exploded in the sky. As we oohed and ahhed, people streamed into the streets below. Some of them must have noticed the archduchess, for they began chanting, "*Viva* Maria Teresa! *Viva* Maria Teresa!"

My heart joined in. *Long live Maria Teresa! May she make all my dreams come true.*

Chapter Thirty-One
Montevecchian Wine

Later that night, I sat in my room brushing my hair. Maria seemed quieter than usual as she prepared for bed, too. I wondered again if she might be jealous. Guilt clenched my heart. I knew too well the grief of feeling second best.

"Is something wrong?" I asked. "You've hardly said a word all evening."

"I've been contemplating what I should do next," she said, "now that God has confirmed the vision I had so long ago."

The beggar. Of course! In the excitement of meeting the archduchess, I'd forgotten about nearly running over the beggar woman. It was uncanny how Maria had foretold every last detail. I wondered if she'd inherited Mamma's gift of prophecy.

I set down the brush. "Did God speak to you today, as he did when you first had the vision?"

"No, and I have been pondering that all evening. I've come to the conclusion that God didn't need to repeat His message." Maria sat down on the edge of our bed. "After completing the booklet of essays for Archduchess Maria Teresa, I felt at loose ends. I wasn't sure what God would have me do next. By confirming my vision today, the very day of our meeting the arch-duchess, I believe God was saying it's time to begin my true calling—a life of service to the poor."

"How will you do that?"

"I will profess religious vows. Padre Gilberto has suggested I join the *Turchine* order."

"The Blue Nuns?" The order's nickname came from their turquoise-colored habits, which made them easy to spot as they distributed food to beggars in the street. "Must it be the *Turchine*? Father might be more inclined to approve if you joined a less conspicuous order."

"God is calling me to serve the poor, not to monastic life," Maria said. "The *Turchine* order is one of the few that allow nuns to do such work. I plan to speak with Father tomorrow to ask his permission to join them."

"So soon? Wouldn't it be better to wait a little longer? He seems confident the archduchess's influence will finally pave the way for his acquisition of the feudal property and its asso-ciated title. He'll be in good spirits when that happens, and more agreeable to your request."

"He's already in good spirits. And this evening, for the first time ever, he showed favor to you over me."

So she had noticed. "I'm sorry, Maria."

"I am the one who is sorry." Maria stood and rested her hands on my shoulders. "The yoke of Father's expectations has been lifted from me and placed onto you."

I thought of Vincenzo's toy puppets, which were manipu-lated by strings attached to the shoulders. I waved away her concern. "You needn't worry about me," I said. "Once Father becomes a nobleman, Antonio Bellini will finally be able to court me."

"How can that be? Didn't Lady Gabriella say Father would want to marry us off to noblemen? Bellini has no title."

I explained to Maria what Gabriella had told me about Mar-quis don Vittore Bellini. "So you see, Maria, all will be well once Father acquires the feudal property at Montevecchia."

"I'm happy for you." Maria squeezed my left shoulder. "But I don't plan to wait that long."

Maria was unable to carry out her plan, however, for we saw little of Father in the following days. Archduchess Maria Teresa and her party quit the city on the eighth of May and Father left shortly thereafter. Adriana told us he and his attorney were going to Montevecchia in the hope of finally completing the purchase of the estate. On hearing the news, I went to the chapel to pray for their success.

Father returned home three weeks later. We had just sat down to eat when he strode into the dining room. He stopped before Adriana and said, "We have cause for celebration, my dear. Our purchase of the feudal property has finally been approved. At long last, we are the official owners!"

Adriana jumped up and clapped her hands. "How marvelous!"

Father took one of Adriana's hands in his. "You must allow me to be the first to kiss the hand of the new Countess of Montevecchia." He pressed his lips to her hand. "My lady."

Adriana giggled. Her free hand fluttered as she curtsied and replied, "My lord."

Father grinned. I couldn't recall the last time I'd seen him so happy. "We must have a toast," he said. "Where is that bottle of wine from the vineyards of the Montevecchia estate?"

"I'll have Naldo fetch it," Adriana said.

The kitchen maid put out a place setting for Father while Naldo went for the Montevecchian wine. But Father remained standing. Naldo soon arrived with a tray bearing the bottle and fresh glasses. He poured wine for all of us.

Father raised his glass and said, "To our good fortune as the new Count and Countess of Montevecchia." He clinked his glass against Adriana's. Before drinking, he held the glass up. "Good color and clarity." He swirled the burgundy-colored liquid, then sniffed it. "Fine aroma." Finally, he tasted the wine. "Mmm," he said. "I shall enjoy being owner of this vineyard." He laughed then took another drink.

Father turned to Maria and me. "Why aren't you drinking, Daughters? Or I should say, *Ladies*?"

I covered my mouth to keep from laughing out loud. It was hard to believe Maria and I were ladies now, as were Isabella and Paola, who sat across from us.

"Drink up, *Ladies*!" Father said. "If not for your hard work, this might not have come to pass, at least not yet." He held his glass out to us. "In fact, I must offer a second toast, to you, Emilia, for winning over the archduchess with your music. No doubt Her Royal Highness expedited our purchase of the estate." Father clinked his glass against mine. "To Emilia!"

"To Emilia!" Adriana repeated.

Father's praise made me blush. I lowered my head. But, inside, my heart leapt, singing, *Alleluia!*

In my joy, I took a large swallow. The wine tasted sweeter than I expected. Almost too sweet.

Between the wine and Father's compliments, my head was spinning. I, Emilia, the second Salvini sister, had been the one responsible for our family's rise to nobility. Not Maria.

At that moment, I could not foresee the terrible repercussions of our change in station.

Chapter Thirty-Two
New Furnishings

A few days later, I was in the harpsichord salon working on a violin concerto when Maria burst in.

"Oh, Emmi, I am heartbroken," she said, her eyes wet. "Father said 'no.'"

"What's happened?" I got up from the harpsichord and stood beside her. "What did Father say 'no' to?"

"He will not grant permission for me to become a nun." Maria seemed unsteady, as though she might collapse at any moment.

"Come, sit." I led her to a sofa. "Now tell me everything."

"Father said I cannot take the veil because he needs me here at home." She swallowed hard. "I must continue speaking at his meetings, and the meetings are to be grander than ever. He said that being granted a title won't be enough to earn the respect of Marquis Volpi and other high-ranking noblemen. We must prove we are worthy of our noble status by showing them how cultured and sophisticated we are. Father said he can't do that without me, and you, too." She blinked back tears. "We must dazzle the most elite members of Milan's aristocracy."

"But that won't take forever," I said. "After hearing you speak a few times, even Marquis don Cesare Volpi will have to admit how extraordinary your talents are. Of course, he and the others will give Father all the credit. But, no matter, for then they will welcome him into their fold with open arms and Father can let you go."

Maria looked down at her hands. "I had the same thought when Father told me his plans. So I asked him, after he was accepted by the elite, could I take the veil *then*." Maria's voice cracked as she went on. "Father said 'no' again." She shook her head. "He said it would be a waste of my God-given talents and my education."

"But you can't live here as a spinster forever. A noblewoman must either profess religious vows or marry a nobleman. To do otherwise would be scandalous."

A tear fell from Maria's face onto her hands. Without looking up, she said in a hushed voice, "Father said he has already been approached by several suitors, but none of them have met his requirements. He wants to use my betrothal to align the Salvinis with one of Milan's noblest families. He just doesn't know which one yet."

"Oh, Maria. No."

Maria nodded. More tears fell onto her hands. She rubbed them away, but she was soon sobbing.

I pulled her close. My poor sister. I wished with all my heart there was something I could do to help her.

In the following days, Maria did not speak again of her situation. In fact, she hardly spoke at all. Her sad demeanor contrasted sharply with Father and Adriana's good humor. In addition to finally acquiring the feudal estate, they had another cause for joy—Adriana was again with child. As soon as she recognized the symptoms, she sent for the midwife, who declared all was well. The midwife promised to monitor Adriana's progress closely.

Father wanted to host another academic meeting right away, but Adriana insisted the harpsichord salon required new furnishings first. With Father now Count of Montevecchia, she said the room needed to accommodate a greater number of guests. In truth, I think she wanted to update the decor to match what we'd seen at Palazzo Visconti.

Adriana replaced our wide, heavy chairs with narrower ones much like those at Count Visconti's. The new chairs had cushioned backs of pale blue fabric surrounded by finely carved mahogany. Adriana also ordered gilt-edged side tables inlaid with marble tops, and porcelain figurines to set upon them. And although the salon's walls were already covered with works of art, my stepmother purchased two new paintings and several mirrors, all in elaborate gilded frames.

I was practicing at the harpsichord the day the paintings arrived. Adriana had Naldo carry them into the salon. He set them side by side on a sofa near the west fireplace.

"Don't let us disturb you, Emilia," Adriana said. "I merely need to decide where to hang these. Perhaps on this wall." She walked around the sofa to face the fireplace. "Oh, dear. We'll have to take something down first."

The painting of the cerulean Madonna holding the infant Jesus hung just to the right of the fireplace mantle. I couldn't have Adriana removing that one.

I hurried to the sofa to examine the new paintings. One depicted the Annunciation, when Archangel Gabriel informed the Virgin Mary she was to be the mother of Our Savior. Halos of shimmering gold encircled the heads of both the archangel and the Blessed Virgin. Archangel Gabriel stood on the left, his flowing, red robes trimmed in gold. The Blessed Virgin sat before him in a humble, attentive pose. She wore a rose-colored gown and a cloak of deep cerulean blue—the same color as in the portrait hanging beside the mantle.

"What rich colors in this Annunciation scene," I said, hoping flattery would help influence Adriana. "And look, the Virgin's cloak is a perfect complement to the Madonna and child already on the wall."

Adriana came to stand beside me. She studied the Annunciation painting for a moment before lifting her eyes to the cerulean Madonna. "Why, they're a perfect match!" she said with a clap of her hands. "Providence destined them to be together. We'll hang the Annunciation to the left of the fireplace, equidistant from the mantle as the Madonna and child on the right." She pointed to the spot where she wanted the new painting. "Remove that boring old seascape, Naldo. This wall shall be reserved for holy scenes."

Relieved, I returned to the harpsichord. I continued practicing while Adriana and Naldo hung the paintings.

After they left, I inspected their handiwork. I glanced from the Annunciation scene to the Madonna and child, and back again. The two did indeed complement each other perfectly and not only in color. The painting of the Madonna and child depicted the fulfillment of the archangel's announcement.

I thought of the *Magnificat* and how I'd sung the Blessed Virgin's song at the reception welcoming Governor von Traun to Milan. That day, I'd so longed to win Father's favor, but Maria had outshone me. Now, two and a half years later, I was no longer the "second sister." All because I'd helped Father finally acquire his title.

I smiled and played the *Magnificat* again, singing,

> *"My soul proclaims the greatness of the Lord*
> *and my spirit rejoices in God, my salvation.*
> *For He has shown me such favor—*
> *me, His lowly handmaiden.*
> *Now all generations will call me blessed,*
> *because the mighty one has done great things for me.*
> *His name is holy,*
> *His mercy lasts for generation after generation*
> *for those who revere him."*

My heart swelled with joy. And to think—our family's noble status would soon allow me to be betrothed to Antonio Bellini. Praise be to God!

My joy would have been perfect if not for Maria's unhappiness. No one else seemed to notice how rarely she smiled now, nor how little she ate. I hoped she'd heal with time, but if anything, she grew even sadder.

One day in late June, I went to Maria's study to express my concern. I was surprised to find the door shut on such a warm day. I knocked. "Maria, are you in there?"

"Come in, Emmi."

Maria's chair sat empty before the desk. I stepped inside and scanned the room. The door to the anteroom stood ajar. There, my sister knelt praying before a painting of Christ on the Cross. She made the sign of the cross then rose and joined me in the study.

"Please, shut the door," she said quietly.

"But it's hot in here," I said. "Wouldn't you rather have it open?"

Maria gestured to the open balcony doors. "I have all the air I need."

"As you wish." I shut the study door.

Maria sat at her desk. I took the chair beside it. The usually cluttered desk was bare except for the inkstand holding Maria's writing quills, inkpot, and pounce pot.

"You're not studying?"

"For Father's next meeting, I am to declaim the same ideas I put forth in the collection of essays for the archduchess. I know those well enough without studying, so I have been spending my time in prayer."

"Wouldn't you be more comfortable praying in the chapel?"

"Of course," she said, "which is why I stay here. It is a greater sacrifice."

Her devotion amazed me, especially in this heat. I could already feel a trickle of sweat rolling down my back. "I've noticed you haven't been eating much lately," I said. "Is that part of your sacrifice, too?"

She nodded. "I'm fasting in prayer that Father will open his heart to God's will and allow me to take the veil."

"Be careful not to fast too severely," I said, "or you shall make yourself ill."

Maria placed her hand on mine. "You need not worry, Emmi. God is watching over me."

Her words did not allay my fears.

From Maria's study, I went to the harpsichord salon. Instead of practicing, I gazed up at the painting of the cerulean Madonna and thought of Mamma. She'd been gone two and a half years, yet her spirit still comforted me often. Mamma had remained true to her promise. I had to find a way to keep mine. "How Mamma?" I said aloud. "How can I help Maria?"

The Madonna's expression seemed to say, "You already know." I recalled the last time Maria had fasted too zealously. All I'd had to do then was bring the problem to Father's attention. He commanded Maria to eat, and she obeyed.

Things were different now. Maria took her commands from a higher master. The only solution would be to convince Father to allow her to take the veil.

Maria's life depended on it.

Chapter Thirty-Three
Il Malocchio

The next morning, I knocked on Father's study door. He usually hated being disturbed, but today he actually smiled when he saw me. "Come in, Daughter." He motioned toward the seat beside his desk. "Sit down."

Once settled, I noticed an envelope addressed to Father lying on the desk.

"I have just received some most gratifying news." Father picked up the envelope. "Marquis Volpi has accepted the invitation to our next meeting."

"Marquis Volpi himself? But he always declines."

"Indeed," Father said. "He has always looked down his sharp nose at the Salvini family. However, now that we are nobility, he dare not snub us." Father raised his chin. "Both he and his son will be here."

"I'd heard Lord Lodovico's marriage had been postponed," I said, "but I thought he was still in Austria, waiting for it to be rescheduled."

Father smiled again. "The marriage has been called off. Apparently, Lady Elizabeth has changed her mind, no doubt due to some misunderstanding. However, as there is no hope of reconciliation, Lord Lodovico has returned to Milan. He is once more an eligible bachelor. And I intend for him to wed your sister."

"Maria? But you can't do that!"

Father's right eyebrow went up. Before he could say anything, I added quickly, "Forgive me, Signor Padre." I fought to keep my voice calm. "Maria is the reason I'm here. I'm worried for her well-being. She's fasting so severely I fear she will make herself ill."

"Fasting? This is not a time of abstinence."

I had to choose my words carefully. Father would not be pleased to know Maria was praying for him to change his mind about allowing her to take the veil. "She feels God desires her self-sacrifice. Since she is unable to serve the poor as a nun, she intends to help them through prayer and fasting."

"Rubbish!" Father said. "I will order her to eat."

"And if she should refuse?"

"She can't refuse," he said. "I'll send her to a convent until she acquiesces."

"But that's where Maria wants to go."

Father's shoulders slumped ever so slightly. "I see." He straightened again. "Such disobedience is a sin. Her confessor will counsel her to submit."

"With all respect, Signor Padre, why not allow Maria to take the veil? She's convinced it's God's will for her."

"It is *my* will for one of my daughters to wed Lodovico Volpi." Father leaned his face close to mine. "I have already mentioned the possibility to the marquis, and he is quite interested in pursuing the matter. Therefore, if Maria refuses to marry Volpi," Father raised his index finger toward me, practically touching my nose, "the obligation shall fall to you."

"Me?" I felt the blood drain from my face. "But I can't." Father's eyes narrowed. "I mean, I already have a suitor."

"What!" Father slammed his hand on the desk. I winced at the sound. "How can you have a suitor without my consent?"

"Pardon me, Signor Padre. I meant to say, someone has expressed interest in becoming my suitor, pending your approval, of course." My voice trembled as I added, "He was merely waiting for the right time to approach you."

"And who, pray tell, is this 'someone'?"

Heaven help me. I swallowed and said, "Antonio Bellini."

"The violinist? Hah!" Father leaned back in his chair. "Bellini is untitled. How can he hope to court you, the daughter of a count?"

"But he will have a title upon his great-uncle's death. Marquis don Vittore Bellini intends to bequeath everything to him."

Father waved his hand as though swatting a pesky fly. "It's a fabrication to win your favor. The marquis disowned the boy's father years ago."

"Antonio Bellini didn't tell me of the inheritance. In truth, he may not even be aware of it. Lady Cavalieri is the one who informed me."

The smugness left Father's face. "How would she know of such things?"

"Marquis Bellini told her husband, Count Cavalieri. The marquis is in failing health and may not be long in this world. His heir is a distant cousin in Padua. According to the count, Marquis Bellini hates the idea of the estate falling into the hands of a non-Milanese."

"Naturally," Father said.

"The marquis said he'll gladly leave everything to Antonio Bellini instead, provided his great-nephew betroths a noblewoman."

"Indeed?" Father placed his hands upright, palms together. Leaning his chin on his extended fingers, he was silent for a long moment.

Please, Lord, I prayed. *Let Father see what's best for Maria and me.*

Father finally lifted his chin and said, "If young Bellini does not know of this, what makes him presume he is worthy to court you?"

"Bellini first mentioned courting me last summer, just before he took a position with the Royal Ducal Orchestra. He planned to approach you after he'd saved sufficient funds from his salary and musical compositions. He didn't know then that our family would soon join the nobility."

"I see." Father still held his hands together as though in prayer. A slow smile spread across his face. "God has blessed me beyond my wildest imaginings. I shall have not one, but two sons-in-law who are marquises."

"But Maria—"

Father held up a hand to silence me. "As I said, it is my will to have Marquis Volpi's son marry one of my daughters. I care not which one. If you wish to marry Bellini, you must convince your elder sister to wed Lord Lodovico first."

I pressed a hand against the nausea rising in my belly. How could I even suggest such a thing to Maria?

"That is all, Daughter." Father dismissed me with a wave of his hand.

Dazed, I left Father's study. I wandered the halls of the palazzo until I ended up in the harpsichord salon. I gazed up at the painting of the Annunciation and thought of the joyful *Magnificat* I'd sung only a week earlier. My show of happiness must have caught the attention of *il malocchio*, for I felt sorely cursed.

———

I said nothing to Maria of my conversation with Father. In truth, I hardly spoke at all.

I spent the following mornings on my knees in the chapel praying for a solution that would allow both Maria and me to be happy. In the afternoons, I practiced in the harpsichord salon.

Time marched on. When only ten days remained until Father's next meeting, I still hadn't discovered any solution to my dilemma. I saw only two possibilities, neither acceptable. If Maria married Lord Lodovico for my sake, guilt would overshadow my happiness at being wed to Antonio Bellini. Yet taking Maria's place would mean giving up the man I loved.

———

One morning as I knelt in the chapel, Isabella rushed in.

"Emmi," she whispered loudly. "I've been looking all over for you." She paused to catch her breath. "You must help me!"

I jumped up. "What is it, Isabella? Are you hurt?"

She shook her head. "I've just come from Adriana."

"Oh, no. The baby!" I turned to flee the room. Isabella grabbed my arm.

"It's not the baby. Adriana's fine."

"Then out with it, Isabella. What's wrong?"

"Adriana told me of Father's plans, that Maria is to marry Lord Lodovico and you will be betrothed to Antonio Bellini. Is it true?"

I sighed. Now Isabella knew.

I took her arm and began leading her out of the chapel. "Yes, those are Father's plans. I don't see how they have anything to do with you, though."

"But they do." Isabella pulled away from me and stood before the chapel door. "Adriana was chattering about how Maria's wedding celebration and yours will have to be at least as grand as Lady Gabriella's, since your husbands will both be marquises one day. So I asked, 'What about me? Will I have a grand wedding celebration, too?' Instead of answering, Adriana tried to change the subject. I badgered her until she finally confessed Father's plans for all of us." Even in the dim light of the chapel, I could see that Isabella's eyes were more gray than blue, just like Mamma's when she was upset.

"After you and Maria are betrothed," Isabella went on, Father is going to send Paola and me to a convent. We are to take the veil."

"What?"

"Adriana said it would require too much dowry money to marry off all four of us. Two of us must profess vows, whether we have a calling or not." Isabella slumped against the door.

Her posture reminded me of Zia Delia slumped in her chair behind the grille at the Convent of the Annunciation. After Mamma's death, Isabella had refused to join Maria and me in our visits to Zia—she'd said she couldn't bear to see our aunt locked away. I realized now there was more to it: Isabella must have shared my own fear of ending up like Zia.

My little sister looked so small and sad. I turned away and my eyes fell on the fresco beside the door—a painting of Milan's patron, Sant'Ambrogio, blessing the kneeling Emperor

Theodosius following his conversion. With a heavy heart, I said, "I'm afraid what Adriana says is true."

"It's not fair!" Isabella said, her voice rising. "I don't want to be locked away in a cloister. I want to live in a palazzo and wear fancy gowns. Maria is the devout one. Why not let her take the veil and let me marry instead?"

A glimmer of hope entered my heart. Perhaps we could convert Father's thinking, just as Sant'Ambrogio had converted the Emperor.

But then I came to my senses. "You're too young, Isabella."

She stretched up her neck. "I'll be fifteen in less than seven months. That's old enough to be betrothed."

Could it be? Isabella always seemed much younger. Of course, there was no denying her age. "But you're not as accomplished as Maria or I."

"That shouldn't matter," Isabella said. "Adriana says I am the comeliest of us girls, and beauty is a greater lure than accomplishments." Isabella twirled in a circle to show off her figure. I hadn't noticed how womanly she'd grown in recent months.

I started to say, "But—"

"Don't you see, Emmi?" Isabella grabbed me by both arms. "It's the perfect solution. I'll simply trade places with Maria. Then she can take the veil as she's always wanted, and you still get to marry Bellini. We can all be happy."

"You'd be happy married to Lord Lodovico? He's so much older than you."

"He's not as old as Lady Gabriella's husband. And Lord Lodovico's never been married so I wouldn't have any stepchildren to raise." Isabella smiled. "Besides, Palazzo Volpi is one of the finest in all of Milan. I will have all the servants I want and dress in the latest fashions. I can't think of anything that would make me happier."

"Hmm. I suppose it could work out, provided—"

"Provided what?" Isabella asked.

"Provided we can convince Lord Lodovico that *you* are the Salvini girl he wants to wed and not Maria."

Isabella batted her lashes and held her hand against her cheek in a flirtatious pose. "I think I can arrange that."

I laughed. Then I remembered where we were and covered my mouth.

Just then, the chapel door opened. Adriana looked startled to see us standing so close by. "There you are, Isabella. Are you all right?"

"I'm quite marvelous, actually," Isabella said. She quickly explained our plan to Adriana.

Adriana said to me, "You're certain Maria has no desire to wed?"

"All Maria desires is to serve God by helping the poor. I tried to tell Father so, but he insists two of his daughters must wed nobility. It hasn't occurred to him that Isabella could trade places with Maria. If Lord Lodovico chooses Isabella of his own accord, Father will have to agree."

Adriana said to Isabella. "Well, then, we'll have to make sure you're the most beautiful Salvini daughter at your father's next meeting. Then Lord Lodovico won't be able to resist you."

"*Grazie*, Signora Madre." Isabella threw her arms around our stepmother.

As I watched them embrace, I felt so happy I could have danced a *saltarello*. Instead, I said a silent prayer of thanksgiving.

Adriana pulled away from Isabella. "With only a week left until the meeting, I think it best we not mention any of this to your father or Maria for now."

Isabella and I answered in unison, "*Sì*, Signora Madre."

Chapter Thirty-Four
True Character

With Adriana on our side, surely all would be well. Maria would take the veil and serve the poor. Isabella would take Maria's place as Lord Lodovico's wife. And I would wed Antonio Bellini.

Yet, one worry still nagged me. I'd had no word from Bellini in over eight months. What if he'd changed his mind, as Lady Elizabeth had changed hers about Lord Lodovico?

I took out the twine Bellini had used to demonstrate the string game. Winding it round my wrist like a bracelet, I considered what to do next. I had to make sure Bellini's feelings had remained steadfast. And I needed to do so soon, for Father had invited Bellini to attend our next academic meeting.

I unwound the twine and slipped it back into the desk. With Father now monitoring all my correspondence, I couldn't write to Bellini directly. I decided to visit Gabriella to ask her help.

A maidservant led me out to the garden, where Gabriella sat in the shade of a pear tree. The branches above her hung heavy with green pears.

"How wonderful to see you, dear Emilia." To the maidservant, Gabriella said, "Betta, bring more ice water right away." She gestured to the empty glass on the table beside her. "And some pastry. I'm craving sweets."

"Yes, my lady."

Gabriella smiled up at me. Her face had grown as round and radiant as a full moon. "Do sit down, Emilia."

"You're looking lovelier than ever, Gabriella," I said, taking a seat in the wrought-iron chair on the other side of the table. "You have a glow about you."

"It's not a glow." She fanned herself vigorously. "It's perspiration from this infernal heat."

I laughed. "I didn't think noblewomen were allowed to perspire."

She pointed her fan at me. "You laugh now. We'll see how you feel when you're in my condition."

"I must wed first, which, in a way, is what I'm here to discuss."

"What? Have you had word from Bellini?"

"No," I said. "I was wondering if you've had any news of him or of his great-uncle."

Gabriella was about to answer when the maidservant returned. Betta held her tray out to me and I took one of the glasses of ice water. The tray also held a plate of puff pastries. Fine white sugar covered the surface of the golden pastry balls. I wasn't in the mood for sweets, though. I sipped my water instead. It tasted faintly of oranges.

Gabriella took the other glass.

The maidservant placed the pastry on the table. "Will there be anything else, my lady?"

Gabriella waved her off. "Not now."

Betta curtsied and left us again.

Gabriella took a long drink. Then, pressing the cold glass to her cheek, she finally answered my question. "All I know is that the old marquis has retreated to his country estate. I assume, to escape this heat. I wish I could do the same." She set her glass on the table and reached for a pastry. "Why do you ask?"

I told Gabriella about Father's plans for Maria, and Isabella's desire to marry Lord Lodovico in her place.

At the mention of Lodovico Volpi, Gabriella suddenly dropped her pastry. Did she still have feelings for him?

"What a waste." Gabriella watched the sugar-coated morsel hit the ground. It rolled under the table and came to a stop near my right foot.

Gabriella's face looked calmer than I'd expected. Perhaps I'd misread her reaction and the pastry had simply slipped from her hand.

She picked up another pastry and took a dainty bite. "I'd heard Volpi was back in Milan," she said between chews, "but I had no idea your father was planning a match between him and Maria." She popped the rest of the pastry into her mouth, then brushed off her fingers. "Your father must be unaware of the reasons behind Volpi's return."

"Father told me Lady Elizabeth had changed her mind and called off the wedding."

"Actually, it wasn't Lady Elizabeth who canceled the wedding. It was Duke von Hildebrandt." Gabriella began fanning herself again. "When Lodovico Volpi tried to call on Lady Elizabeth to see if there was any hope of a reconciliation, the duke had him forcibly removed from the premises."

"Forcibly removed? Why?"

"I don't like to repeat such things," Gabriella said, "however, considering your father's intentions, I feel bound to tell you."

She leaned toward me. "My brother warned me long ago that Volpi was a notorious gambler, but I thought he was exaggerating. Well, Raffaele happened to be in Austria when Volpi's betrothal to Lady Elizabeth was first announced. Almost immediately, Volpi left for Paris, saying he had business there. Turns out his 'business' was conducted at the gambling tables, with notes borrowed against the generous dowry he would soon receive by marrying the future Duchess von Hildebrandt. However, Lady Luck was not with Volpi. He sustained heavy losses."

"And the duke found out?"

"That's not all the duke found out." Gabriella lowered her voice. "Volpi is the worst kind of scoundrel. He has numerous mistresses, of *all* classes, scattered in cities across the empire."

I gasped. "Are you sure?" My hand trembled as I set my glass on the table.

Gabriella nodded. "I overheard Raffaele tell Father all about it—while Volpi was in Paris, he visited his mistress there, a married noblewoman, no less! When the woman's husband walked in on them, he challenged Volpi to a duel. Instead of giving the man satisfaction, Volpi ran back to Austria with his tail between his legs. The husband, being a persistent man, had Volpi investigated and learned not only of his engagement to Lady Elizabeth, but also his other liaisons. Unable to travel to Austria himself, the man sent word to Duke von Hildebrandt, informing him of Volpi's true character."

"Incredible!" I knew Volpi was a flirt, but I'd never imagined him a womanizer. The idea of such a man marrying my sister made my stomach sick.

"I'm sorry, Emilia."

"You're not to blame."

"Someone must tell your father," Gabriella said. "Do you want me to ask Raffaele to speak to him?"

"No," I said. "Father would be ashamed to have anyone outside the family know he'd been planning to marry his daughter to such a scoundrel. I'll have to tell him myself." How would I even bring up such a subject? My cheeks burned at the thought.

Gabriella didn't seem to notice. She reached for another pastry. "These are quite delicious. You must try one."

The feeling of nausea resurged. "No, *grazie*."

After finishing the last of her pastry, Gabriella said, "Really, you should have one. Something sweet will improve your humor."

I shook my head, but her words gave me an idea. "Father will certainly be outraged when I tell him about Volpi. But perhaps I can share some good news to counterbalance the bad." I took a sip of ice water. The nausea eased a bit. "In truth, that is what I came to discuss with you."

Gabriella licked the sugar from her lips. "How can I be of service?"

"I need to know if Bellini is ready to court me, but I cannot write him directly." I didn't mention that I also needed to confirm Bellini's feelings had remained constant. "I was wondering if you might help me get word to him."

"Well, I don't see why you can't speak to him here, in person, with me as your chaperone." Gabriella gestured toward the palazzo. "I'll tell my husband I have an urgent desire for musical entertainment." She smiled, patting her abdomen. "The count has been most indulgent of my whims lately."

Chapter Thirty-Five
Ticking Clock

Gabriella arranged for Antonio Bellini to perform a private concert at her home on the morning of July 15, two days before Father's meeting. Meanwhile, I told no one of the scandal surrounding Lord Lodovico. After confirming Bellini's intention to court me, I would speak to Adriana. She'd know how to approach Father about Volpi.

The night of the fourteenth, I could hardly sleep. Even so, I rose early the next morning and arrived at Palazzo Cavalieri well before the appointed time. The maidservant Betta greeted me at the door. "My lady asks that you wait for her in the harpsichord salon, Lady Emilia. She will join you shortly."

"*Grazie*, Betta." It still felt odd to be called "Lady Emilia." I was the same person as before, yet I'd noticed people did indeed treat me differently.

In the harpsichord salon, I was too anxious to sit. I strolled about studying the paintings on the walls. When the brass mantel clock chimed the hour, I walked over to it. Two fat-cheeked cherubs framed the clock's face, one on each side. I tried to focus my attention on the clock's steady *tick-tick-tock, tick-tick-tock*, hoping the rhythmic sound would calm me. I'd had no word from Bellini since his letter last fall following the death of Adriana's baby. What if he'd lost interest in me after all these months? What if he'd found someone else? The questions created a discordant melody that played over and over in my mind. Finally, I moved from the mantel and sat down at the harpsichord. Perhaps I could chase away the tune with a more pleasant one.

Instinctively, I began playing my most calming composition, the lullaby I'd sent the archduchess. I sang softly:

"I am so blessed to have you as my own,
my precious, precious one.
I will love you my whole life long.

My love will be the sun that shines on you by day
and the moon that caresses your cheek at night.
For your health and happiness, daily I will pray
and that you'll always walk in God's light.
No matter what pain or hardship life may bring
I'll be ever near, ready to kiss your tears away.
Rest easy now, dear one. For you alone I sing.
Your place in my heart is secure, come what may.

"I am so blessed to have you as my own,
my precious, precious one.
I will love you my whole life long.

When I finished, I looked up to see Bellini standing beside the harpsichord, his violin case in hand.

"Oh," I said. "I didn't hear you come in."

He bowed. "I'm sorry if I startled you. I didn't want to interrupt." He gestured toward the keyboard. "That was lovely."

My cheeks flushed at his words. "*Grazie.* It was one of the pieces I wrote for Archduchess Maria Teresa." I couldn't bring myself to tell him I'd originally composed it as a love song to him.

He nodded. "I didn't know you would be here today." He took a step closer and lowered his voice. "It seems an eternity since we last spoke. Much has happened in that time."

Bellini's eyes were the same deep blue I remembered. I tried to read his thoughts in them, but he averted his gaze.

"You must forgive me, Lady Emilia." He bowed low before me. "I'm not used to your new station."

"Please don't," I said. "There's no need for you to be so formal. Unless ..." My heart tightened. Was the formality his way of freeing himself from his promise to me?

His eyes met mine. "Unless what?"

"Unless your feelings have changed and you no longer wish to court me."

"My feelings *have* changed."

"Oh." I clutched the harpsichord bench for support. "I see."

"No, I don't believe you do. These past months, I've thrown myself into my work, writing cantatas, sonatas, and even a symphony, to earn enough to feel worthy of approaching your father. Then, just as my goal was in sight, I learned from Maestro Tomassini that your father was made a count." Bellini fell into a chair and laid his violin case across his knees. "It's all been for nothing."

My head was swimming. "I don't understand. If you still care for me, how can it all be for nothing? *My* feelings haven't changed."

"Your feelings may not have changed," he said, "but your social station has. You're the daughter of a count now." Bellini's shoulders sagged. "Yet I'm still the son of a wine merchant. Your father'd never accept me as your suitor."

"I expressed the same concern to Gabriella months ago," I said, "but she has discovered a solution."

He sat up. "She has?"

Gabriella appeared in the doorway. "Here she is now," I said. "I'll let her explain."

Bellini stood. We all exchanged greetings as etiquette demanded. Then Gabriella eased herself into a chair near the harpsichord. It seemed to take a moment for her to catch her breath. Finally, she said to Bellini, "Won't you sit down?"

He pulled up a chair to face her and sat with his violin case again on his lap. I remained at the harpsichord.

"Gabriella," I said, "please tell Signor Bellini what you told me about how we can resolve our ..." I paused, trying to think of the right word. "Our predicament."

"With pleasure," Gabriella said. She began by saying that her husband had visited Antonio Bellini's great-uncle a few months earlier. Bellini stiffened at the news but said nothing.

Gabriella explained how Marquis don Vittore Bellini's health was failing and he was in a quandary regarding his successor. She looked directly at Antonio Bellini as she said, "When my husband told him you, his great-nephew, wished to wed a noblewoman, the old marquis was relieved. He said that upon confirmation of such a betrothal he would gladly change his will to make you his heir." Gabriella smiled. "So you see, Emilia's new status as a noblewoman solves everything."

Covering his face with his hands, Bellini shook his head. "No, it doesn't."

"Of course it does," Gabriella said. "Emilia has already explained the situation to her father. Count Salvini is quite pleased at the prospect of having a marquis as his son-in-law."

Bellini jumped to his feet. "You don't understand, Lady Cavalieri. I cannot be the next marquis. To accept such an inheritance ..." His voice trailed off.

"I know of the quarrel between your father and his uncle," Gabriella said. "But surely your father would not begrudge your happiness."

"You don't know the whole story," Bellini said to Gabriella. He came over and stood beside the harpsichord. "And neither do you, *Lady* Emilia."

I cringed at the way he said "Lady."

Bellini continued, "Do you recall my telling you that Father never spoke to the marquis again after my parents wed?"

"Yes, I remember."

"Father did write to him, though." Bellini looked down at the violin case in his hands. "Once. After my mother took ill. About four years ago." Bellini rubbed the neck of the case as he went on. "The physician had prescribed an extended stay at the hot springs of San Giuliano as a remedy for my mother. We couldn't afford the journey, let alone the accommodations. Faced with no other recourse, my father swallowed his pride and wrote to his uncle for a loan. Father hoped that even if the marquis refused, he might at least offer the use of a carriage for the trip. Lord knows, the marquis has plenty of carriages to spare."

"And his response?" I asked.

"The marquis not only refused the loan request," Bellini's voice rose as he spoke, "he berated Father again for marrying my mother in the first place. The marquis wrote in his reply, 'He who makes his bed must lie in it.'"

I'd never seen Bellini like this. He gripped the violin case so tightly his knuckles turned white.

When he finally spoke again, his words were slow and measured. "The waters of San Giuliano might not have healed my mother, but they could have eased her passing. Instead, I watched her suffer a slow, painful death."

A tiny gasp escaped my lips. Bellini's eyes met mine. I saw hurt and sorrow and anger in them. Any sign of love was gone, or at least buried.

"So, you see now why I can never forgive the marquis," Bellini said. "Or accept his inheritance?"

I swallowed the cry that rose in my throat. I wanted to shout, "No, this can't be!" I turned to Gabriella and opened my mouth, but no words came out.

"Well," Gabriella began then fell silent. The mantel clock's *tick-tick-tock, tick-tick-tock* filled the room.

No one spoke for several long moments. Suddenly, Gabriella said, "Oh, my!" She clutched her abdomen.

I hurried to her side. "Are you all right?"

She took a long breath. "I think so, but perhaps I should go lie down."

As I helped Gabriella to her feet she said, "Emilia, your father might still consider a marriage between you and Bellini. After all, he is a respected musician and—"

I cut her off. "I doubt it matters to Father how respected Bellini is if he doesn't possess a title."

"Perhaps your stepmother can help you," Gabriella said. "After all, her father allowed *her* to choose her own husband."

"Adriana? What could she do?"

"If your father is anything like my husband, he is most anxious to keep your stepmother happy right now." Gabriella rubbed her abdomen as if to remind me that Adriana was also with child. "She might be able to convince your father to permit you to marry Bellini despite his lack of title."

"I suppose I could ask her," I said. But my heart held little hope.

Chapter Thirty-Six
Bubbling Fountain

As soon as I returned home, I went in search of Adriana. I found her on the balcony of her sitting room, embroidering a gown for her baby.

"Ah, Emilia," she said. "How is Lady Gabriella today?"

"She is well, though she has little tolerance for the summer heat."

"I understand that's normal for women close to childbirth. I suppose I should be grateful my baby isn't due until winter." Adriana pointed at the chair beside her. "Please, sit down and tell me the latest gossip."

The request seemed a sign from Heaven that I should indeed confide in Adriana. "What I have to tell you isn't mere gossip," I said as I sat down. "Have you heard the reason for Lord Lodovico's broken engagement?"

"Only that there was some misunderstanding between him and Lady Elizabeth."

"It was much more than a misunderstanding." I told Adriana about Lord Lodovico's gambling, his love affairs, and his cowardice when challenged to a duel.

"Oh, my!" Adriana set her needlework on the table. "Are you certain this is all true? You know how rumors can be."

"They aren't just rumors. Lady Gabriella's brother witnessed the scene between Volpi and Duke von Hildebrandt. When Lord Raffaele returned to Milan, he told his father to count it a blessing that Lord Lodovico was not *his* son-in-law."

"*Santo cielo!*" Adriana raised her hand to her cheek. "We must tell your father right away." She started to get up.

"Wait," I said, placing my hand on her arm. "There's more."

"About Lord Lodovico?"

"No, about Antonio Bellini."

"Don't tell me he's a scoundrel, too!"

"No, not at all." I told Adriana of Bellini's refusal to accept his great-uncle's inheritance as a matter of pride. While sharing Bellini's story, I thought of how terrible it must have been for him to watch his mother die so painfully knowing the marquis could have helped. I didn't blame Bellini for his feelings—were I in his shoes, I'd hate the marquis, too.

"In spite of everything, Bellini's become a respected musician and composer," I said. "He's worked hard to prove himself a worthy suitor. But all will be for naught if Father insists I marry a nobleman."

"You still wish to wed Bellini despite his lack of a title?"

"With all my heart."

Adriana patted my hand. "Perhaps I can convince your father to give his consent if we find some other high-ranking nobleman to replace Lord Lodovico as a suitor for Isabella. However, I haven't yet spoken to your father of her wish to exchange places with Maria."

"Do you really think Father would allow Maria to take the veil if I married Bellini without a title? Wouldn't that make Father even more determined to have *her* wed a nobleman?"

"I don't know." Adriana was quiet for a moment. Finally, she said, "Your father returns from Montevecchia tomorrow. Let me see what he says when I tell him the real reason behind Lord Lodovico's broken engagement. Perhaps he himself will suggest someone to replace Lord Lodovico. Then you and I can discuss how to proceed. For now, though, we best not say anything to your father about Bellini's situation, or of Isabella's wishes."

"Very well," I said.

The next morning, I received a note from Count Cavalieri with surprising news. Gabriella had gone into labor during the night and given birth to a healthy baby boy. The baby had arrived earlier than expected, but both he and Gabriella were doing well. Praise be to heaven! Not only was I thrilled and relieved for them, I hoped the news might be a good omen for me. The count wrote that Gabriella was anxious for an update regarding my situation. I responded with my congratulations and promised to send more information soon.

I went to the harpsichord salon to distract myself by playing while I waited for Father's return. After an hour or more had passed, Nina brought word that Adriana wanted me to meet her in the garden.

"Has Father returned?" I asked Nina.

"Yes, my lady," Nina said. "He was just leaving Lady Salvini's sitting room as I entered."

Outside, I found my stepmother admiring our hedge of blooming red oleander. "What did Father say?" I asked immediately.

She took my arm. "Come, let's find a spot far from any ears."

Adriana didn't speak again until we'd passed the end of the hedge. "I told your father the information about you-know-who. He admitted he'd heard rumors, but your father said he was certain the events had been greatly exaggerated. To which I replied, 'Even if that's the case, wouldn't you rather have Maria wed a worthier suitor?'"

"And Father's response?"

"Let's sit first." Adriana pointed to a nearby bench.

We sat facing the fountain at the center of our garden. Two winged cherubs stood on opposite sides of the fountain, one holding a lute, the other a violin. Water gurgled up from a spout at the center of the pool separating them. The cherubs reminded me of the pair on the mantel clock in Gabriella's harpsichord salon. It was hard to believe less than a day had passed since I'd seen that clock.

I asked again, "So what was Father's response?"

"He said he has a most specific reason for wanting a marriage between the Salvinis and the Volpis." Adriana glanced around to make sure no one was nearby. "Your father didn't want to divulge it, but I persisted until he finally confessed. He told me that years ago, when he was a boy of only four or five, he spent much time in his father's silk shop."

"The shop on Via Pantano?"

"Yes," Adriana said. "Your grandfather was known for providing the finest silks in the city, and so he attracted the richest clients. One day, Marquis Volpi came into the shop."

I could hardly believe her words. "Marquis Volpi?"

"Himself. He was a young man then, preparing to wed. He came to select the fabric for a new wardrobe. Your grandfather was occupied when Volpi entered the shop. Having to wait for service must have irritated the marquis, for when your grandfather finally greeted him, Volpi reprimanded him for not bowing low enough. The marquis placed his walking stick on your grandfather's back and pushed down until his head practically touched the ground. Volpi rebuked your grandfather, saying, '*This* is the posture you must bear before nobility. Take care to never forget it.'"

"Goodness!" I sat up straighter, as though the gesture might somehow restore my grandfather's dignity after all these years. "Nonno often says his rudest customers were noblemen. Now I understand why."

Adriana went on. "Unbeknownst to your grandfather, your father was a witness to this scene. He vowed then and there to raise his station in life so no one would ever treat him in the manner Marquis Volpi had treated your grandfather."

"That's why Father was so determined to become a nobleman all these years."

"Precisely," Adriana said. "And when he learned Lord Lodovico was an eligible bachelor after all, your father took it as an act of Providence. What sweeter revenge could he have than for Maria to wed Marquis Volpi's only son and for her children to be born into the house of Volpi?"

I slumped back against the bench. "Then, short of getting hauled off to prison, there's probably nothing Lord Lodovico could do that would break Father's resolve to have him as a son-in-law."

"I'm afraid you're right," Adriana said. "And given Bellini's lack of title, your father would never agree to allow Isabella to marry before you." Adriana put her hand on mine. "I don't see any way to spare Maria."

We sat in silence as the fountain gurgled a sad melody. My thoughts bubbled and foamed like the water. I recalled Father's words to me in his study: *If Maria refuses to marry Volpi, the obligation shall fall to you.*

I considered telling my sister of Father's ultimatum. Knowing Maria, she would willingly sacrifice herself to save me from such a scoundrel. But I knew in my heart that was wrong. Maria had a calling from God. She shouldn't have to marry at all, let alone to marry someone as despicable as Lodovico Volpi.

As I turned away from the fountain, the red oleander blooms in the distance caught my eye. I'd hidden behind that very hedge the day of Maria's first speech. Thanks to her success that evening, Maria was able to convince Father to hire a music tutor for me. If not for her, I'd never have become a musician and composer. I'd never have played for the archduchess. And I'd never have won Father's favor.

Mamma's long-ago words came to mind. *Maria's destiny will one day rest in your hands, Emilia.*

That day had finally arrived.

I looked back at the two stone cherubs perched on opposite sides of the fountain. I had to harden my heart if I was to bear what lay ahead. *Help me, God.*

Still staring at the cherubs, I said to Adriana, "There is one way to save Maria."

"How?"

"I'll take her place."

"What? You? But what of Bellini? Once Maria weds Lodovico Volpi, your father's triumph will surely make him more open to your marrying Bellini."

"I doubt Father would ever allow me to wed a man without a title." Adriana opened her mouth to argue, but I raised my hand to silence her. "And even if he did, I could never be happy knowing I'd kept Maria from her calling." My heavy heart weighed down my chest. I leaned into my little step-mother.

Adriana put her arm around my shoulders. She asked softly, "You would make such a sacrifice?"

My breaths grew shallow. It hurt too much to breathe. I nodded.

"We mustn't give up all hope just yet." Adriana gave me a sideways hug. "Your father *was* quite distraught when I spoke with him. I believe he's gone to confront Marquis Volpi regarding his son's scandalous behavior. Perhaps God will provide a solution we haven't envisioned."

I nodded again, not because I agreed, but because I could no longer speak.

Chapter Thirty-Seven
Two Squirrels

I dragged myself to the harpsichord salon and sat staring at the keyboard for the longest time. My mind couldn't accept what my heart knew: I had no real choice. I was like one of Vincenzo's puppets.

I thought of the puppet show we'd seen in Masciago. The tale of Filadora and the Prince had dramatized the old adage "Love conquers all."

But the adage was a lie.

My anger made me sit up straighter. The day after tomorrow, at Father's meeting, would be my last chance to show Antonio Bellini how I felt. Once his intention to refuse the marquis's title became known, Father would never welcome him in our home again. I resolved to make the performance my best ever.

I'd just finished working through my entire program when I looked up to see Adriana in the doorway. Reading her expression, I knew immediately she had bad news. I waved her over. "Come, tell me what you've learned."

Adriana shut the door, then stood beside the harpsichord. "Your father has returned," she said. "I was right. He did call on Marquis Volpi." My normally energetic stepmother spoke slowly, as though tired. She rested her arms on the harpsichord frame. "Your father said the marquis acknowledged his son's gambling debts. However, Marquis Volpi claimed to know nothing of Lord Lodovico's other transgressions."

"Did Father believe him?"

"The marquis was very convincing," Adriana said. "He called his son into the room and interrogated him in your father's presence. Lord Lodovico confessed all in rather dramatic fashion. He fell to his knees and begged his father's forgiveness. He vowed to denounce his former habits and live up to the responsibilities of his position."

"Hah," I said. "And did the marquis forgive him?"

"Of course. Well, at least in front of your father. Marquis Volpi is a shrewd man. He knows Lord Lodovico's actions could impact his eligibility to marry a noblewoman. The marquis assured your father that since his son has seen the error of his ways, he is still a worthy suitor."

"What did Father say?"

"Only that he needed to consider the matter further." Adriana rubbed her hands along the top of the harpsichord frame. "He obviously relishes having an advantage over the Volpis. Your father is shrewd, too. The situation will allow him to negotiate a smaller dowry."

"It will also allow Father more freedom in choosing which daughter he'll betroth to Lord Lodovico."

"My thought precisely. So I said to your father, 'There's no need to betroth your eldest daughter to Lord Lodovico now. Why not allow Maria to follow her calling to take the veil and betroth her younger sister to Lord Lodovico?'" Adriana paused, then added, "Your father still anticipates your betrothal to Bellini, and thus assumed I was speaking of Isabella."

I rose and stood beside Adriana. "What was Father's response?"

"He was quiet for so long I feared he would yet insist upon Maria marrying Lord Lodovico. When your father finally spoke, it was as though he was thinking out loud. He said, 'I suppose Maria could put her learning to good use in a convent. She would make an excellent Mother Superior. I will wait until after Emilia is betrothed to Bellini to begin negotiations with Volpi. With my two eldest daughters situated, Marquis Volpi will have no choice but to match his son with the third and least accomplished. That should take the high and mighty marquis down a peg.'"

"Father knows nothing of Bellini refusing his great-uncle's title, then?"

"Since it would be improper to disinvite Antonio Bellini and his father at this late date, I thought it best not to say anything until after Friday's meeting."

"Good." I fought to sound calm. Meanwhile, puppet strings wrapped themselves around my heart. "And you're certain Father won't enter into a marriage contract with Marquis Volpi before you're able to explain everything?"

"Quite certain," Adriana said. "Your father plans, as he put it, 'to let Volpi and his son dangle on the hook awhile before reeling them in.'"

The strings around my heart tightened.

Adriana must have sensed my feelings, for she placed a hand on mine. "Your mother would be proud of you."

I glanced over at the painting of the cerulean Madonna. *I hope you're watching, Mamma.*

—

That night, after Maria went to bed, I stayed up writing the letter I'd promised Gabriella. I told her of all Adriana had learned and of my decision to take Maria's place. I let my tears flow, though I was careful to keep them from falling onto the page. Better to let them out now than during my performance tomorrow.

But even as I folded the letter and pressed my monogram into the wax seal, my mind searched for some other remedy for the situation. I thought of what Adriana had said in the garden: *Perhaps God will provide a solution we haven't envisioned.* I looked up at the crucifix hanging above my dressing table, barely visible in the shadows of the flickering candelabrum.

Despite knowing it would take a miracle, I prayed, "Please, Lord, let there be some other way."

I woke early the next morning, my eyes burning from all my tears. I wet a cloth at the basin and pressed it to my face. As the coolness seeped into my skin, I heard the mournful cooing of doves coming from outside, followed by skittering sounds.

I went to the window. A flash of red in the courtyard below caught my eye—two young squirrels were chasing each other. From their playfulness, I guessed they were siblings. The first one, which was a darker shade of red than his brother, jumped onto a small cypress tree. The second scurried after. I lost sight of them among the branches. Then the darker squirrel suddenly emerged at the top of the tree. He chirped down as if to say to his sibling, "Hah, see! I'm faster and smarter than you."

The lighter squirrel seemed unperturbed. He scurried back to the ground and scampered away. Still perched atop the cypress, his brother stared down, apparently surprised by the abrupt end to their competition. He cried out in frustration, *screech, screech, screech.*

The cry must have woken Maria, for she stirred then. The morning light filtering through the window gave Maria's face a gentle glow. For the moment, there was no sign of the sickly pallor that had come over her the last few weeks.

As Maria rubbed the sleep from her eyes, I thought of easing her mind by telling her I planned to wed Lord Lodovico in her place. But I held my tongue. She might try to interfere to spare my sacrifice.

Maria stretched her arms and smiled. "Oh, Emmi," she said, "I just had the most wonderful vision. Mamma was here, in our room." She glanced around as though expecting to see our mother.

My mouth went dry. "I'm the only one here, Maria." My words came out in a whisper.

She sat up. "I tell you, Emmi, Mamma was here, standing beside the bed." Maria gestured to her right. "She caressed my cheek and said, 'My dear Maria, I've come to tell you that God has heard your prayers. Tonight will be your last performance. Soon, you will be following your true calling.'"

How uncanny, I thought. If all went as planned, tonight would indeed be Maria's last performance. "What a lovely dream."

"Wait, there's more." Maria came to stand before me. "Mamma had a message for you, too. She said, 'Tell Emilia God has also heard *her* prayers. All will be well for both of you.'"

"It was only a dream, Maria." I turned to the window again, shutting my eyes against my tears.

"No, I tell you. It was real."

I sighed. There was no point in arguing. The future would soon reveal itself.

Chapter Thirty-Eight
Final Meeting

That evening, Maria, Isabella, and I stood beside Father and Adriana greeting our guests in the recently refurnished harpsichord salon. Antonio Bellini and his father were among the first to arrive. Benedetto Bellini bowed to Father and said, "I am most honored to be invited to your meeting, Lord Salvini."

"We are most happy to have you here." Father's eyes scanned Signor Bellini from head to foot. Bellini's suit was not of the finest fabric, but his posture was proud and noble enough. Father said to him, "Allow me to present my wife."

Signor Bellini bowed again. "A pleasure to meet you, Lady Salvini."

"The pleasure is mine," Adriana replied.

As Father continued the introductions, I held my breath. I feared that when Father got to me, he'd say something about betrothing me to Antonio Bellini. Heaven intervened, though, for just as Father said my name, Governor von Traun arrived. Father's face lit up at the sight of the governor. It was his first visit to our palazzo.

"Excuse me," Father said. "I must welcome Governor von Traun."

"Of course," Signor Bellini said. Then he said to me, "We meet at last, Lady Emilia. I have heard a great deal about you from Antonio. My son has much praise for your musical talents." Signor Bellini's eyes were the same azure blue as his son's, but I saw a profound sadness in them.

"*Grazie*," I said with a curtsy. "But I fear your son exaggerates." I glanced at Antonio. His eyes bore sadness, too, but also a hint of hope. He didn't know yet of my decision to take Maria's place.

"*Buonasera*, Lady Emilia." Antonio looked down at his hands. As he clasped and unclasped them, I thought of the string game and how he'd ensnared my wrist in his loop of twine. Just before tonight's meeting, I'd slipped the flax-colored twine into my pocket. I intended to return it to him before the night was over.

"Good evening," I replied. Before I could think of something more to say, Father called us over to greet the governor.

By the time Marquis Volpi and his son arrived, Maria had already left to prepare for her presentation. The marquis approached slowly, leaning heavily on his walking stick. He seemed to have aged greatly since I'd last seen him, no doubt due, at least in part, to the embarrassment caused by his son. Lord Lodovico, on the other hand, walked with his usual proud stride.

Father stood tall as he exchanged greetings with Marquis Volpi and presented us all to him. The marquis was polite but brief. He soon hobbled away.

Lord Lodovico, however, lingered. He said to Adriana, "You are especially lovely this evening, Lady Salvini."

"You are too kind, Lord Lodovico." Her voice had an icy edge that contrasted sharply with her words, but Lord Lodovico didn't seem to notice.

He turned to me and said, "And who is this enchanting young woman?"

"Why, Lord Lodovico," Adriana said, "have you forgotten our Emilia? I believe you've heard her perform several times."

"Forgive me, Lady Emilia," he said with a bow. "You have changed much since our last meeting." He smiled and added, "in ways I find quite becoming." The curl of his smile and tilt of his head reminded me of the long-ago conversation I'd had with Gabriella regarding the signs of flirtation. No doubt Volpi's pretend memory lapse was part of an act to charm me.

I swallowed back the bile rising in my throat. For Maria's sake, I had to join in the playacting. I fluttered my fan in front of my face. "I believe you're trying to make me blush, Sir."

"Not at all," Lord Lodovico said. "I speak only the truth."

Adriana then gestured to Isabella. "And this is our third daughter, Isabella."

"My heavens," Lord Lodovico exclaimed. "How can so much beauty exist in one family?" He bowed to Isabella. "A pleasure and honor, Lady Isabella."

Isabella tilted her head and said coyly, "So you have forgotten that we have met before, too, Lord Lodovico?"

"I beg your pardon, my lady." He stroked the black beauty patch on his left cheek. "I must have been so intoxicated by your loveliness that the memory of our meeting was wiped away."

Isabella laughed. "You do have a way with words, Lord Lodovico."

I hadn't told Isabella yet that I would be the one to wed Volpi and not her. No matter. She'd learn of it soon enough. And now that Father planned to let Maria become a nun, Isabella could be betrothed to some other nobleman. Perhaps she'd be lucky enough to marry someone she could be happy with, as Gabriella had.

I glanced over at Count Cavalieri. His face beamed as it had on his wedding day. He'd already reassured me that Gabriella was doing well and couldn't wait to introduce me to their new son.

~

Maria's talk for this, her final meeting, would be different from all the others. Instead of discussing new theories, she would present a summary of the booklet she'd dedicated to Archduchess Maria Teresa. Father had planned tonight's meeting to demonstrate that my sister, who was nearly seventeen now, had completed her studies. Thanks to Adriana, the next step in Maria's life would be to take the veil and not Lord Lodovico's hand.

Father announced the news as part of his introduction to Maria's talk. He must have told Maria first, though, for her face was aglow even before he began to speak. It soothed my heart to see her so happy.

As Maria reaffirmed the notion that women could and should be educated, I scanned the room. I spotted Antonio Bellini seated in the front row, his back to me. I planned to speak to him right after my performance. My head grew heavy at the thought of telling him of my impending betrothal to Lord Lodovico. But Bellini deserved to hear the news directly from me.

I looked away and my eyes fell on Lord Lodovico and his father. While Marquis Volpi sat perfectly still, transfixed by Maria, Lord Lodovico fidgeted incessantly. He raised his handkerchief to his mouth to hide a large yawn, then glanced about. His gaze caught mine before I could avert my eyes. Lord Lodovico smiled. If I hadn't known of his exploits in Austria, I might have been flattered. Instead, my stomach sickened at the thought of marrying such a scoundrel. Yet I managed to make myself smile sweetly just the same.

Maria came to the end of her talk. Everyone rose to their feet and applauded enthusiastically, especially the governor. When the applause died down, Governor von Traun signaled Maria toward him. I watched as he spoke to her, no doubt complimenting both the content of her speech and her eloquence.

In that moment, I realized that the envy that had smoldered in my heart all these years had finally died out. I was filled with only pride for my sister, as on the day of her first public speech. Maria had followed in the footsteps of Lady Elena Cornaro, one of the learned women she'd praised that day. Like Cornaro, my sister had mastered seven languages and studied philosophy, mathematics, and astronomy.

Maria's intelligence had won her renown throughout the Duchy and beyond. Yet she'd remained incredibly humble through it all. And now she was giving up everything—marriage, wealth, acclaim—to serve the filthy beggars who lined the streets of the city. My own sacrifice seemed paltry in comparison.

Chapter Thirty-Nine
Farewell

After a break for refreshments, it was my turn to perform. Antonio Bellini again seated himself in the front row, with his father beside him.

The guests grew silent as I took my place at the harpsichord. I adjusted my skirts, drew back my shoulders, and began. I went through a repertoire of my best sonatas and songs, playing with such enthusiasm that perspiration soon trickled down my spine. I cared not. I was determined to express myself as fully as I could, through both the words and music. The audience applauded warmly following each piece. That mattered not either. Today I played for an audience of one.

Finally, I came to my last piece—the lullaby the archduchess had liked so well, my love song to Antonio Bellini. He'd heard me play it at Gabriella's, but tonight I wanted him to really *feel* the music, to be touched by the emotions that had inspired it.

I took a deep breath. I would need to keep tight rein on those emotions to sing without faltering.

I played the prelude *molto teneramente*, as tenderly as I could. Then I began:

"I am so blessed to have you as my own,
my precious, precious one.
I will love you my whole life long ...

As I sang, I recalled telling Bellini I'd written the lullaby for the archduchess. He knew not that I'd originally composed it for him.

I glanced up and found him in the audience. His eyes met mine. The rest of the room fell away.

No matter what pain or hardship life may bring
I'll be ever near, ready to kiss your tears away ...

My vision blurred. I could never fulfill those words now. I shifted my gaze upward and struggled to keep my composure.

Rest easy now, dear one. For you alone I sing.
Your place in my heart is secure, come what may ...

Finally, I came to the last line:

I will love you my whole life long.

I prayed for Bellini to understand—I *would* love him my whole life long. No matter that we'd never be together.

I slowed the tempo as I played the final chords. With an aching heart, I looked over at the portrait of the cerulean Madonna. A sad smile crossed my lips. *I'm keeping my promise, Mamma.*

The audience's applause pulled me from my reverie. They were on their feet now, clapping vigorously. I stood and curtsied, brushing the tears from my cheeks.

When the applause died down, Governor von Traun waved me over as he had Maria. The governor remained standing while he congratulated me in his heavy German accent. "Your songs are among Archduchess Maria Teresa's favorites," he said, "especially that lullaby. She sings it to her children often. The archduchess asked me to tell you she looks forward to receiving more of your compositions."

I curtsied low. "Thank you, Lord Governor." His words eased some of my heartache. My one consolation at having to marry Lodovico Volpi was that I'd be able to continue composing for the archduchess. I said to the governor, "I hope to soon have some new pieces to send Her Royal Highness."

Father appeared beside me. The governor said to him, "Thank you, Count Salvini, for a most enjoyable evening."

"Thank *you*, Lord Governor, for gracing us with your presence." Father bowed low. "But you are not leaving already?"

"I'm afraid so," the governor said. "I must depart the city early in the morning to tend to an urgent matter." To me, he said, "I hope to have the pleasure of hearing you perform again soon, Lady Emilia."

I curtsied again. "I would be honored, Lord Governor."

As Father escorted the governor out, old Marquis Volpi approached. He gave me a slight nod and said only, "*Brava*, Lady Emilia," before hobbling over to the refreshment table.

His son, on the other hand, praised me effusively. "I have never witnessed such musical genius in one of the fairer sex. Such virtuosity, such style, such grace!"

I knew Lord Lodovico was just flattering me, but I couldn't help smiling. After we were wed, I would remind him of his praise and the archduchess's comments, if need be, to ensure I'd be allowed to continue making music.

Stroking the beauty patch on his cheek, Volpi went on and on while Count Cavalieri and Benedetto Bellini stood waiting nearby. When Lord Lodovico finally paused for a breath, Count Cavalieri said, "That's enough now, Volpi. There are others here who also wish to congratulate Lady Emilia."

Lord Lodovico's eyes widened. Either he hadn't noticed anyone was waiting, or he took offense at the interruption. He didn't reply to the count. Instead, he bowed to me and said, "Forgive me if I have monopolized your attention, Lady Emilia." He glanced about then headed toward Isabella.

I curtsied to Count Cavalieri. "I am in your debt, my lord."

"Nonsense," Count Cavalieri said. "I am the one indebted to you for your stupendous performance this evening. It is unfortunate my wife could not be here to enjoy it as well. Perhaps you can come to our home soon and give her a private concert."

"That would be my great pleasure."

Benedetto Bellini said, "I congratulate you, Lady Emilia. My son did not exaggerate your talents one iota. You are an outstanding composer, musician, *and* singer." He smiled, and for a moment the sadness seemed to fade from his eyes.

"*Grazie*, Signor Bellini." He bowed and stepped away. I'd expected his son to be behind him, but it was another guest. Then I realized it was best I not speak to Antonio in front of his father. I didn't know what, if anything, Benedetto Bellini knew about our relationship.

I wore a polite mask as I accepted congratulations from one guest after another. Finally, I couldn't take any more. I excused myself, grabbed a goblet from a passing servant's tray, and escaped to the balcony.

The air outdoors felt almost as warm as in the harpsichord salon. I took a long drink of iced lemon water, but it did little to relieve the tightness in my throat. I pressed the cool goblet to my cheek. In a moment, I'd seek out Antonio Bellini for what would surely be our last private conversation.

A large moon several days short of full lit the night sky. How right that a misshapen moon, rather than a whole one, should mark this new beginning.

I thought of the squirrels I'd watched this morning. For so many years I'd chased after my sister, seeking to surpass her. Now, in my triumph, I would be undone.

Even though my jealousy was gone, I couldn't help wondering if my life would have been different had I been born before Maria. Would I still have been envious of her? Or would I have sought to protect her from the start?

Strangely enough, I suddenly felt grateful for my destiny. Had I not been the second sister, I might never have studied music. Nor met Antonio Bellini. And I couldn't imagine a life lacking either one.

Yet such a life was about to become my fate.

———

I heard footsteps then a voice behind me said, "I've been searching for you, hoping we might speak privately."

My heart quickened.

"And so you've found me, Signor Bellini," I said, facing him.

He bowed. "Lady Emilia, words cannot express my admiration for both your compositions and your performance this evening." His formality belied the look in his eyes. The lullaby had touched him, just as I'd hoped. The accomplishment tasted bittersweet.

"*Grazie.*" Now that we were finally face-to-face, I didn't know how to tell him all that was in my heart. "I selected the pieces with you in mind," I said, "as a farewell."

"A farewell? Are you going away? Was your stepmother unable to help?" The formality had disappeared from his voice.

"She did help." I considered explaining how Adriana and I had worked together to get Father to let Maria take the veil. But I feared Bellini might think I *wanted* to marry Volpi. So I said only, "Adriana found out the reason behind my father's lifelong quest to join the nobility. From what she told me, I'm certain he'd never allow me to wed someone who wasn't a nobleman."

"I feared as much." Bellini took a step closer, though he was careful to maintain an appropriate distance between us. For a moment, I wished he were less honorable. But then I wouldn't care for him as I did.

I resisted the urge to move toward him. "Father is determined to betroth one of his daughters to Lodovico Volpi. With Maria joining the convent, that responsibility will now fall to me."

"I wish there were some way," Bellini said. "But even if I could put aside my hatred of my great-uncle, I still couldn't accept his inheritance for fear of what it would do to my father."

I'd seen the profound sadness in Benedetto Bellini's eyes. If Antonio accepted the marquis's inheritance, his father would no doubt see it as a terrible betrayal. "Does your father know of his uncle's desire to leave everything to you?"

"Yes, though I hadn't planned to tell him. When the invitation for tonight's meeting arrived, Father thought it had been addressed to him in error. I deduced otherwise. Your father'd obviously assumed I'd soon be an eligible suitor. He might even have intended to speak to my father tonight of our betrothal. So I had to explain everything to Father. If he'd returned the invitation as being sent in error, it would have caused us all a great deal of embarrassment."

"I'm surprised your father didn't simply decline the invitation." New hope flickered in my heart. "You did tell him of your resolve to turn down the marquis's inheritance?"

"Yes," Bellini said, "and Father was visibly relieved at the news. His reaction reinforced my resolve. I encouraged Father to send his regrets for tonight. However, he didn't want to miss what might be his only opportunity to see you perform."

"Oh. I understand." My hope extinguished, I turned away. "Of course, you were correct—my father doesn't know of your decision yet. He may indeed intend to discuss plans for our betrothal with your father this evening."

"If so, Father's determined to avoid the topic," Bellini said. "At any mention of it, he'll suggest they make an appointment to discuss it later. That will give you time to explain."

I nodded. In the silence that followed, I gazed up once more at the misshapen moon. Could it really be God's desire to part us now? If so, for what purpose had He brought us together in the first place?

My eyes still on the moon, I said, "I originally wrote it for you, you know. The lullaby."

"So I guessed, or at least hoped," Bellini said. "It's a haunting melody. I'll never forget it. Nor will I ever forget you."

Something in his voice made me turn to him again. "I expect we'll still see each other from time to time," I said. "I look forward to one day watching you conduct your own opera at the Ducal Theatre."

He shook his head. "I can't stand the thought of seeing you wed to someone else. I'd rather leave Milan."

"Leave Milan? Where would you go?"

"To any city with an orchestra that will have me. I'll apply to Padua, Bologna, even Rome if need be."

"But what of your family? How will your father manage his business without you?"

"I've already saved enough for my sister's dowry. And she's found an admirable suitor who will be happy to take over the business. Father can choose whether to live with them here in Milan or join me in whatever city I make my new home."

A new thought sprang to mind: *Could this be God's solution to my problem, for me to leave Milan with Bellini?* I could pretend to agree to a betrothal to Volpi. Then, after Maria had made her religious vows, Bellini and I could elope.

Then I recalled Governor von Traun's words. If I disgraced myself by running off with a poor violinist, the archduchess would have little interest in me or my music and neither would anyone else. Save for Bellini. Would that be enough?

I reached into my pocket and ran my fingers along the loop of twine, but I couldn't find the tiny knot that held it together.

Finally, I said, "Then this really is farewell."

"Yes, I suppose," he replied. "I pray Volpi will prove a worthy husband."

His voice gave no hint that he knew of Volpi's true character. For that I was grateful.

Bellini bowed. "*Addio*, Lady Emilia."

"Wait." I pulled the twine from my pocket. "I have something of yours." When my hand touched his, a familiar shiver went through me. His eyes met mine, and I knew he'd felt it too.

I pressed the twine into his palm. I blinked back tears. What more could I say to him?

"God be with you, Antonio Bellini."

As he walked away, I braced myself against the balcony railing to keep from slumping to the floor.

My heart would never sing again.

Chapter Forty
News of Great Import

The following morning, I woke when Maria rose from bed, but I pretended to sleep on. I soon slept again in truth. When I next awoke, it was to the sound of the basilica bells chiming.

I lay staring at the ceiling, my whole body heavy, as though held down by a millstone. The mere thought of moving made me weary. Was this how I'd feel every morning for the rest of my life?

Someone knocked at the door. "Emilia, it's Adriana. May I enter?"

"If you must."

"Why aren't you up yet?" Adriana said, shutting the door behind her. "Are you ill?" She hurried to my bedside and reached for my forehead.

I brushed away her hand. "My sickness is of the heart, not the body."

"Then brace your heart," Adriana said, "for I have news. Two visitors are here to speak with your father."

"So?"

"They're Count Cavalieri and Benedetto Bellini."

I bolted upright. "What are *they* doing here? Have you told Father yet about Antonio Bellini disclaiming the marquis's title?"

"No. I decided to wait until today," Adriana said. "But the visitors arrived before I had a chance. They're meeting with your father in his study right now."

"Oh, no." I leapt out of bed. "Quick! Help me dress." I pulled off my nightclothes.

"I don't understand," Adriana said. "What's this all about?"

While Adriana helped me, I told her of my conversation with Antonio Bellini the night before. "His father must have assumed I would have explained everything by now. Otherwise, Signor Bellini would never have agreed to an appointment so soon. I need to speak to Father immediately."

"It's too late," Adriana said. "Your father would be furious if you interrupted their meeting."

"Father's going to be furious with me anyway."

"Well, truth be told, this is all my fault," Adriana said. "*I* was the one who suggested we wait until after the meeting to explain the situation. I'll tell your father so."

I fell into a chair. "*Grazie*, Signora Madre."

"It's nothing," she said. "He won't stay angry long, especially when I remind him that Marquis Volpi is still waiting to arrange a betrothal. Since your father has made no promises, the daughter will be of his own choosing."

"Well, at least that daughter will be me now, and not Maria." Then a horrible thought crossed my mind. "Father *is* still planning to let Maria take the veil, isn't he?"

"Indeed," Adriana said. "He spoke with Padre Gilberto at last night's meeting, after Maria's presentation. Your father was none too pleased with Maria's desire to join the Blue Nuns, of all orders, but Padre Gilberto convinced him God would reward him well for such a sacrifice." Adriana placed a hand on my shoulder. "I trust God will reward you even more, for you are making a true sacrifice. Now come, you need to finish dressing. Then I'll fix your hair."

Adriana was still arranging my hair when Nina came to the door. "Pardon the interruption, my lady," she said to Adriana.

"Lord Salvini would like to see you and Lady Emilia in his study right away."

"*Grazie*, Nina." Adriana quickly finished my hair. "*Andiamo*," she said. "We mustn't make your father wait."

We found the door to Father's study wide open. He sat writing at his desk.

I hung back as Adriana entered the room. Despite my stepmother's assurances, I still feared Father's wrath.

Adriana said, "You sent for us, my lord?"

"Yes, indeed." Father set down his quill and waved us in. "I have news of great import." His smile puzzled me. He wasn't angry?

"Please, sit down." Father got up to shut the door then returned to stand between us and the desk.

Adriana and I seated ourselves in the two chairs facing him.

"I have just met with Signor Benedetto Bellini and Count Cavalieri." Father addressed his words to Adriana, his voice filled with excitement. "They have confirmed what Emilia told me: Marquis don Vittore Bellini wishes to leave his estate and title to his great-nephew, provided the young man is betrothed to a noblewoman." Father turned to me. "And I have agreed to such a betrothal between you and young Bellini." He gestured to the letter on the desk behind him. "I am writing to the notary now, asking him to draft the necessary documents immediately."

Adriana clapped her hands and jumped up. "This is marvelous!"

I was still confused. "But I thought ... How can this be? Last night, Antonio Bellini told me his father could not abide his accepting the inheritance."

Father's smile widened. "So I learned this morning. Signor Bellini did not explain what brought about his change of heart. Perhaps it was Count Cavalieri's offer to act as intermediary, thus sparing Bellini and his son any contact with the marquis." Father leaned against his desk. "I am not surprised by Cavalieri's success in this matter, given the Old Bulldog's reputation as a diplomat. However, I have no idea why he should take any interest in it."

Of course, I knew the reason. It was Gabriella's doing.

"In any case," Father said, "the marquis's ill health requires swift action. Unfortunately, since tomorrow is Sunday, we must wait an extra day. Count Cavalieri and Signor Bellini will return Monday morning. I'll have the notary bring the nuptial agreement here and serve as official witness to its signing. Then Count Cavalieri will take the documents with post-haste to the marquis, who has promised to sign his revised will immediately upon sight of the contract." Father rubbed his hands together. "By Monday evening you, Daughter, shall be officially betrothed to the future Marquis don Antonio Bellini."

"I can scarcely believe it," I said.

Adriana clapped her hands again. "We must give praise and thanks to God." She put her hand out for mine. "Let's go to the chapel together, Emilia."

"Oh yes, Signora Madre." I took her hand.

"Be quick about it," Father said. "I will not allow the midday meal to be delayed. I have an appointment at the Convent of the *Turchine* this afternoon to discuss the arrangements for Maria."

"Rest assured, my lord," Adriana said, "we will be punctual."

We hurried downstairs. Outside the chapel door, I said, "I fear I am sleepwalking, and this is all a dream."

Adriana pinched my arm.

"*Ouch!* What did I do to deserve that?"

Adriana laughed her cricket laugh. "Nothing. I was simply proving you are indeed awake."

I rubbed the spot where she'd pinched me, smiling despite the pain. "You didn't have to be quite so convincing."

"Forgive me," she said. "I wanted to be expedient. There's no time to waste. Now come." She opened the chapel door, and we stepped inside.

To my surprise, the chapel was already occupied—Maria was on her knees before the altar. When we reached the pew, she rose and said, "Oh, Emmi, God has answered my prayers. Father will be making the arrangements today for me to join the Blue Nuns. Isn't it wonderful?" Her face radiated joy.

"God has answered my prayers, too," I said. "I will soon be betrothed to Antonio Bellini."

Maria grabbed my hands in hers. "I'd told you all would be well for both of us." Maria glanced at Adriana, then whispered in my ear, "just as Mamma said."

I'd forgotten about Maria's dream, or actually, her vision. Maria had indeed inherited Mamma's gift. I should have had more trust.

"Come, Emilia." Adriana pulled me into the pew. "I promised your father we wouldn't be late."

I knelt beside Adriana. Maria stood waiting at the end of the pew. My stepmother said a quick prayer and was soon on her feet again. She took Maria by the arm. "*Andiamo*."

"You two go on ahead," I said. "I need a moment more."

"Very well," Adriana said. "But hurry."

Alone at last, I stared up at the mahogany crucifix above the altar. My mind still struggled to accept the truth: Maria was to be a nun. I was to wed Antonio Bellini. All would be well for both of us.

The only prayer that came to mind was, "Thanks be to God."

Chapter Forty-One
Butterfly Wings

I met Isabella on the stairs to the dining room. She greeted me with a grin. "Isn't it wonderful, Emmi?" She waited on the landing for me to join her. "Everything's working out just as we'd hoped. With Maria taking the veil, I can be the one to wed Lodovico Volpi!"

Heaven forgive me. In my excitement, I hadn't thought about Isabella. Now I cringed at the idea of my little sister marrying such a despicable man. "That remains to be seen," I said. "Father said nothing of Volpi today."

Yet even as I spoke, I recalled Father's earlier words, "It is my will that one of my daughters marry Lodovico Volpi." After what Adriana had told me about Father's motives, I knew it would be impossible to change his mind, especially after Volpi had vowed to mend his ways.

"I shall suggest it to Father myself then," Isabella said.

I started to say, "Why would you do such a thing?" but I knew the answer. Isabella longed to avoid poor Zia Delia's fate, just as I had all these years.

"There's no need for haste," I said. "Your turn will be here soon enough."

Isabella's face brightened. Despite her joy, I still loathed the idea of her marrying Lodovico Volpi. But there was nothing I could do about it.

Later that afternoon, I sat in the garden doing needlework beside Adriana when Naldo announced the arrival of Antonio Bellini. On hearing his name, my heart quickened.

"Good day, Lady Salvini," Bellini said, bowing to Adriana. "And to you, Lady Emilia." He smiled, exposing the elusive dimple I loved so much. I couldn't keep from smiling back.

"What a pleasant surprise, Signor Bellini," Adriana said. "I didn't expect to see you today."

"I hope you'll forgive the intrusion," Bellini said, "but I wondered if I might have a word with Lady Emilia."

"I don't see why not." Adriana reached over and squeezed my hand. "It's such a lovely day, why don't you show Signor Bellini about the garden, Emilia?"

"That's a splendid idea, Signora Madre."

Bellini put out his right arm, and I took it. "You must see our oleander hedge, Signor Bellini. The blooms are quite abundant this year."

As we approached the hedge, its masses of ruby red flowers came into view. "You weren't exaggerating," Bellini said. "I've never seen so many blossoms! And look, they've attracted butterflies." He gestured toward two yellow swallowtails fluttering nearby.

My heart fluttered like the butterflies' wings—I could hardly believe I was walking in our garden on the arm of my beloved.

When we were out of earshot, Bellini said, "After you and I last spoke, I never expected to see you again. And now ..." He stopped and turned to me. "And now, we'll soon be betrothed." His smile lit up his eyes.

"It's an answer to my prayers, though God does move in mysterious ways. I'd never imagined Count Cavalieri would approach your father regarding Marquis Bellini's will."

Bellini's brow wrinkled in puzzlement. "The count said nothing of the will to my father."

I let go of his arm. "I don't understand. Then what made your father change his mind?"

"Well, it was a conversation *I* had with Father that led him to give his blessing. Though I confess Count Cavalieri played a role in prompting that discussion."

"You? You didn't want to have anything to do with the marquis."

Bellini nodded. "Quite true. But last night, as I was leaving the meeting, Count Cavalieri pulled me aside to tell me what a scoundrel Lodovico Volpi really is. The thought of you wed to someone like him set my blood to boiling. When I asked the count if you knew the truth about Volpi, he told me you did, and that you had in fact volunteered to take your sister's place so *she* wouldn't have to marry him. That was incredibly unselfish of you."

"Not really." I looked down. "Since I couldn't marry you, it made little difference whom I married."

"Nonsense! There are other, more honorable, noblemen you could have married if you hadn't sought to spare your sister. Indeed, it was your willingness to sacrifice yourself that opened my eyes to my own selfishness."

I lifted my face to his. "I still don't understand. What of the pain it would cause your father for you to accept the marquis's inheritance?"

"On our way home from the meeting, I told Father how much I hated the idea of your marrying Volpi, especially given the unselfishness of your motives. Father said you were 'noble' in the best sense of the word. I told him I wished I could be half as noble. He was quiet the rest of the way home. This morning, he came into my room and said that if I wanted to accept the marquis's inheritance, I had his blessing."

Bellini's eyes seemed bluer than ever as he said, "Father's exact words were, 'Despite all the hardships we've faced, I've never regretted marrying for love. My conscience would give me no peace if I kept you from doing the same.'"

Bellini took my hands in his. His warmth set my fingers ablaze, spreading up my arms and through my whole body. "You were right about one thing, though. God *does* move in mysterious ways."

As if to confirm that Heaven was watching, one of the butterflies flew over to us, fluttering just above our heads. We both laughed.

Bellini let go of my hands and reached into his pocket. He pulled out some twine—the same flax-colored piece I'd returned to him just the night before.

I laughed once more. "You don't think I'll let you ensnare my wrist again, do you?"

He shook his head. "I want to show you something." He looped the twine around his hands and began weaving it back and forth between his fingers. When he was done, he raised his hands and said, "See, a butterfly." Sure enough, he had shaped the twine into a series of triangles that formed a butterfly's body and wings. He held his creation out to me as though offering a precious gift. "For you."

When I tried to take the butterfly from him, the twine caught and tangled between us.

We giggled like children as we struggled with the jumble we'd created. Working together, we finally managed to disentangle the twine.

I held up my hands with the smooth loop laced between them. "You're going to have to teach me how to do it myself."

"It will be a small return for all you've taught me."

My heart sang at his words.

About the Author

Carmela A. Martino is an author, speaker, and writing teacher who lives in the Chicago area. She wrote the middle-grade novel, *Rosa, Sola*, while working on her MFA in Writing for Children and Young Adults at Vermont College. The novel was named a Booklist "Top Ten First Novel for Youth" and received the Catholic Writer's Guild Seal of Approval.

Her other credits for children and teens include short stories and poems in magazines and anthologies. Her articles for adults have appeared in such publications as the *Chicago Tribune*, *Catholic Parent*, *Writer's Digest*, and multiple editions of the annual *Children's Writer's and Illustrator's Market*.

Carmela has taught writing workshops for children and adults since 1998, and she blogs about teaching and writing at www.TeachingAuthors.com. You can read more about her at www.carmelamartino.com and follow her on Facebook at www.facebook.com/carmelamartino.

To download Book Discussion Questions for *Playing by Heart* or a Teacher's Guide containing book-related student activities, visit //smarturl.it/PlayingbyHeart or see www.carmelamartino.com.

Acknowledgements

I am especially indebted to Professor Robert L. Kendrick of the University of Chicago for answering my questions about the music of 18th-century Milan, and to Dorothy Strening, musician and composer extraordinaire, for catching the errors that crept into the manuscript despite all my research.

My heartfelt thanks also go out to:

Harpsichordist Diana Malon, for helping me understand what it might have been like to play a harpsichord in the 1700s.

Italian teacher Bijou D'Arpa, for proofreading my use of Italian.

The Windy City Romance Writers of America Chapter, for selecting *Playing by Heart* winner of the Young Adult Category of their 2013 Four Seasons Romance Writing Contest.

The Hive, my Vermont College classmates, for their encouragement and support.

My critique group, the SWLs, for their insightful feedback.

The Whole Novel Workshop teammates Leanne Pankuch, Karen Halvorsen Schreck, and Mary Sandford.

Amy Cattapan, for connecting me with my publisher via the Catholic Writers Guild's online conference, and to Karina Fabian and the other CWG members who helped me polish my pitch.

Finally, undying thanks to my family for always being by my side, especially my husband, John.

Author's Note

This story was inspired by two amazing sisters who lived in eighteenth-century Milan: musician and composer Maria Teresa Agnesi (1720-1795) and linguist and mathematician Maria Gaetana Agnesi (1718-1799). Their wealthy father, Pietro Agnesi, regularly held academic meetings in their home to show off the girls' talents as part of his efforts to gain a noble title.

I first learned about the older sister, Maria Gaetana, after reading an article on little-known women of history. Since my undergraduate degree is in mathematics and computer science, I was surprised I'd never heard of her before. I set out to write a non-fiction biography of Gaetana for young readers. While researching her life for that yet-to-be-published book, I began to wonder what it must have been like for Maria Teresa to live in Gaetana's shadow. That's how I came to write *Playing by Heart*, basing the main character, Emilia Salvini, on Teresa Agnesi.

Unfortunately, I couldn't find any book-length biographies of Teresa. Much of what I know of her comes from my research of Gaetana (see below). I used that research to incorporate aspects of both sisters' lives into the novel. For example, the Latin speech my fictional character Maria Salvini gives defending the education of women is modeled after Gaetana's first known public speech at age nine. My character has Gaetana's knack for languages, too—Gaetana was fluent in seven languages by her teen years. She also studied philosophy, astronomy, and mathematics. She eventually wrote the first mathematics textbook that covered everything from basic mathematics through algebra, geometry, and the relatively new calculus. In 1750, the pope offered Gaetana a position as a mathematics professor at the University of Bologna. She would have been the first woman mathematics professor, but she turned down the position. She preferred to stay in Milan to focus on charitable work.

I modeled my main character, Emilia Salvini, on what we know of Teresa Agnesi, who was a gifted musician, singer, and composer. Teresa was one of the first Italian women to write a serious opera, though there's no record of it ever being performed. We do know that several of her other compositions were performed in Milan's Royal Ducal Theatre, predecessor to Milan's famous *La Scala* Opera House. Unfortunately, much of her work has been lost, including a collection of arias she dedicated to Milan's ruler at the time, Empress Maria Theresa of Austria. The Empress reportedly liked the arias so much that she sang them in her home at the Royal Palace in Vienna.

Empress Maria Theresa visited Milan only once, while she was still an archduchess. The scenes in the novel depicting that visit are based on firsthand historical accounts. The then-archduchess participated in the ritual of the Holy Nail in May 1739. The ritual is still performed annually in Milan. (You can watch video clips of the ceremony on YouTube.)

Both Agnesi sisters were well-known in their day. However, that fame did not bring them happiness. Gaetana disliked her celebrity status. She was devoutly religious and longed to serve the poor. Around age 18, she asked her father's permission to become a nun, but he refused. Her sister, Teresa, wished to marry a poor nobleman named Pietro Antonio Pinottini, but their father refused her as well. At the time, the only respectable position for an upper-class Italian woman was either as a wife or as a nun. Some members of Milan's aristocracy considered Pietro Agnesi's failure to make such arrangements for his two eldest daughters scandalous. When the governor of Milan confronted Pietro Agnesi with the rumors, the men had a terrible argument. According to one of Gaetana's biographer's, the incident led to Pietro Agnesi's death from a heart attack less than two weeks later.

Pietro Agnesi's death in 1752 made it possible for his daughters to finally live lives of their own choosing. By then, Gaetana was nearly 34 years old. She quickly traded her inheritance for a small annual stipend and devoted the rest of her life to help-ing the poor.

Thirty-one-year-old Teresa married Pietro Antonio Pinottini three months after her father's death, a rather rebellious act, given that she was supposed to still be in mourning. She re-mained active in Milan's music scene for many years. In 1770, she was among those who welcomed a barely fourteen-year-old Mozart on his first visit to Milan. Little is known of her life after that, except that she and her husband struggled finan-cially. After his death, Teresa had to sell everything she owned to pay the bills. They had no children.

A great deal of misinformation has been published about the Agnesi sisters, both in print and online. I've created the website www.MGAgnesi.com to dispel some of the myths about Maria Gaetana Agnesi and her family. The site includes information about Teresa and links to websites where you can hear and watch musicians performing her work.

In researching the life of Gaetana Agnesi, I found the follow-ing books the most helpful. Both works mention Teresa, too, though briefly.

A Biography of Maria Gaetana Agnesi, an Eighteenth-Century Woman Mathematician by Antonella Cupillari

The World of Maria Gaetana Agnesi, Mathematician of God by Mas-simo Mazzotti

The best information I've found regarding Teresa Agnesi and her music is in Volumes 3 and 4 of *Women Composers: Music through the Ages*, edited by Sylvia Glickman and Martha Furman Schleifer.

Glossary

(words are Italian, unless otherwise indicated)

adagio	(musical term) slow tempo
addio	goodbye (typically when you don't expect to meet again)
allegro	(musical term) lively tempo
andante	(musical term) moderately slow tempo; between adagio and allegro
andiamo	let's go
arrivederci	goodbye (until we meet again)
Ave Maria	(Latin) Hail Mary
basso continuo	(musical term) bass harmony
bellissima	beautiful
brava!	well done! (feminine form)
buon giorno	good morning or good day
buona fortuna	good luck
buonasera	good evening
cadenza	(musical term) skillful passage near the end of a movement
carnevale	period between Epiphany and Lent; the celebrations during this time
cassone	chest, particularly a hope chest
chiacchiera	crispy fried cookie eaten during *carnevale* (plural is *chiacchiere*)
ciarlatani	charlatans or frauds
coda	(musical term) concluding passage of a piece of music

commedia dell'arte	improvised theatre based on a set of stock characters
concerto	(musical term) musical work for a solo instrument accompanied by an orchestra
concerto grosso	(musical term) musical work for a group of soloists accompanied by an orchestra
delizioso	delicious
don	nobleman
donna	noblewoman; may also mean simply "woman"
dono divino	(Latin) gift from God
duomo	cathedral
eccellente	excellent
grazie	thank you
il malocchio	the evil eye
innamorati	pair of lovers in the *commedia dell'arte*
maestro	master or teacher, especially of music
maestro di cappella	music director for a specific church or chapel
mea culpa	(Latin) through my fault; an admission of sin
mille grazie	thank you very much
molto teneramente	(musical term) very tenderly
movement	(musical term) section of a musical work, usually differing in key or themes from other sections
musica lieta	(Latin) joyful music

nonna	grandmother
nonno	grandfather
omnia vincit amo	(Latin) love conquers all
ora pro nobis	(Latin) pray for us
panettone	dome-shaped bread containing raisins popular at Christmastime
per favore	please
perfetto	perfect
prescienza	precognition; ability to foresee the future
presepio	Nativity scene
porta romana	gate on the road to Rome
saltarelli	plural of *saltarello*, see definition below
saltarello	(musical term) lively piece of music often used for dancing
Santo cielo!	Good heavens!
sì	yes
signor	may mean Sir, Lord or simply Mr., depending on context
signora	madam or Mrs.
signorina	unmarried girl; miss
sinfonia	symphony
sonata	(musical term) instrumental piece of music, typically containing three or four movements
sorbetto	sorbet
terrazzo	terrace

viola d'amore	a type of viola that typically has fourteen strings: seven playing strings and seven resonating ones
Viva!	Long live!
zia	aunt

Dear Reader,

If you enjoyed reading *Playing by Heart*, I would appreciate it if you would help others enjoy this book, too. Here are some of the ways you can help spread the word:

Lend it. This book is lending enabled so please share it with a friend.

Recommend it. Help other readers find this book by recommending it to friends, readers' groups, book clubs, and discussion forums.

Share it. Let other readers know you've read the book by positing a note to your social media account and/or your Goodreads account.

Review it. Please tell others why you liked this book by reviewing it on your favorite ebook site.

Everything you do to help others learn about my book is greatly appreciated!

Carmela A. Martino

Plan Your Next Escape!
What's Your Reading Pleasure?

Whether it's captivating historical romance, intriguing mysteries, young adult romance, illustrated children's books, or uplifting love stories, Vinspire Publishing has the adventure for you!

For a complete listing of books available, visit our website at www.vinspirepublishing.com.

Like us on Facebook at
www.facebook.com/VinspirePublishing

Follow us on Twitter at
www.twitter.com/vinspire2004

and join our announcement group for details of our upcoming releases, giveaways, and more! http://t.co/46UoTbVaWr

We are your travel guide to your next adventure!